P9-CQW-442

Bloomington Public Library

NOV   2013

17 : mp,

THE MEMORY OF TREES

Recent Titles by F G Cottam

BROADMAW BAY
THE COLONY
DARK ECHO
THE HOUSE OF LOST SOULS
THE MAGDALENA CURSE
THE WAITING ROOM

THE MEMORY OF TREES

F.G. Cottam

This first world edition published 2013
in Great Britain and the USA by
SEVERN HOUSE PUBLISHERS LTD of
19 Cedar Road, Sutton, Surrey, England, SM2 5DA.

Copyright © 2013 by F.G. Cottam.

All rights reserved.
The moral right of the author has been asserted.

British Library Cataloguing in Publication Data

Cottam, Francis, 1957–
 The memory of trees.
 1. Forests and forestry–Wales–Pembrokeshire–Fiction.
 2. Billionaires–Fiction. 3. Folklore–Fiction.
 4. Fantasy fiction.
 I. Title
 823.9'2-dc23

ISBN-13: 978-0-7278-8315-5 (cased)

Except where actual historical events and characters are being
described for the storyline of this novel, all situations in this
publication are fictitious and any resemblance to living persons
is purely coincidental.

All Severn House titles are printed on acid-free paper.

Severn House Publishers support The Forest Stewardship Council [FSC],
the leading international forest certification organisation. All our titles that
are printed on Greenpeace-approved FSC-certified paper carry the FSC logo.

MIX
Paper from
responsible sources
FSC
www.fsc.org   FSC® C013056

Typeset by Palimpsest Book Production Ltd.,
Falkirk, Stirlingshire, Scotland.
Printed and bound in Great Britain by
TJ International Ltd, Padstow, Cornwall

For Susan Searle 1924–2004
Much loved, greatly missed

ONE

The letter was printed on a plain sheet of A4 paper and signed at its conclusion with an old-fashioned fountain pen. The signature was legible. The writer was a man named Samuel Freemantle, who described himself as the estate manager. The estate in question, when Curtis subjected it to a Google Earth search, was not so much substantial as it was vast. He thought that Freemantle, despite his courteous tone and the formal approach the letter signified, must be a man with a job that kept him pretty busy.

The estate was owned by Saul Abercrombie and Curtis had, of course, heard of him. Self-made business successes tended to be more flamboyant than those who had inherited their money and Curtis thought of Abercrombie, whenever he saw the tycoon's picture or heard his quotes in the media, as someone happily addicted to the celebrity status his enormous wealth had brought him.

Curtis thought he shared the general view of people who knew Saul Abercrombie only through headlines and sound bites and photo opportunities. He was the warts and all entrepreneur with a business empire embracing everything from a Hollywood film studio to a prestigious brand of single malt whisky. He ran enterprises ranging from a bespoke software company to a road haulage fleet. He had been to prison in his twenties, and in middle age confessed, once he'd conquered it, to a couple of years of enslavement to an almost fatal crack cocaine habit.

He had survived that, unapologetic to the point of defiance about his personal extravagance and ravenous appetite for the good life. And good luck to him, people tended to think. He's fallible and honest and, in common with too few people with the talent for becoming rich, he genuinely enjoys what his money buys him.

There was the charitable foundation and the commitment

to ecology and a collection of rare Beatles and Rolling Stones material. McCartney and Mick Jagger had tried and failed to buy back some of the acetates of their early recordings he owned. There was the priceless collection of Pre-Raphaelite paintings. There was an aircraft hangar-sized garage replete with trophy cars. And, not least, there was a beautiful daughter he very publicly doted on.

Saul Abercrombie's wife, the mother of his jewel of a daughter, had taken her own life. The press account of that event was still vivid a decade on because the manner of the suicide had been so lurid. She had paid the toll and driven halfway across the Severn Bridge and brought her convertible E-type Jaguar to a halt. It had been a beautiful spring day and witnesses said she had been driving in a pink headscarf with the roof down. She clambered up the bridge railings and, without apparent hesitation, threw herself off.

Impact injuries killed her the moment she hit the water. She didn't leave a note. An autopsy report established that she had been in good health. She wasn't taking any medication and, when she jumped, Susan Abercrombie was completely sober.

Curtis folded the letter back into the envelope it had arrived in, rose from his desk and opened the blind to look at the morning as light gathered and strengthened in the sky. He listened to the traffic on the street seven stories below as it swelled in volume towards the beckoning rush hour. And he remembered that Abercrombie's daughter was named Francesca. He couldn't remember where he had seen her picture and he couldn't remember what it was that she did. That was, if she had an occupation. It didn't matter much. With a father like hers she didn't really need to do anything.

The estate Freemantle managed stretched inland from a ragged spread of cliffs on the Welsh Coast. It was sufficiently substantial for parts of it to own individual place names, when Curtis looked. There was Raven Dip and Gibbet Mourning and a place called Loxley's Cross. There was nothing on the map to signify settlement, but the names sounded old. They belonged to places that lived wholly in a past no one had bothered to document. They were of a time remote from factual detail. Maybe they were translations originally from the Welsh. Even what myths they might have engendered had perished through neglectful centuries.

Again, it didn't really matter. Down on the ground there might be a few scattered stones but the walked by-ways of these lost hamlets would have vanished entirely. And if Abercrombie's scheme, the scheme described in Freemantle's letter, proved to be feasible, they would be obscured and then consumed and forgotten forever.

Those cliffs at the edge of Abercrombie's domain had an average height of over a hundred feet. They were a vast rampart against the corrosive powers of the sea. But were they a formidable rampart? The practical part of Curtis' mind was already turning to the subject of coastal erosion. He needed to discover whether the cliffs were granite or chalk or predominantly quartz. They might be limestone, but he hoped they weren't. He returned to his desk and his computer but before he could switch it on, his mobile in his pocket rang.

'Sam Freemantle,' a voice said. 'Did you get my letter?'

'It arrived this morning.'

'Much maligned, the Royal Mail.'

Curtis looked at his watch. 'It's not yet seven thirty.'

'Postmen start work early.'

'I didn't mean that.'

'We rise early too, Mr Curtis, those of us who're slaves to the land.'

'I've no cows to milk or crops to tend, Mr Freemantle. Just because my profession is trees, it doesn't oblige me to live in a wood.'

Freemantle chuckled. He was not a Welshman, Curtis didn't think. There was a curl to the vowels, a slight suggestion of the West of England in his dialect. He said, 'I know exactly where you live. I posted you the letter. But you're up with the larks, nevertheless.'

Curtis nodded to himself. This was true.

'Should you have such things as larks, in Lambeth.'

Curtis didn't know whether he did or he didn't. Ornithology was not his speciality.

Freemantle cleared his throat. The small talk had come to its conclusion. He said, 'Do you think it practical, Mr Abercrombie's scheme?'

'Depends on what you mean by practical,' Curtis said. 'It can be done. It can be successfully achieved.'

'It's sustainable?'

'It can be made sustainable, yes.'

'I'm sensing a "but".'

'It'll be hugely expensive, even if the conditions are ideal. It could be colossally expensive if they're not.'

Freemantle paused. 'With or without you on board, he'll do it,' he said. 'Mr Abercrombie is someone with a lifelong habit of fulfilling his dreams. This dream is going to be no exception.'

'Except in scale,' Curtis said.

'He's totally committed.'

Maybe he should be committed, thought Curtis, who'd detected more than a touch of megalomania to the plan baldly mapped in Freemantle's letter. He glanced at his desk, at the mail that had arrived but had not been opened that morning, at the brown envelopes containing bills he knew he would struggle any time soon to pay. It was almost the end of March and he had not worked except in fits and starts since the Salisbury commission of the previous September.

'Will you assist Mr Abercrombie in achieving his dream?'

'I'll come and take a look,' Curtis said.

'Excellent. When can you get here?'

Curtis bit his lip. There was no point in standing on ceremony. Cash was a far more important imperative at this point in his life than point scoring. 'I could come up tomorrow.'

'Today would be better,' Freemantle said. 'But I suppose tomorrow will have to do. And you'll need to stay the night.'

'You can't treat this as something doable in the blink of an eye,' Curtis said.

'I know that,' Freemantle said. 'I've spent the bulk of my life outdoors. I've never come across a scheme remotely like this one. It's almost a reversal of nature.'

'It's more in the way of restoration,' Curtis said.

Freemantle's tone, when he replied, was suddenly more

relaxed. 'That's how Saul sees it too. I'm not sure I agree. Do you really restore something after a thousand years? Surely you recreate it,' he said.

'I'm not a philosopher,' Curtis said, scratching the stubble on his jaw. 'Not at seven thirty in the morning I'm not.' So the land manger was on first-name terms with the man employing him.

'One more thing,' Freemantle said. 'Keep all of this to yourself.'

'It won't be a project you can exactly hide. Not if it goes ahead. It'll practically be visible from space.'

'Just the same, please speak of it to no one. Scheme, scale, logistics, projected cost – all of it remains a secret. Are you someone capable of discretion?'

'This isn't espionage we're talking about.'

'Answer the question.'

'I've never courted gossip in my life.'

'Good. I'll email you a set of map coordinates. There's an eight-foot barbed-wire fence strung along the entire landward perimeter. There are gates for access, obviously.'

'Go on.'

'The coordinates will put you outside the western access point. I'll have keys to the gate there couriered to you this afternoon.'

'All the way from Pembrokeshire?'

'Saul Abercrombie has a London office. And we were fairly confident you'd take the job.'

'Why not just meet me at the gate?'

'Don't want to prejudice your first impressions. When you've had a bit of time to have a good look around, we'll come and find you.'

Curtis calculated that he could comfortably arrive at his destination by 11 a.m. the following morning. Freemantle said, 'At the wheel of a Land Rover, I assume?'

'You'd be disappointed if I was driving anything else,' Curtis said.

But he drove down in the Saab. It was quicker and less thirsty. The Land Rover was garaged, having failed its MOT, and he hadn't had the money since it failed to put right the faults. He assumed Freemantle would be equipped anyway with the sort of off-road vehicle suited to a thorough tour of the site. If the weather was fine – and the forecast was good – they'd probably do it on quad bikes. Nouveau-riche landowners generally had a stable full of those.

Evidently Saul Abercrombie was an impatient man. He would have to get used to the fact that his dream couldn't be realized as quickly as he seemed to wish. He would have to accommodate a huge workforce and massive material disruption. On the other hand, the timing, seasonally, could not really have been better. It was spring, the time of growth and life and regeneration in nature; the time of warmth and fecundity returning to the land and the warming and softening soil beneath its surface.

Curtis had his sample and analysis kit in a canvas grip on the seat beside him. He would need that gear. He also had a freshly pressed suit in a suit bag carefully folded into the Saab's boot. He didn't know whether Freemantle's invitation to stay the night at the estate involved dinner with its master. But he thought it might and wanted, if it did, to observe the necessary courtesies. His formal shoes were polished and he'd even packed a necktie. The truth was that he needed this job pretty desperately.

He drove with the picture in his mind of dinner, of a candelabra-lit baronial hall; Abercrombie and the lissom Francesca seated at a huge table heaped high with dishes, cooling under glittering metal domes as an army of discreet staff served them, Freemantle a red-faced figure in hairy tweeds, blushing as he twisted his cap between ruddy hands, standing awkwardly on.

It wouldn't be like that, of course. Saul Abercrombie was self-made and the land manager referred to him by his Christian name. He was a man with a bohemian history and a famously common touch, and his daughter would be busily occupied in some exotic and exclusive part of the world a cultural universe away from rural Wales. But the speculation passed the time, diverted him from the motorway monotony of the journey. And Curtis was more relaxed during the four hours his journey took for having packed his suit and scrupulously polished shoes.

He naturally wondered why they had selected him for the job. It was possible he was among a handful of arboreal specialists shortlisted and that this was just a preliminary audition. But his phone conversation with the land manager had suggested otherwise. He was their man, wasn't he?

He did have some experience of large projects, carried out on-budget and with successful results. Despite this track record, he had no real media profile, which apparently suited Freemantle and, given the nature of the project, the frankly absurd condition of confidentiality insisted upon by his boss.

But he thought probably his bloodline had been the clincher in getting him the job, rather than any professional qualification or career achievement. That would have been the deciding factor when they looked at their shortlist and selected his name from the three or four he imagined would have been written down there.

His father had been Welsh, born in Barmouth in the autumn of 1948. And his father, in common with his own ancestors, had been a fisherman who lived and died in the Kingdom of Wales. Tom Curtis had not been born in Wales, but he could have played rugby for the country had he possessed any aptitude or appetite for the game, and that tended to be the populist qualification on which the nationality of Welshmen was these days judged.

You could not transform the character of so vast a tract of Welsh land in the way that the Englishman Saul Abercrombie intended to. Not without the person orchestrating that transformation having a blood bond with the land undergoing the upheaval, you couldn't.

The days of burning weekend cottages owned by English visitors seemed thankfully to have gone. But Wales was still a nation in some important regards and it would be only pragmatic for Abercrombie to employ a Welshman to oversee this job. Some would see it as a violation, however handsomely the justification was dressed up. It would be a provocation too far for some of the local population for that violation to be committed by an Englishman.

*   *   *

He reached the western gate on foot. The Saab was fine until the narrow road he was on petered into a lane and then a rutted track. But when the track became rough ground the car didn't have the clearance for the terrain. By that point the fence securing Abercrombie's land was in sight, a quarter of a mile distant. He could see the evenly placed wooden stanchions and the sunlit glitter of its steel thorns. He picked his workbag off the passenger seat and locked the car door behind him.

He used the single key couriered to him the previous afternoon to open the heavy padlock securing the gate. Having entered the estate, he paused and looked around and listened, but there was no one there to meet him. He would have seen them over the flat expanse of wild grass rippling greenly in the breeze.

Curtis was aware of how quiet it was. Birdsong came with hedgerows and bushes and the branches of trees in which to nest and perch and there were none of those here. The land was not exactly flat, however. That was an impression given by the openness and scale of what he viewed from where he stood, an illusion strengthened by the vacant expanse of the sky. He was in Wales, not Kansas. The ground undulated beneath its verdant carpet of grass. There were no trails, though, beaten and worn by trampling feet as clues to which direction to take.

He walked for about half an hour. He'd walked in Wales before, but in Snowdonia and the Black Mountains and on the coastal stretch of land between Barmouth and Cader Idris. They were locations characterized by dramatic and even majestic landmarks. This was a wilderness – empty, almost featureless. When eventually he stopped, it was because, practically speaking, he was lost.

He looked around. Slightly to the north-west of where he stood, on a bearing that he reckoned would eventually take him to the cliffs and the sea, he noticed then the smudge of something that looked man-made. It was slate grey and solid and unmoving, but the lie of the land prevented him from seeing more than a fraction of it, low and perhaps a couple of miles distant. He began to walk towards it. It seemed the logical thing for him to do.

He was quite close to this building before the contour of the land exposed more of it and it was finally resolved into a small chapel or church. It was too plain to be a folly. He was only five hundred metres away when it revealed its detail fully as a place of worship built from stone in what he assumed were Saxon times. It was square in shape and a squat single storey only in height.

The studded oak wonder of a door looked original to this building when he reached it. It was blackened by time and exposure but still carried the scars of the primitive tools that had fashioned it in faith. When he pushed it, it creaked open on iron hinges and the cool smell of the church interior was a sudden, stony contrast to the sweet grass smell of the spring morning outside.

Gloom enveloped him. His eyes adjusted to it. He became aware of the one light source in there, beyond the gaps cleaved as narrow as archery slits at even spaces in the masonry.

This was a stained-glass window. It was high to his left and the angle of the sun through it cast shimmering lozenges of light on the wall opposite. There was enough light, now his eyes had grown accustomed, to see that the interior of the church was denuded of any furnishings. There was no altar, no pulpit, no benches in cramped rows or bolsters on which to kneel and pray. There were no lamps. There were no pictures hung or candles in holders to light. The church interior lacked a font. There was just the flagged stone floor and that one ornamental window to look upon, and so he did, studying its detail.

It was not religious in subject matter. If anything, Curtis thought, it might actually be construed as slightly blasphemous.

The window was tall and narrow and arched. It pictured a knight, bareheaded, clad in silver armour. His war horse stood tethered to a sapling with its head bowed to his rear. From his right hand, a bloodied broadsword trailed, its tip buried in the ferns growing lushly around his feet. In the grip of his left fist, his arm extended, he held a severed head by its hair. Its eyes had risen to white blankness in its face in death. It was not human, this grisly trophy displayed by the knight in the stained-glass window. It was twice as large as any human head

Curtis had ever seen. And its skin was ridged and coarsened with scales.

'Man, that's one ugly motherfucker,' a voice from behind him said.

Curtis jumped at the sound of the voice and turned and recognized the facial features of Saul Abercrombie contorted into a grin. He looked pleased with himself at the shock he'd just inflicted. 'Relax, brother,' he said. He nodded up at the window. 'The bad guy looks pretty dead to me. Dude in the steel suit saw to that.'

'Do you know who they are?'

'It's a thousand years ago,' Abercrombie said. 'People float theories. But guesswork is bullshit. Truth is, nobody knows.' He put out a hand and Curtis shook it. 'Saul,' he said.

'Tom Curtis.'

'Yeah, I know. My tree guy.'

'Only if I pass the audition.'

Abercrombie was slightly shorter than he looked in pictures. He was grey-bearded with white, wavy hair he wore at the same shoulder length he had in the famous picture of his arrest at the Red Lion Square demo back in the early seventies, when his tresses had been a youthful shade of brown. He was wearing a wrinkled blue linen suit, the trousers belted with a knotted club tie. His feet were laced into sneakers. He looked like he always looked, except that on his head was perched a pair of old-fashioned leather aviator goggles, their round glass lenses framed in circles of brass.

He said, 'I already like the vibe you give off, Tom. I'm rarely wrong about people. We're simpatico, the two of us. Everything is going to be cool, trust me.'

Curtis heard an engine approaching outside. Because he owned one himself, he knew it belonged to a Land Rover.

Abercrombie cocked his head at the sound. 'My principle gofer, Sam,' he said. 'Quad bikes on the trailer. You and me, Tree Man, are going to take the tour.'

Thus the steampunk goggles, Curtis thought, smiling to himself. There was something slightly pantomimic about Saul Abercrombie. But the man could afford to play the fool, couldn't he, having proven so conclusively over the years he was anything but. And he was likeable. Curtis realized with surprise that despite all of the reservations and prejudices he'd brought with him to Wales, he'd liked his potential new employer immediately.

'What is this place, Saul?'

Abercrombie adjusted the goggles over his eyes before answering. Outside, Curtis could hear Freemantle lower a ramp or running boards from the trailer to the ground to unload the bikes.

'The church is nameless,' Abercrombie said, blinking. 'It's lost, like the identity of the guy who won the argument up there in the window. The spot we're on is known as Raven Dip. It's a natural depression, the reason you have to get up close to recognize the building we're in for what it is.'

'I saw Raven Dip on the map,' Curtis said. 'I studied the lie of the land on my laptop yesterday. I didn't see any sign of buildings at all.'

'Google Earth?'

'Yes.'

'You're shitting me.'

'I'm not.'

'Which goes to prove, you can't trust anyone,' Abercrombie said, slapping him on the back and steering him towards the door in a single deft movement of his hand.

The quad bikes gleamed like alien and bulbous toys on the ground outside the old building, the Land Rover already distant, its trailer sashaying when Curtis looked, over the bumps and through the depressions of the ground on the route back to wherever it came from.

The estate occupied a tract of land that stretched seaward to an area of the Pembrokeshire coastline between Fishguard and Aberaeron. That finite boundary was made up of eight miles of cliffs. They ranged in height from about seventy feet to over 200 in a couple of places, undulating smoothly rather than raggedly because this part of the coastline was not prey to the erosion, Abercrombie told him, that plagued the eastern shoreline of Britain, ravaged as it was by the North Sea.

They toured the perimeter, travelling counter-clockwise. They stopped only when they reached what Abercrombie announced was the tallest of his sea-facing promontories, the one offering the best view out west over the water in the direction of Ireland and, beyond that, six thousand miles away, the Eastern Seaboard of the United States.

They were quiet for a moment, seated on the bikes, Curtis enjoying the relative peace after the belligerent roar of their engines, aware after a few moments of the rhythmic wash of the surf on the shore a fairly remote distance beneath them.

Abercrombie sniffed and lifted his goggles up on to his head. He looked skyward and said, 'Is salt a serious downer? In the rain, I mean, at the edge of the sea?'

'It's a common enough fallacy,' Curtis said. 'But most of your clouds coming from offshore will have gathered above the Irish land mass. Even if they hadn't, clouds don't carry salt in damaging concentrations. Drench would be a problem. Persistent sea spray could afflict the soil. But everything on your land is so far above sea level it nullifies all that.'

'Anything else that should be costing me sleep?'

'The depth and pH balance of the soil. Mature root systems will undermine the cliffs if the soil isn't there to sufficient depth.'

'You'll measure all of that shit, right?'

'I'll do all the testing necessary,' Curtis said. 'But I'm reasonably confident, having seen what you've shown me, that your plan's achievable. The scale is pretty awesome. But we're only really putting back what was originally there.'

Abercrombie was quiet for such a long time that Curtis thought perhaps he hadn't heard this last remark. There wasn't much wind to snatch away his words. But men of his new boss's vintage were sometimes a little deaf. Then, quietly, Abercrombie said, 'When was the last time you were allowed to see your daughter?'

'It'll be four months on Tuesday.'

'Bummer.'

'I'm surprised you know about that.'

'You shouldn't be. I like to know everything significant about the guys I hire.'

'Is it significant?'

'On a project this size, everything is that could put it in jeopardy. Anyway, it sounds like a bitch of a problem.'

'It's my problem.'

'And the reason you want this gig so bad.'

'I thought we were simpatico?'

'Tree Man, it's not confined to you and me.'

'I want access to my daughter. Her mother's putting every possible obstacle in the way of my seeing her. We're unmarried, so my rights are limited. Litigation is expensive and I've no savings. You're right, I need this job. I need it far too badly to be likely to fuck it up.'

'My worry is you'll convince yourself the project's feasible, even if it isn't,' Abercrombie said. 'You've just admitted you're desperate for the bread.'

'I'll do my tests. I'll tell you the objective truth when I've done them. Right now, things look promising, but I won't lie to you, Saul. What would be the point? If we begin this and it fails, I'll be unemployable.'

'You got that right, Tree Man.'

'What's your budget?'

'It stretches somewhere slightly north of fifty million pounds.'

'You won't need anywhere near that much.'

'It's there if I do,' Abercrombie said. He turned to look behind them, at all the grassy wilderness he owned.

'It's an awful lot of what you call bread.'

'Yeah, it's a chunk of change, all right. What can I tell you, Tom?' Abercrombie said, laughing. 'I like trees.'

He liked them so much that he was going to oversee their planting across every part of this vast Welsh acreage. He was going to return to it the character the land had possessed in the Dark Ages, when England and Wales and Ireland too had been covered in dense, deciduous forest.

They had cleared it first for their settlements and then for their by-ways and then for cultivation. In the end, they had cleared it because cleared land seemed to them a symbol of civilization and forests the home of outlaws or just the gloomy refuge of magic and barbarism. They had chopped

and hacked and burned in the name of progress until only
a few areas of forest remained as a precious legacy to be
nurtured and preserved in modern times by professional
conservationists.

Saul Abercrombie wanted to reverse that process. He wanted
to restore his domain to the virgin woodland it had been a
thousand years ago. And he didn't want to do it by planting
saplings and watching them grow through patient decades.
The stealth approach didn't work for him. He was seventy
years old. He had neither the decades nor the patience in him
for stealth. He wanted a mature forest rightfully restored on
a gigantic scale and had set aside north of fifty million pounds
to see this ambition realized.

'Ash and elder,' Abercrombie said. 'Yew, chestnut, oak,
sycamore and beech.'

He talks like a hippie, Curtis thought, *and this is his mantra.*
He wants to build something profound and unprecedented. It
will be wild and beautiful and his spectacular legacy. That
was what Curtis supposed he had meant when he'd said the
project went beyond whether the two of them could rub along
all right together. He was a man for whom getting what he
wanted was a lifelong habit. And he wanted nothing more than
for his forest kingdom to be successfully realized.

As though reading his mind, Abercrombie said, 'Broadleaf,
brother, as far as the eye can see.' Then, 'Where will you
source the trees?'

Curtis had thought about that. Of course he had. There were
plenty of heavily wooded areas of British coastline doomed
by erosion caused by the sea. Blackgang Chine on the Isle of
Wight was one such spot. If someone was prepared to take
the physical risk and organize the engineering and logistics,
who would not be pleased to see those threatened trees on the
precipice there saved and re-planted?

More cynically, there were lumber companies in Canada
and the United States who would do almost anything to
improve their compromised ecological credentials. They
would get the same tonnage dollars from Abercrombie that
they would get from customers looking to turn the wood
into floors and furniture and roof joists. They wouldn't get

the same kudos, though. They'd bend over backwards to facilitate him.

Curtis explained all this. He did so once the quad bikes had taken them back to Abercrombie's house, located about half a mile from the sea, towards the southern extremity of his land.

The house would have been a surprise had he not Google-Earthed it the previous day. It was modern, made mostly of wood from what Curtis assumed was a sustainable source. There were solar panels on the gentle slope of its roof. It was a spacious, handsome, two-storey affair, but even the most hyperbolic of estate agents would have blushed when calling it a mansion.

Abercrombie had mansions. He had homes in Barbados and London and British Columbia and they were far grander than this one was. Curtis had the intuition it might be razed and obliterated when the forest reached completion. The integrity of the forest would not be compromised by something modern and man-made. What a lonely construction that would make of the Saxon church, with its gory, stained-glass mystery, six or seven miles to the north-east of where they sat, the sun descending, on lawn chairs at a garden table to the rear of the property.

Unless Abercrombie planned to have the church razed too, of course. The church was an ancient monument and its stones had once been sanctified. But you could do such things, couldn't you, when you were in the business of playing God.

They were sipping beer. That had turned out to be the second and less pleasant of two surprises. The first, welcome surprise had been Saul's daughter, Francesca, exiting the house through the kitchen door and delivering their chilled bottles and iced beer glasses on a tray. She smiled and was introduced to Curtis, who stood and shook her hand. She was dressed in jeans and a blue cardigan he thought was probably cashmere over a plain white shirt. The breeze blew a tress of her hair across her face and she lifted a languid hand and brushed it away. She was one of those tall and slender women who move like liquid.

Her father asked her if she would join them, but she said she was working on something she was vague about in what she called the studio. She was as beautiful and as graceful in life as her pictures suggested she would be. With his counter-cultural phraseology and Artful Dodger manner of delivering it, there was something of the East End still about Saul. Francesca, by contrast, sounded like the product of a Surrey boarding school.

The unnerving surprise was the brand of beer Francesca had delivered him. Abercrombie's was a Heineken. Curtis was served a Hoegaarden.

'How did you know?'

Abercrombie chuckled. 'That you have a taste for Weiss beer? Knowledge is power, friend.'

'I'm flattered and all,' Curtis said. 'But really, how did you know?'

'If you value your privacy, brother, don't shop online.'

'You've had me spied on?'

'Assessed,' Abercrombie said. 'Secure Internet connectivity is an oxymoron, Tree Man. When it comes to privacy, the web is one faithless fucking bitch.'

A man exited the house and joined them, then. Dusk was gathering and he looked huge before he got close, loping over on light feet to where they sat and the detail of his clothing and features were properly resolved. He was shaven-headed and about six-four, dressed in camouflaged fatigues. And Curtis endured a third surprise, because he suddenly knew he'd had Sam Freemantle all wrong.

Deliberately so, he thought. Freemantle on the phone had just played on his preconceptions, planting assumptions, toying with him. He was nothing to do with tweed and twelve-bores; with partridge shoots and baiting traps to catch hares. His prey, should he hunt, was much more likely to be of the human variety. His claim to having spent the bulk of his life outdoors was probably true but had also been deliberately ambiguous.

He was Saul's security and didn't look to Curtis of the cut-price variety that gave the trade a bad name. Physically, he looked like he could create some serious carnage in the second row of a rugby scrum. But his body language suggested ex-military. Curtis would have bet what little money he had on that.

He nodded and smiled at Curtis and said, 'Everything OK, Saul?'

'Go and grab yourself a beer,' Abercrombie said to him.

To Curtis, Freemantle said, 'I took the liberty of locating your car and bringing up the things you left in the boot. In case you need them, I mean.'

'I left my car locked,' Curtis said. But this remark went ignored.

'I assume you'll stay the night?' Abercrombie said.

'I'd be delighted to stay.'

'Go and grab that beer,' Abercrombie said to Freemantle. 'And bring me and Tree Man here another fresh one apiece.'

The three men talked. Curtis learned that his host had started buying the land he owned here in parcels twenty years ago. The bulk of it had belonged, ironically, to the Forestry Commission. They had planned to cultivate conifers on it but had enjoyed such success with their planting in Snowdonia and the Scottish Highlands that the site had never been brought into productive use. There had never really been sufficient demand.

Ten years ago, when he finally owned the whole area that was originally covered by the forest he wanted to re-create, Abercrombie had everything on it ploughed under and then just left it to lie fallow for a full decade before embarking upon his scheme.

Curtis said, 'How do you know the size and shape of what was here a thousand years ago?'

'There are written accounts. There are illustrated maps. They contain place names. The places haven't moved. There's enough information to feed into a computer for fairly exact analysis. There are 3D software packages that can model to scale.'

'And computers are one of your strengths.'

'They are, Tree Man; it would be futile to deny it.'

'Raven Dip is kind of self-explanatory,' Curtis said. 'Ravens were common enough in medieval times.'

'If an omen of bad luck,' Freemantle said.

'And there's a depression there in the ground,' Curtis said. 'Gibbet Mourning intrigues me, though. It sounds positively ominous.' To Abercrombie, he said, 'Could you tell me about it?'

'I can do better than that, Tree Man,' Abercrombie said, squinting at the descending sun. There was still some light in the sky but it was diminishing at a stealthy creep. 'Sam here can treat you to the guided tour.'

'Now?'

'Sure.'

'It's going dark.'

'Be cool, Tree Man. It's ten minutes away, a stroll in the park. Sam knows the land like he knows his favourite lady of the night, every curve and hollow. The quads have headlights and you'll be back in time for dinner. Chill, baby, is my advice. Take the trip. Go with the flow.'

Curtis didn't know why he lacked the appetite to the extent he did for this excursion. He'd liked Abercrombie on meeting him and the initial impression hadn't really altered. A man investing the money he was, in the project he planned, had the right to learn what he could about his prospective project manager. It was disconcerting that he'd learned the personal stuff he had, but not sinister or offensive, given the circumstances. A lot was at stake.

And he was comfortable enough in Freemantle's company. The man was probably expert in half-a-dozen methods of killing an antagonist silently and unarmed. He was huge and oddly nimble in his movements. But he was intelligent and possessed a sly sense of humour and he'd been courteous so far to the point of genial. Curtis knew he didn't pose a threat to Freemantle; to the esteem in which Abercrombie obviously held his to-do guy on the ground, or to his position in the general scheme of things. He wasn't the enemy.

So what was it?

It was that stained-glass window in the tiny church. More specifically, it was the dripping trophy held by the knight who had despatched whatever the severed head had belonged to in life. It was grotesque and oddly real. Medieval artisans had been schooled in allegory, were well versed in the power of myth. But there was something about that giant, scaly head that looked authentically taken from life. It had spooked him.

They were about fifteen minutes away from the house when Freemantle signalled with a wave of his hand that they should stop and killed his engine. Here we go, Curtis thought, with a flutter of trepidation in his heart and his lovely daughter's face imprinted, smiling, on his mind.

They took off their helmets. Freemantle tossed his on to the ground, where it bounced silently and then lay still. Curtis cradled his own helmet in his lap. He hoped this pause in their progress would not be a long one. Gibbet Mourning awaited them and the darkness was gathering all around.

'He's dying,' Freemantle said. 'Cancer of the throat. Inoperable. He's been given eight months. He's a stubborn bastard and will probably stretch that out to a year, knowing him. But his number's up. He'd love to go out on something substantial. That's why you're here.'

'You're attached to him.'

'I'd take a bullet for him. He's full of shit, but then you get to know him, and I have. Fuck him around, Tom, and you'll have me to deal with. I can be nice. I can also be the opposite of nice.'

'I need the money.'

'I know.'

'I'm good.'

'I know. Saul thinks you're the best and I wouldn't argue.'

'And I'm Welsh.'

'Kind of Welsh,' Freemantle said. 'Welsh enough.'

'Anything else?'

'Keep away from the daughter. I watched her from the house doing her barmaid cameo earlier. She likes you. At least, she's intrigued. Why wouldn't she be? You're a good-looking young bloke and you've got that bruised thing going on some women find appealing. Steer clear, Tom, is my advice.'

'Well. Thanks for your advice.'

'Take it.'

Curtis put his helmet back on, fastened the chin strap and kicked the bike under him back into life.

There was little light left now and when he noticed the

object growing in size and solidity in the middle distance he thought it might be a farm beast, a horse or bullock lying in the wilderness on its side. When they got closer, he saw that it was both much bigger and less dense than a living creature. The object was the whorls and twists of a thorn bush, a vicious spread of pain waiting to inflict itself on anyone who got too close to it.

'We're here,' Freemantle said. 'Welcome to Gibbet Mourning.'

A wary dozen feet away from where its barbed tendrils reached out to him, Curtis studied the bush. He said, 'I thought the land had been ploughed under a decade ago?' Some of the branches were as thick as his fist. The thorns were curved and cruel, sharp, horny protrusions two or three inches long. He said, 'How did this thing get here?'

'You're the agricultural expert. You tell me.'

'Air-borne pollen,' Curtis said, sniffing the air, looking around at the dark spread of land. It stretched featureless in every direction.

'If you say so,' Freemantle said.

'Except that it looks like it's been here for a long time,' Curtis said. 'Nothing could grow to that size in a single decade, I don't think. Nothing indigenous, anyway. It looks mature.'

What it looked, he thought, was ancient. And malevolent. He shivered. He didn't think he liked Gibbet Mourning very much. There was something dismaying about the spot. Isolated places did sometimes feel desolate just after sunset, a feeling that was really just momentary grief in the person stranded in them for the light recently lost. It was probably a human instinct survived from prehistoric times, when primitive man was not confident when darkness fell that the sun would ever return.

But it was more than that. Something impended in the silence there, like an unresolved threat. And Curtis felt the self-consciousness of a man being watched. But the scrutiny he sensed did not come from Freemantle, who was looking, like he was, at the great, squat complication of the bush.

'Watch this,' Freemantle said. He took a few slow steps forward, towards the bristling thorns. And the bush at once began to rustle and shiver, its horny weaponry glimmering under the moonlight with movement. Freemantle pressed on. And the thick limbs of the bush trembled and stiffened with a sound weirdly similar to an intake of breath.

Freemantle stopped. He was close enough to touch the tips of the foremost thorns. But he didn't do that. He walked away from the bush, backwards, warily, until he was parallel with Curtis, where he stopped. When he spoke, his voice was low and had a confidential quality, as though he was afraid of being overheard.

'I was on a manoeuvre back in the day when the objective was to evade capture living rough. This was in rural Lincolnshire. I found some outbuildings on a derelict airfield and, beggars not being choosers, bedded down for the night in one of them, an old Nissen Hut. I was woken by weeping, Tom, and there was nobody there to do it. The sound was terrible, like agony stretching back from someone wretchedly dead. I fled the place, ended up sleeping in the rain in a dry drainage ditch under a stolen tarp, having put some serious miles between me and the weeping.

'I later learned the airfield was used by fighter pilots in the Battle of Britain. The Few?'

'Go on.'

'Average age nineteen. Average flying time before they clambered into a Spitfire cockpit on a combat mission, ten hours. Mortality rate at the height of the battle, sixty per cent.'

'Your point?'

'They were kids. They weren't ready for death. And I heard one of them lamenting his own short life, nearly seventy years after it was taken from him.'

'You think this place is haunted?'

'I think some places have trouble escaping their own past. I don't like it here. I don't much care for Raven Dip. I don't think you did, either.'

Curtis thought Freemantle had got that about right. He wasn't surprised, particularly, at the line taken by the man. Most old soldiers were superstitious and most of the ones that were, when encouraged, could tell a personal story or two to substantiate what they believed.

Gibbet Mourning was an uncomfortable place. The thorn bush was ugly and odd and its great size alone would make it seem sinister. But take to it with a flame-thrower and in twenty minutes there'd be nothing left but a large scorch mark on innocent ground. And anyway, the conversation Freemantle was steering him towards was not one he was prepared to have.

He didn't need spectral setbacks. He needed the money to be able to go to court and win the right to see his seven-year-old daughter. He needed this commission, which was of so high profile a nature it would make his name and propel him to the forefront of his esoteric profession. He would fulfil a dying man's dream in the process.

And hadn't Freemantle said that was what he wanted, too?

The bush bristled noisily across its entire substantial length and height, rattling and shifting in a sinuous way the wind could never accomplish. There was no wind. The fancy capered into his mind that it had heard him think about burning it and was bristling now in an ugly show of defiance.

'Come on,' he said to Freemantle. 'Let's go back. I'm done with Gibbet Mourning.'

Dinner was a relaxed affair after their quad bike jaunt. It was cooked by a pretty young oriental woman Abercrombie introduced as Jo. Judging by the number of dishes and the speed with which they were produced, Jo had some assistance in the kitchen. Either that or she was a magician. The food was fusion in character and the wines accompanying it expensive, and it occurred wryly to Curtis that he hadn't been asked whether he had any special dietary requirements because his host already knew the answer to that question.

They ate in a spacious dining room. It was stark and rather modern, the only suggestion of flamboyant wealth provided by the paintings hung on the walls. They were originals and some of them were very recognizable, even to someone as ignorant about art as Curtis considered himself.

Francesca joined them. She hadn't changed out of what she'd worn earlier, but she had put her hair up and her pearl earrings lustred bluely in her lobes when she moved her head on her elegant neck. The whole effect was pleasing enough to remind Curtis of the warning Freemantle had earlier given him. The bodyguard – except he was more than that – proved the point by eating with them too. And when Curtis dragged his eyes away from Francesca and looked at him across the table, he was treated to a glower he thought he probably deserved.

Saul Abercrombie entertained them until the meal was finished with episodes from his life. They were raucous tales of Jagger and Richards and Bonham and Plant and other members of the rock aristocracy from the debauched period of their pomp. Hollywood figured in Nicholson and Dunaway and De Niro, except he referred to everyone by their first names and you had to work out from the time frame and locations the person he was talking about.

It wasn't hard to do this. But it was scandalous and shocking stuff; at least to Curtis. He was entertained and genuinely amused but couldn't help wondering how often Freemantle had been forced to endure these boastful anecdotes. And Francesca must have grown up with it all. She would probably be able to recite her father's outrageous stories by heart.

When the coffee had been drunk, somehow, gently, they got on to the subject of his daughter.

'She's called Charlotte,' Curtis said.

Freemantle said, 'Are you one of those Fathers for Justice?'

'No. There are strategies other than protesting on top of a crane in a Superman suit.'

Francesca smiled at him when he said that and said, 'Come with me, Tom. There's something in my studio I want you to see.'

He followed her out of the dining room, Freemantle's eyes burning like twin lasers into his back in his mind. He followed her all the way to a door at the rear of the house and then into a separate building with a roof made entirely of glass.

'I paint using natural light,' she explained, switching on a row of fluorescents so that they could see in the darkness. Her work was figurative, he saw from the drawing half completed on her easel. It was a boy flying a kite on a beach and to Curtis it looked very accomplished. She began to flick through a pile of stretched canvases leaning against the far wall.

'Mostly I paint from photographs,' she said. 'The one I brought you here to see, I did from life.' She paused, then pulled out a smallish canvas, a picture about three feet high and two across in size. It was a portrait, the head and shoulders of a man, and if the hair had not been so long, Curtis would have been looking at a mirror image of himself.

'You don't recognize it?'

'It looks like me.'

She frowned. 'I understood you went there today. It's the knight from the window in the church at Raven Dip.'

'I'll take your word for that,' Curtis said. 'I didn't really scrutinize his features. I was paying more attention to the head he was holding in his fist.'

'You could be twins,' Francesca said. 'It struck me straight away. I'm amazed my father didn't comment on it.'

'Maybe he missed it.'

'Don't be fooled by the stoner vocabulary. He misses nothing. And it's an uncanny likeness.'

'Uncanny,' Curtis said, the word sounding as hollow as he suddenly felt.

TWO

Curtis spent the whole of the following morning busily engaged with his tests. The soil was as nutrient-rich as he'd expected it to be. Most of it, for most of its life in the millennium since the clearance of the original forest, had been wilderness. The land had not been worked to exhaustion under rotated crops.

It was rich in minerals and moist, a dark, loamy earth that would support the root systems of mature trees ideally. The cliffs, geologically, were a spine separating the sea from the land. A few metres inland from their granite bedrock the stone gave way to clay. And it was clay that lay under the thirty feet or so of soil covering the entirety of the area to be re-forested.

Even at the cliffs, the soil was six or seven feet deep a stride inland from the edge. Good enough for yew trees. The forest would flourish to their very brink, as it had, apparently, in ancient times, when he imaged one or two huntsmen chasing deer or boar perhaps, experiencing surprise as their last living emotion as they blundered upon the sheer drop down to the shore.

He'd have to brush up on his climbing skills. Recovery of the raw materials from the threatened places at the coastal areas he'd talked about meant abseiling and he hadn't abseiled in a few years. His head for heights was cool enough. The rest was just checking and re-checking your gear because most abseiling fatalities were caused by carelessness in failing to notice that pitons weren't securely hammered home or that ropes had frayed.

He surveyed the land from the seat of a quad bike, stopping occasionally, still somewhat numbed by the sheer scale of the enterprise envisioned by Saul Abercrombie. He began to calculate in his mind the manpower and machinery that would be required, the plant and the living quarters they would need to build and the logistics of recruiting and briefing and feeding the army of arboreal workers needed to transform a dream into something living and real.

It was ambitious and exciting. And it was lucrative. The previous evening Abercrombie had told him he wanted everything accomplished over a ten-week time frame. Three months at the outside, he said, joking that the extra fortnight was only available if they had to factor in some major catastrophe. Curtis' fee for this was £250,000. If he delivered on the nail he qualified for a bonus. It was considerably more money than he had managed to earn over the past five years of his working life.

His criss-cross route across the site brought him at one point in his progress close to Gibbet Mourning. He stopped and from the saddle of the bike saw that the great thorn bush possessed in daylight almost the same menace it had in darkness. It was squat and baleful and ugly. Its branches were almost implausibly thick and fibrous and there was something anthropomorphic about them in the sunshine. They seemed like strong and sinewy limbs twisted and contorted with the promise of the pain they could inflict.

He looked at the thorns. He noticed with a shudder that in daylight several of them had the corpses of birds impaled on them. They must have flown into the horny talons of that revolting growth over the course of the night. Their feathers fluttered as they lay skewered there, sparrows and thrushes and finches hung like bloodied trophies.

For some reason he remembered then Freemantle's joke of two mornings earlier about being up with the larks. A lot had changed since that phone conversation, but one thing hadn't: he still wouldn't know what a lark looked like. Maybe there was an example present in the gory tableau in front of him. But he didn't really feel like further studying the bush.

He decided he would visit Loxley's Cross. He calculated that it lay about four miles to the north-east of where he stood. He had seen Raven Dip and he had visited Gibbet Mourning and he wondered whether the third ancient location mapped on this wilderness would have the same sinister character of the other two. It didn't matter, really. In a few weeks these places would be obliterated forever as the forest returned to claim its place and restore the character of the land to how it had originally been.

There was a signpost when he got there. It was so stark and solitary an object in the surrounding grassy expanse that it possessed the character, to him, of some sort of man-made anomaly. It was made of cast iron and looked as though it dated from the early nineteenth century. It was painted black and its surface was pitted by time and weather. The places it pointed to were picked out on vanes placed at right angles to one another.

The first of the vanes pointed him back towards Gibbet Mourning. The second pointed coastward, towards some forgotten destination that had once been named Puller's Reach. Who or what a puller was, Curtis had no idea. He was a bit mystified by Loxley's Cross. It was enigmatic and so solitary and redundant it seemed almost surreal. It pointed to nowhere anyone might ever wish to go. But it was not sinister, which was something.

Looking at it, still and black and staunch, he wondered whether the function of the signpost at Loxley's Cross might actually be the opposite of what would generally be assumed. It might exist to warn the wary traveller against places they should not visit. He smiled to himself at that contrapuntal bit of reasoning. Then he looked at his watch. He was due back at the house for lunch at one o'clock. He had ample time. He would head for Puller's Reach and check personally on whatever it was the sign was warning people to avoid.

He was almost at the edge of the sea and had practically given up, was on the very brink of the land before he saw what he supposed must be the Reach. It was a construction. It was modest, but it was unarguably man-made.

Only a small cairn of stones marked the spot, at a place indistinguishable otherwise from anywhere else on the cliff top. It was very still, the sea was calm and it was almost noon when he got there. He dismounted and switched off the quad bike's engine, listening to the somnolent rhythm of the waves lapping eighty feet below on the beach as he studied the conical pile.

The cairn had been assembled from large pebbles. This careful work had been completed a long time ago. The quantity and age of the moss and lichen suggested decades. The stones were stained a deep, enduring green with what had grown over them in their enduring stillness there through the years. The whole construction was about a yard across at its base and reached to a flat pinnacle only a little higher than his waist.

The wind had got up, unless it was just that bit fresher anyway in the exposure of the cliff top, so close to the expanse of the open sea. It whistled through the cairn. Curtis listened. The sound crooned and insinuated, like some sly and secretive melody half reluctant to let you hear it. It was as though some spirit inhabited the stones and he was hearing it at play, making music partly to entertain itself, partly to signal the fact of its presence, invisible there.

Curtis tried to enjoy the boundless view out over the sea as the waste of water glittered and toiled. He searched the horizon for ships, but there were none. Ordinarily a view such as this one would have lifted him, the way endless vistas were apt to do to anyone, freeing them from the bondage of their daily concerns with the sight of something naturally exhilarating, timeless and in the truest sense, free. He inhaled the pure air.

But his mood did not lift. The whistle through the cairn had grown harsh and insistent. There was something restless and febrile about the sound. It scratched and mauled at the senses. And the air did not seem pure. It smelled sourly tainted, as though something had spoiled on the spot. He thought that it might be the moss on the stones. Then it occurred to him that some small mammal might have sickened and sheltered at the cairn's stone heart and perished there. He could smell its decomposition.

He decided he would attempt to descend the cliff to the beach. He would try to discover a route that could take him down without risk of falling and breaking his neck. The cliffs were not sheer. There were routes. They were goat-narrow but he was young and agile and he felt a compulsion to breathe clean air at the edge of the water. He wanted the smart of salt in his nostrils, suddenly, the prick of sea spray on the skin of his face.

Ten minutes later he was at the tide line. The smell of brine was strong and invigorating and the tumble of waves hissing into shingle an innocent sound that brought back, as it always did, a rush of tumbling childhood memories – each of them warm and innocent. He felt the strengthening sun on his face and was reminded that soon it would be April and the earth would surrender its spring life in tremulous buds reaching for light above the soil.

Then his eyes alighted on something else man-made. He saw a pattern imposed on the beach and not randomly, by nature. It was two parallel rows of pilings, the wood ancient and petrified, the planks of the landing stage they must once have secured at the spot long rotted away. He remembered the name on the sign he had seen pointing in this direction and thought that boats would be hauled ashore and that Puller's Reach was a more logical name for a landing stage on a shore than it was for a pile of whispering stones on a cliff top.

He was studying the pilings, engrossed in his study of them, when he experienced the sudden and unmistakeable sensation of being watched. It wasn't subtle this time, like it had been the previous evening at Gibbet Mourning with Sam Freemantle. It was almost overwhelming, so much so that he had no alternative but to turn around and look at the direction his senses strongly insisted this unwelcome scrutiny was coming from.

There was a figure above him at the cliff edge. It was a quite tall and slender man. He was attired in a belted tunic and leggings. He was not clad in armour as he was having slain his monster in the stained-glass depiction at Raven Dip. He was older and his hair was shorter and he wasn't armed. He was looking directly at Curtis with an expression that was impossible to read and Curtis had the giddy thought that if he lived to see the age of forty, this was what he would look like. The clothes would be different. Physically, the likeness would be exact.

He was looking at a ghost. Reason told him that. Reason dictated that conclusion to him and so did the gooseflesh crawling over his skin and the tingle of terror invading his scalp. The warmth of the sun was forgotten. His childhood memories were suddenly at a bleak remove. He stood stranded in a stark winter of fear and incomprehension for a moment and then the courage and nerve returned to him and he thought, *I'm being toyed with here. I'm the victim of an elaborate joke. There are no ghosts. It's broad daylight and that's a costumed actor up there.*

He ran for the path he had descended. He climbed, agile and furious, his heart hammering with effort and indignation until he reached the top.

There was no one there. The stones of the cairn were silent. All he could hear was his own heavy breathing and his own thumping heart until he heard the sound of an engine and saw a quad bike at the horizon to his left coming towards him. The rider was tall and long-limbed and riding out of the saddle, like someone galloping astride a racehorse might. The rider was too young to be Abercrombie, far too slight to be Freemantle. The bike was still half a mile away when Curtis realized its rider was Francesca.

'Did you follow me?'

She said, 'Don't flatter yourself. I've better things to do.'

'I think this place might be haunted.'

She shrugged. She was still astride the bike. She'd taken off her helmet and shaken out her hair with a toss of her head. It moved in wisps at its edges with what little wind there was. There wasn't enough now to summon any noise at all from the stones of the cairn. Looking at him, she said, 'Why did Charlotte's mother leave you?'

'I might have left her.'

'But you didn't.'

'I was unfaithful.'

'Habitually?'

'No. A brief affair, last summer. I should have told her.'

'Big mistake.'

'My big mistake was in cheating in the first place.'

'You've paid a high price.'

'Present tense. I'm still paying it. How did you find me?'

She held something up. It looked like a walkie-talkie receiver but was only the size of a mobile phone. 'The bikes all have tracking devices attached. It's only practical. Dad invites senior management to his places sometimes.'

'And they can bring their families and that means teenage sons and daughters. Teenagers have no sense.'

'Are you not curious as to why I've come to find you?'

'We'll ride back together,' he said. 'I'm sure you'll tell me on the way.'

'What did you mean just now? About this place being haunted?' She was putting her helmet back on. She looked unconcerned.

'I thought I saw my doppelgänger, right here, a minute before you arrived.'

'Don't they steal souls, in fairy stories?'

'I'm not sure what they do. This one scared me. It looked like the stained-glass guy. Do you know who he was?'

'Nobody does. Only that he was gentle.'

'He doesn't appear gentle in that window. He's just used a sword to sever a monster's head.'

She laughed, then said, 'Gentle in the medieval sense, which means of noble birth. He was a knight.'

'I knew that.'

'No, you didn't.'

Curtis grinned back at her. She had arrived at a good moment. He'd been rattled and relieved to see her. And he liked her. She was a reminder that women could be warm and funny as well as beautiful. It was something he'd forgotten.

Abercrombie had a set-piece planned for him. That was what she'd ridden out to warn him about. It was the planting of the first tree and it was to take place that same afternoon. There was something symbolic about it and there would be a little ceremony to follow, she said. They would celebrate with drinks afterwards. It would certainly require his staying on the site a second night.

'It makes no difference to me,' Curtis said. 'I'll be based here anyway for the work pretty much from now on. I'll be travelling to source, obviously, but I'll be on site the rest of the time until completion.'

'You don't have any other obligations?'

'You mean do I have a life? Not really. It's all on hold until I get access to Charlotte. There's a rented flat in Lambeth. There's a gym membership. There are a few acquaintances I meet up with now and then for a beer.'

'You sound like quite a solitary man.'

'Why did you think you needed to warn me about this afternoon? It's what I'm here for.'

'The ceremonial element,' she said. 'My dad can be a bit odd about trees. He had this mystical experience with them, this epiphany a few years ago. He was experiencing a big drugs come-down back in his partying days. He kind of came-to in a square in Soho. The sun was coming up. He was having a very bad moment, and credits the trees lining the square with saving his sanity.'

'I see.'

'I wanted to give you a heads up on how to behave if he gets all teary or starts quoting poetry when the tree is planted. Don't laugh at him. He'll be offended and you'll lose the job.'

Curtis thought this warning unnecessary. He liked Saul Abercrombie, who had earned the right to his eccentricity. He would not have laughed at him, he did not think. But he was flattered that Francesca had taken the trouble to caution him.

'Allen Ginsberg.'

'What?'

'The poetry, if your dad quoted it. I'd bet money.'

'You don't have any money, Tom.'

'What about you?'

'What do you mean?'

'I didn't think you'd be here. Whenever I've seen you in the papers you've been in some exotic part of the world.'

'That's because the photographers get sent to the exotic parts of the world to get their pictures,' she said. 'They want you on the beach at Rio or in a Monte Carlo cocktail bar, where you reinforce the celebrity myth. You're no good to the paps reversing out of a Waitrose car park in Pembroke. Who'd want to goggle over that?'

'You actually live here?'

She was silent before answering. When finally she did, her tone was sombre. 'My father has been given seven months to live,' she said. 'I'm here for the duration. I want to share as much time with Dad as he's got left.'

He thought it crass not to have realized that. Freemantle had told him the previous evening that Abercrombie's cancer was incurable. Freemantle, who would probably see them now arriving back together and draw entirely the wrong conclusion if he did.

'What type of tree does your dad have for me?'

'An English yew, the type used for the bows that won the English victories at Agincourt and Crécy.'

'The forest here was cleared hundreds of years before those battles were fought. And this is Wales.'

'Well,' she said, distracted, because they were almost there, 'I'm sure Welsh yew was used to carve Welsh bows to use in Welsh battles.'

'I'm sure it was.'

'In the time of your doppelgänger,' she said. In a time before recorded history, the era they called the Dark Ages, when myths were created that became legends. And Curtis had his first inkling that Francesca might know more about the noble subject of the portrait she had painted than she was letting on.

There was no sign of Freemantle. They joined Abercrombie for an open-air lunch. Curtis became aware for the first time of the telltale signs as Jo, the industrious cook, served them a tuna pasta salad: of how drawn and hollow-eyed his host looked in the glare of the spring sunshine, of how little he ate and the deliberate way each morsel of food he did manage was chewed and swallowed.

'Got a tree for you to plant, brother.'

'So this is the audition.'

'No. You got the gig. I told you that.'

'Then I'll be planting a hundred thousand trees.'

'Only one of those comes first. This is special, the breaking of the ground.'

'Have a particular spot in mind?'

'Should I?'

'No. Everywhere's good, Saul. The ground is so nutrient-rich you could probably grow giant red-woods here.'

'It's a mature yew tree. It's forty years old and comes from a copse in the Black Mountains. That's where this baby was born and raised. I thought the first planting should be Welsh.'

'I'd suggest beside the cairn at Puller's Reach,' Curtis said. 'We're going to have to work inland from the cliffs anyway, once the heavy diggers arrive. That seems like as good a spot as any.'

Abercrombie frowned. 'You're not thinking of destroying the cairn?'

'I'm not, but if it came to practicalities, why wouldn't I? You can't make an omelette without breaking eggs.'

'You're not engaged in cookery,' Francesca said. 'You'd be no competition for Jo. You're here to create a forest. I'm sure a forest can accommodate a pile of old pebbles.'

'Is there some significance to the stones?' He saw father and daughter exchange a swift glance at the question.

Francesca said, 'Nothing's written from the time that little monument was built. The stories pass down the generations. There's a saying about it to the effect that if you safeguard it, it will safeguard you.'

'Bad, bad karma, Tree Man,' Abercrombie said. 'You're bringing it on if you total the cairn, inviting heavy karmic retribution. And fate-wise, with this project, I'd say we need the breaks.'

'I'd no intention of destroying it,' Curtis said. 'I've as much respect for an ancient monument as anyone.' This was true, so far as it went. But what he was thinking was that they were wary of the cairn, maybe even scared of it. Perhaps they knew something they weren't sharing about the capering spirit that caused it to whistle and croon. It was his second such intuition in less than an hour.

Freemantle emerged from the house and marched over to them. *He's been for the tree*, Curtis thought. It was obvious from his determined stride and the clothing and industrial gloves he wore and the smirk of triumphalism spread across his face.

The yew was lashed to a low-loading trailer behind a Land Rover at the front of the house. Its foliage was an intense green rising from its gnarled trunk but its roots looked pale and somehow loathsome exposed to the light, more than anything like the trailing innards of a mortal creature.

'We need to get it into the ground as quickly as possible,' Curtis said.

Freemantle said, 'Where do you want it?'

'Puller's Reach.'

'There's another vehicle with a small digger on its trailer in one of the garages at the back of the house,' Abercrombie said. He rubbed the dry palms of his hands together. 'This is an auspicious moment,' he said.

It took just over two hours to get that first tree successfully into the ground, once they had reached the site. It was a small tree and rose to a modest height, no more than eight feet at its tip when it was firmly anchored in the willing earth. It looked much bigger, of course, because it stood so solitary in the surrounding flatness of the grass. Curtis planted it about thirty feet from the cairn, which it dwarfed in its size and vibrancy.

The cairn was a monument. The tree was a living thing, its leaves responding to the caress of the wind with a shiver there in the exposure of its new-found home. It wouldn't be alone for long, Curtis thought. But Abercrombie was right, wasn't he? It was the first and would always have that distinction.

The yew was positioned a dozen feet from the cliff edge. A person could walk around it without risking a fall. And Saul Abercrombie did this, six or seven times, pausing at the start or the conclusion of each circuit – for it was both – before striding around it again. There was a ceremonial or ritual character to this progress that made it seem much more dignified than ridiculous. It occurred to Curtis that the last thing he felt like doing was laughing at the man.

Freemantle opened a bottle of champagne and produced four flutes. Abercrombie raised a toast. It was four o'clock in the afternoon. Curtis took only a token sip of his drink. His mind was on the magnitude of his task. He was thinking about personnel he could recruit and plant equipment he could hire and trees he could source at short notice. He was wondering how much stuff he could delegate to Freemantle, a smart man with a substantial ego with whom he felt already he could very easily clash.

He'd had no alternative but to accept the job. The pay was going to enable and secure his future, legitimate access to his daughter. The ten-week time frame, though, was ridiculous. He knew it and suspected that his new employer did too. But when you'd been given seven months to live it was probably only human nature to try to accelerate the achievement of a life's ambition.

They'd do it before he died. If his condition didn't deteriorate and the prognosis proved correct, he'd live to see his forest realized. They might by then have to carry him on a stretcher through the permanent twilight of its leafy glades, but they'd do it. It wasn't a reversal of nature. That lonely yew looked firmly rooted, very much at home despite its isolation. They would collude with nature to restore something that should never have been taken from the land in the first place. Nature would be their ally and friend.

To Abercrombie, once the tycoon had completed his ceremonial laps of the yew, he said, 'Do you own this copse in the Black Mountains?'

'I've made some good buddies in the Kingdom of Wales.'

'With a view to buying trees?'

'It was probably at the back of my mind.'

'How many can you personally deliver?'

'I'd say at least a thousand, perhaps as many as twice that. It's nowhere near enough, Tree Man.'

'It's a start,' Curtis said. 'I'd suggest you get Sam on it right away.'

When they returned to the house he went back to the room he'd been given the previous night and switched on his laptop and began work in earnest, contacting potential suppliers, recruiting manpower, arranging plant hire.

He emailed Dora Straub, with whom he'd worked on a project in the German Black Forest two years earlier. She was engaged in academic research, attached to the Ecology Department at Hamburg University. He thought that she could probably arrange a short-notice sabbatical for work as challenging and interesting as this was likely to prove to be.

He phoned Pete Mariner and reached him, as expected, in the pub. Pete was totally focused on the job in hand when he was working and totally intent on spending what he'd earned when he wasn't. The fact that he was in a boozer in Tottenham was great news for the Pembrokeshire project, as far as Curtis was concerned.

He'd only just got Pete on board when Dora's emailed reply reached him. She was very interested, she said. She was ninety per cent sure she'd be able to do it and would let him know for certain in a couple of days.

He worked solidly for two hours, then answered a soft knocking on his door and discovered Jo outside it, carrying a tray with coffee and biscuits. She asked whether he would be joining them for dinner and he said he didn't think he would – he'd scavenge something from the kitchen later, if that was OK.

Francesca ate dinner with her father. His mobile rang as they were finishing and he retrieved it from a pocket and answered it with a frown. He didn't say anything, just listened and stared absently at one of the paintings on the wall opposite where he sat before grunting an acknowledgement and breaking the connection.

'Bad news?'

'Nothing to get hung about,' he said. 'Sam's in the comms room. Satellite's picked up a fog coming in. Dense, localized.'

Francesca put down her knife and fork to either side of her plate. 'Is this the start of it?'

He smiled at her. 'Is this the start of what?'

'Even if I was a believer,' she said, 'one tree wouldn't do it.'

'Sam says—'

'Sam,' Francesca said. 'You put a lot of store in a man you buddied up with in rehab, Dad. Sam's a coke-head.'

'Was, sweetheart. Past tense. And so was I, when I met him.'

'You should tell Tom Curtis.'

'That I met my do-do guy in rehab?'

'You know what I mean.'

'Sam thinks you have the hots for our tree man.'

'For Christ's sake. I only met him yesterday.'

'Honey, even I can see he's easy on the eye.'

'I think you ought to tell him. Not just because he's picturesque, either. He's obviously decent and conscientious. He deserves to be told.'

'He'll find out,' Abercrombie said, 'in the fullness of time, if there's anything to tell, if any of it turns out to be anything other than weird Celtic bullshit. You're not really sold on it, so what exactly would you tell him anyway?'

'I think this place affects people in strange ways. You hear and see things here that aren't real.'

Her father laughed. 'Hallucinations?'

'It's to do with scale and remoteness. It's a wilderness. All that space and isolation plays on the senses.'

'You're talking about creative people, wild imaginations, tuned to atmosphere in a way most people aren't. He won't be sensitive to the same vibes you are. You're a painter. He's a guy who plants trees. It's a practical skill. Artist versus artisan, honey.'

'Curtis thought he saw something down on the shore this morning. He thought he saw a man who looked like his twin, staring at him.'

'He seemed pretty chilled this afternoon.'

'The stare was hostile. He felt threatened.'

Her father shrugged.

'Who would you say it was?'

He didn't say anything for a long time. He put his fingers to his throat and stroked the place housing the tumour that would end his life when it erupted and he drowned in his own haemorrhaging blood. That was Francesca's thought and she could see her father read her mind, seeing it there.

'I'd say it was a ghost, baby,' he said. 'But you don't believe in those. Yet you'd still like me to share a bunch of myths about this place with Tom Curtis that risk freaking him out and scaring him away when he's planted only a single tree. Women are such contradictory creatures.'

'I don't actually think anything would scare him away,' Francesca said. 'Folklore certainly wouldn't do it.'

'Because he's brave?'

'Because he's desperate. He needs the money too badly. You know he does. It was one of the reasons you gave him the job.'

'He got the gig for a whole stack of reasons. But I do think it sort of cool that he's so broke. It makes him keen. God loves a trier and so do I.'

There was a knock at the door and Freemantle entered the room. He did so on silent feet. Francesca thought you didn't need to see or hear him to know who it was. You could smell his aftershave and sense his bulk and eagerness.

Without turning, Abercrombie said, 'What you got, Sam?'

'Cold spots are still registering low temps. Raven Dip's about five degrees below ambient, Loxley's Cross the same.'

'Puller's Reach?'

'Just the fog bank. It came in low and it's dense.'

'Well,' Abercrombie said, 'you want the sea, you gotta take the weather. Mother Nature's sometimes a bitch.' He stood, signalling that the meal and conversation were both over. 'That's the deal, people,' he said.

Francesca got up and walked past where Freemantle stood without a word or a look and went to her studio. Night was descending. She would work on the painting she was close to having completed for an hour and then have an early night. An early night still seemed a paradoxical thing in her father's company, a kind of contradiction in terms. He had lived all the way up, as the saying had it. But he was dying now, his strength depleted, and the nights were ending earlier all the time for him.

She could see the contradiction in the position she had taken over dinner with her father. She knew from her own experience that the place they were in evoked sensations in people that were unfamiliar and unnerving. At least, they did in her. She thought they did too in her father and in Freemantle, whom she suspected was thoroughly spooked by the whole domain.

She refused to accept the myths as the cause of these sensations. The stories were scary. But they were monstrous and outlandish and only an ignorant medieval mind convinced of a vindictive God and dark magic and a flat earth with an edge to fall off if you ventured too far could take them as anything other than gory folkloric metaphors. They were a thousand years old, the stories. They were impossibly remote from the real world.

Yet she wanted Curtis told about the mythic history of the place when it had been thickly forested. She wanted him told about the creatures abiding in its permanent twilight and the things legend insisted they had done.

Her father would have spotted this flaw in her reasoning. He hadn't pointed it out, as he would have in the old days. Instead, he had diverted her with some flattering guff about her distinguishing artistic status and heightened creativity. The cancer had mellowed him into this approach to verbal conflict. Where once there had been the ferocity of clashing wills, now there was gentle cajoling. It was just avoidance.

She felt nostalgic for one of the blood and thunder rows between them of the old days. But to have one of those would mean her dad was getting better and he wasn't and wasn't going to. Those dramatic conflicts were a part of their shared past. The curtain had been drawn on them. The theatre was dark.

She looked at the painting on the easel and sighed because she knew she couldn't paint. She had told Tom Curtis the truth when she had told him that she painted only in natural light. What she'd actually done, she realized, was taken refuge in the studio to get away from Sam Freemantle because she found it so difficult to tolerate sharing space with the man.

Curtis being around made things more endurable. It was one of the characteristics that she liked about him. But she knew that he was going back to London the following day to sort out his affairs before the start of the project proper. He'd be back before long. He was in his room now translating the challenge into practical terms and it was necessary. He was putting the wheels in motion and they were gigantic wheels that would turn slowly at first but gather unstoppable momentum really fast.

Francesca went over to the pile of canvases leant against the wall and fingered through their stacked edges until she came to the representation of the knight from the stained-glass window in the church at Raven Dip. When she got the opportunity, she resolved there and then that she would inform Curtis of his real identity. She would tell him who he was and what it was said that he had done. That much at least, he surely had the right to know.

Curtis worked till midnight. He wasn't disturbed again. He slept soundly but rose just after six thirty, fully alert, rested enough but strangely eager to see how the tree he had planted had fared through its first night on this remote and secretive domain. The sun was just creeping over the eastern horizon as he zipped on his jacket and fired up a quad and set off westward, chasing his own shadow, towards Puller's Reach and the edge of the new world he was now involved in creating.

Fog had rolled in off the sea. It lay opaque in a low bank in front of him. It was uniform in its density, the low sunlight unable to pick holes or fissures in it anywhere so that it gave the impression of being solid. It was unmoving, like it had settled there forever, obscuring the land, making a sudden, lurching trap of the cliff edge for anyone blundering into it.

Curtis didn't blunder. He ditched the bike before the fog bank enveloped him and felt his way into a grey and uniform universe that felt damp and cold on the skin and smelled intensely of the sea. It whitened the ground under his feet, the blades of grass dim and petrified. He held out his own hand and looked at it: the flesh was pale, corpse-like and indistinct, a memory summoned from a sinister dream, right there in front of him.

For no reason he could have rationalized, he began to feel a chill of foreboding. He told himself it was the silence imposed by the mist, which deadened sound, as mist is apt to. He told himself it was the chill and the fact that, unable to see what it was he might share the mist with, he felt suddenly vulnerable.

He progressed. And the world he knew retreated at his back. The fog seemed to thicken, slyly increasing in density. And the silence became more profound, deadening his tread over the earth and the noise of his breathing.

It seemed an eternity before he saw the tree. His sense of

direction had always been excellent and the fog had thrown him off only a few degrees so that he came first upon the dim green cluster of pebbles that was the cairn, before looking to his left and seeing the green cone of the tree, anaemic and still in its solitary spot on the cliff top.

The cairn made no sound. The stillness of the fog had silenced it, he thought, grateful to be spared its shrill and gleeful crooning. He tried to make out the sea, but there was nothing in the space where the land ceased but greyness. Fog filled the void with its dumb emptiness. The sight and the thought made him feel momentarily lonely. Then he went back to feeling the trepidation that had grown with every step taken towards his destination since he'd climbed off the bike.

It had got worse, hadn't it? He recalled the feeling he'd had after clambering down the cliff face to the beach. Such a climb would likely be fatal in these conditions, but he felt it again, didn't he? He felt scrutinized, watched. And he did not think the study friendly or even neutral. The watcher felt to him wholly like a powerful physical threat.

He eased through the pale blur of the yew's branches and felt the solidity of its trunk. He ran fingers over the wrinkles in the bark. The tree was substantial and secure, something real and solid in a world reduced by the fog to speculation and whatever menace it hid. He felt it in the raised hair and chill on his skin.

The cairn emitted a sound, then. It was sudden and short and sounded to Curtis' ears like a chuckle of laughter. He shivered, his hand recoiled from the rough surface of the tree he stood next to and he tried and failed to rationalize what his ears had just registered. He hadn't imagined it, had he? No, he hadn't. The spirit evoked by the cairn, the capering phantom it stood in stone tribute to had judged him and found him absurdly wanting. It had laughed at him; at his blindness and at the terror gripping him.

Something splashed below him on the shore, at the edge of the sea. It sounded large, whatever was doing the splashing. He heard a sort of sucking noise as something that sounded bulky and soft blindly gained the shore and clambered closer over the shingle.

Curtis sank to all fours and crawled the six feet to the brink of the cliff. He could see nothing below him when he reached it. There was that weird sucking sound and a rising smell of something so foul it made him retch and stung his nostrils. Then there was a scream and the scream was altogether inhuman, a wet wail too deep and savage to emanate from any human throat; too prolonged in the mournful outrage of its fury and pain.

The world went silent again. Curtis rolled on his back in frustration. He turned his head to his left and thought he saw the outline of the cairn, silent and innocent now, more clearly than he had before. The fog was lifting. When he turned back to the view from the cliff edge – where the view ought to be – he could make out white foam on anaemic pebbles where the waves broke below him. But as the view gained detail, there was no beast to see crawling, reeking from the sea.

The fog disappeared. The world clarified.

Freemantle did four sets of twenty bicep curls to end his workout in the gym. The gym was one of three rooms occupying the basement of the property the new guy hadn't been shown. It was the biggest of the three. The others were the comms room and the armoury.

He dropped his dumbbells to the rubber floor with a thud and decided on a couple of rounds on the heavy bag. It was an addition to his usual routine but he felt like throwing some leather. He pulled on a pair of bag gloves and did three rounds, shaking the 100lb bag with each heavy blow on the chain it hung from, the staccato thud of his punches echoing around the room.

When he finished and pulled off the gloves, he saw that friction had rubbed raw the skin from the two most prominent knuckles of his right fist. He should have wound bandages to prevent the friction from doing that but he hadn't. Hitting the bag had been a spontaneous urge. Wrapping bandages was a laborious task. The lost skin was an only slightly painful tribute to the weight of his shots.

The gym was there because Saul Abercrombie had not really believed the prognosis when his specialist had determined it.

Instead, he'd sought a second opinion that transpired to be just as bleak.

He still didn't believe it. Most people thought that doctors were somehow God-like. They had the power, didn't they, of life over death? Surgeons were especially God-like because in the operating theatre they presided over modern-day miracles.

But Saul, by contrast, didn't really buy any man's superiority over his own human capabilities. He had achieved staggering wealth. He had provided a workforce of thousands in a dozen different countries with their livelihoods. He had given millions away. To him a doctor was only a specialist in the same mechanical way a software designer or an actuary was. They had a set of professional credentials and a given area of expertise. There was nothing really awe-inspiring about them. They could as easily be right as wrong.

So before the disease really gripped, he had the gym built; as though exercise could counter a lifetime's contempt for routine physical exercise and heavy indulgence in bad habits. Of course, it hadn't worked.

But it was good news for Freemantle, who took his responsibilities to his employer very seriously, who liked to keep in shape and who believed very strongly in checks and balances. There wasn't a man born who didn't have a few bad habits. But you could counter the damage they were likely to cause unchecked by compensating for them with some good ones.

The gym was one of his good habits. It kept his cholesterol and blood pressure down and helped with his resting pulse. It made him physically strong and sharp and it countered the natural aggression that could sometimes cause him to act regrettably when someone chose to provoke him. He liked how his gym work made him look. He had been given a pretty good start genetically, but had built on that foundation over the years.

The comms room was necessary to the smooth running of Abercrombie Industries. Freemantle didn't know how Saul managed to juggle so many balls with the skill and enterprise he did. Even sick, he kept everything in the air. It would have a second use now, of course, that the planting was to begin.

They would get accurate meteorological information. Weather prediction was pretty crucial in so vast a challenge as planting a mature forest of the size they intended.

Some of the info the comms room provided was sort of freaky. Saul had taught him how to use the monitoring equipment and made it his task to take regular readings. He didn't really understand the motive for this. Nor did he understand the anomalies thrown up. Why were some parts of the estate persistently cold? Pockets of ground fog could reduce the temperature of low-lying spots, particularly at night. But while that wouldn't be exactly random, it would be more arbitrary than the puzzling consistency of the readings he got.

The fog bank, though, was a new one on him altogether. It had been like nothing he'd seen before in the weeks that they'd been here. And he hadn't seen the thorn bush move with quite the same barbed restlessness as it had when he had shown it to the tree guy. It had shifted in the past. It hadn't seethed. In a funny way, it seemed to him as though the place was preparing for something. It was a ludicrous thought, held up to the light. But it was also kind of unnerving.

The armoury was the smallest of the rooms in the basement of the house. It was little bigger than a walk-in cupboard. But it was well-stocked with rifles and shotguns and half-a-dozen automatic pistols of a very recent vintage.

Some of this ordnance was what a seasoned countryman might expect. Most isolated farms had a shotgun and rifle to hand. They were necessary tools and with the increase over recent years in violent theft from remote properties, it was only really common sense.

There was some heavy calibre stuff too though, that might have raised a rural eyebrow, lubed and gleaming on the armoury's racks. Freemantle considered this equally necessary. Saul was one of the wealthiest men in the Britain. That made him a potential target for kidnap. Kidnap gangs arrived heavily armed and in numbers and were not easily deterred from plans painstakingly put together. Freemantle was confident he could deter them if it came to it. He was vigilant and willing and with the hardware and ammo in the armoury room, his boss had provided him with the means.

People made assumptions based on appearance. He'd seen the assumptions the tree guy had made on meeting him and encouraged them with that bit of fiction about his 'manoeuvres' in Lincolnshire back in the day.

Lincolnshire hadn't been drill. It had been running. He had been a fugitive. He really had experienced that ghostly encounter taking refuge for the night in a Nissen hut on the abandoned airfield. He knew about weapons too. He had handled them often and used them to lethal effect. But his experience in their use had not been acquired in quite the way Tom Curtis would be likely now to assume.

He showered after his workout and changed. He sauntered into the comms room, switched on a screen, tapped coordinates into a keyboard and saw that the fog bank had all but lifted. He looked at his watch. It was 10 a.m. With no pressing duties till lunchtime, he decided he would spend a couple of hours oiling and cleaning the guns.

Francesca spent the early part of the morning in her studio. It was a much more productive period than her flustered visit of the previous evening. She cleaned oil paint off her fingers with turpentine at the end of it, thinking that two more sessions might see the picture she was working on completed. It was an inexact science. They were done only when they announced to you that they were done. But this one almost was now and she was pleased with it.

She joined her father for coffee on the terrace just after 10 a.m. and he had only just poured for her when they heard the buzz of Curtis returning from wherever he'd been aboard the quad bike.

'Went to check on his handiwork,' her father said.

'Into that fog bank?'

'Yeah, if the grey stuff was still with us this morning.'

'Oh, I think it probably was.'

'An experience,' he said.

'What you'd call a bad trip, Dad?'

He smiled at that. She knew that he liked it when she teased him but thought the joke a bit callous of her. She didn't think there was anything really dangerous out there to threaten Tom

Curtis. On the other hand, she would not have ventured into the fog herself. Not to the cliff top, by the cairn, where the yew tree was now planted. Certainly not alone.

He was getting closer to them. She couldn't make out his features clearly yet, but he looked pale. 'What if he's just experienced something that's really freaked him out? He did yesterday. He seems to be quite sensitive to atmosphere, for a guy who deals in practicalities.'

Her father shrugged. She couldn't see his eyes. They were hidden by his sunglasses. She suspected a bad night. He said, 'Curtis won't just quit and take off. Not the type. Anyway, Jo told me two hours ago that he wasn't in his room, after she knocked on his door with a breakfast tray. Gave me time to arrange something.'

'A little surprise for him?'

'An incentive for him to stay.'

He'd reached them. He got off the bike, took off his helmet and finger-combed his hair. Abercrombie gestured for him to join them. He unzipped his jacket, took it off and hung it across the back of his chair. Francesca poured him coffee. He smiled a thank you and raised the cup to his lips. She noticed a slight tremor in his hand. It could have been caused by the vibration of the bike, but she didn't think it was.

'How's our yew?'

'Lonely.'

'But healthy? Flourishing?'

Curtis paused before replying. He said, 'It looks like it belongs there. It looks at home.'

'No downside, Tree Man?'

'Not with the yew. I think you might have a wildlife issue, though.'

'No way,' Abercrombie said.

'Something large and feral.'

'A beastie? We're a long way from Bodmin Moor, brother.'

'I'd take the Beast of Bodmin over whatever it was I heard in the fog this morning.'

When her father next spoke it was in his real voice, the one underneath the hippie vernacular, the one Francesca remembered having heard maybe half-a-dozen times in her adult life.

The last time, it had been to break to her the news of her mother's death. And that had been five years ago.

'I'm dying, Tom. This project is important to me. It will very likely be the last thing I ever do.' He reached for his daughter's hand. 'Don't run out on us.'

'I'm going to London,' Curtis said. 'I'll be back tomorrow evening. I'm not running out on anyone, but when I get back, I'd like answers to some of the questions this place is posing.'

'You'll have them,' Abercrombie said, 'if I know them. Word of honour, you will.'

Curtis nodded and rose to go. To his retreating back, Abercrombie said, 'There's a little something in your room, Tree Man, in a bag on the bed. Let's call it a down payment.'

THREE

S he said, 'I'm surprised you haven't asked to see her yet. It's almost twenty minutes since you arrived.'

'She isn't here.'

'Your self-control is quite something. Don't you want to see your daughter?'

'She isn't here, Sarah. You wouldn't have agreed to see me if she was.'

'I probably would have, just not here. I would have insisted on neutral ground.'

'What do you think of my proposal?'

She looked at the open bag on the table between them, at the money it contained. It was so quiet in the sitting room of the home they used to share that Curtis could hear rain beat on the window almost one heavy drop at a time.

'Where do you think she is?'

He stood and went over to the window. What used to be his family were housed in a gated development. The view outside was sterile, rows of parked cars in identical drives, white paintwork and trim lawns and sycamore saplings in a tame row, everything wet. He said, 'It's half-term. I expect she's enjoying a sleepover somewhere with a friend. Not here, not a neighbour. You'll have put her a safe distance away.'

'How much is in the bag?'

'Nineteen thousand pounds. Walking around money, he calls it. I kept a thousand for the actual walking around. That's the balance.'

'What's he like?'

'You've heard of him?'

'Everyone has. He went to prison after that student protest in Red Lion Square. He was fashionably militant, back in the day. They tried to link him in court to the Red Brigades and the Baader-Meinhof Group. But it was the seventies, the days when police routinely fitted people up. He's certainly proven since he's no anti-capitalist.'

'What else?'

'What I just said. Conspicuous consumption is the phrase, isn't it? Drugs, hostess bars in south-east Asia, casinos, mansions, all the paraphernalia of being rich when you're not a family man.'

'He has a daughter.'

'So do lots of men. Paternity is different from parenting. It's just biology.'

'He's dying.'

'What are you doing for him, exactly?'

'It's a secret. I mean, I've signed a confidentiality agreement.'

She nodded, smiled slightly and looked at her perfectly shaped fingernails, which were lacquered a deep shade of red. 'It involves trees. If twenty grand is walking around money for his pet planter, it must involve some really esoteric and valuable trees, species that have to be stolen and smuggled. Or it involves a huge number of trees, planted on a vast scale somewhere. That second option would be my guess. This is Saul Abercrombie you're working for. He's spent his entire adult life empire building.'

From his position by the window, Tom Curtis looked back towards the woman with whom he used to share his life and tried to view her objectively. She was blonde and slender and, even though she was seated, the length of her legs suggested she was quite tall. She was dressed in engineer boots, Earl jeans and a white fitted shirt, and had a high-boned hauteur which the cool appraisal of her green eyes emphasized.

He couldn't do it. He couldn't see Sarah objectively at all. He could acknowledge that she was physically attractive and knew that she was successful at what she did. But she had the power to break his heart and she had used it in a way he thought both calculated and cruel, and in doing so had harmed their daughter. Charlotte was the most precious person to him in the world.

'What about my proposal?' he said again.

She smiled. Her smile was complex, not good-humoured or

accommodating, but a cold warning of what was to come. 'You can't buy access to your daughter.'

'I'll spend every penny he pays me on legal fees if I need to. Don't make me take that route, Sarah. It's so wasteful.'

'I won't be bribed, Tom.'

'This way we both benefit.'

'I won't be bought.'

He nodded. He would have to pass Charlotte's things on the coat rack at the foot of the stairs on the way out. Her school coat and her satchel hung there on a peg. He would inhale for a breath the sweet aroma of his daughter's hair and skin and, this close, not seeing her would be unbearable.

Sarah stood. She spread the fingers of her elegant hands to dust imaginary debris from where it might have gathered in her lap had they eaten anything. They hadn't. He was the debris. She was brushing him away. It had become a gesture she performed now every time they were obliged to meet. He thought that she was completely unaware of it.

'Charlie has written you a letter.'

He hated their daughter's name abbreviated. 'When did she do that?'

'She's been working on it for a week. She finished it yesterday. She's been quite stressed about it, actually.'

'Then let me see her. I'll put her mind at rest.'

'It's addressed and stamped in the envelope. You might as well take it, since you won't be in Lambeth to get it through the post.'

Outside, he walked through the rain for a while. He couldn't bring himself to read Charlotte's letter just yet. He needed to recover from his encounter with Sarah. He walked along the chestnut-lined path at the rear of the development that led to the river. Over to the right, through the dripping tree trunks, was the park in which he had played with his daughter on the infant rides in the years before she was old enough for school. He could see their shapes in bright pastels through the prevailing gloom.

He reached the river. The surface was stippled in places with the current and dimpled everywhere with rain. It was still quite early in the morning and the boat houses opposite were brick follies in lingering mist where the far bank reached down through grand sweeps of garden from great detached houses no more in this light than ghostly suggestions of stone. At the water's edge, willows bowed and wept. Kingston was a lovely place in which to live. The richer you were, the lovelier it became for you.

He would go back to his flat and pack what was necessary for a prolonged stay in Wales. He wouldn't need much. He wanted a couple of pairs of boots and his climbing cleats, abseil gear and some foul weather clothing.

He wanted too the bag of sea shells he had collected with Charlotte during their week in Swanage of the previous summer. She had presented them to him almost ceremonially at the end of their little holiday. He had come to regard them in the period since, despite the obvious evidence to the contrary, as his hoard of lucky charms.

Swanage had all the charm a coastal resort on the Dorset coast should properly possess. That's why he'd picked it. There was a tiny fairground and a crazy golf course on its pretty, banked promenade. There was a seafront museum. Fishermen caught crabs from its short wooden pier. Out over the shimmering July sea, the Needles announced the presence of the Isle of Wight in pillars rising as pale and distant as a mirage. Charlotte had built her sandcastles and collected her shells against their distant backdrop.

And there had been nothing at all sinister about it, he thought, staring now at the Thames in the rain, remembering his encounter of the previous day with whatever had lurked in the Welsh mist at the edge of Saul Abercrombie's ancient domain.

Wales wasn't England. It had a bloodier history in which oppression figured fairly large. But the seaside was a British tradition and there were Welsh Coastal towns sharing the wholesome charms that Swanage possessed in such happy abundance. They had whitewashed cottages, welcoming quayside pubs, lettered rock and shrimp fleets crewed by men with smiling, ruddy faces.

The Welsh Poet Dylan Thomas had written his verse masterpiece about just such a Welsh port. Curtis remembered studying *Under Milkwood* at school. Maybe it was people. You needed the presence of people to humanize a place, to give it compassion and humour and a soul.

It wasn't just that Abercrombie's Pembrokeshire tract was wilderness though, was it? There was more to it than its barrenness and the absence of a resident population. He had to admit to himself that it was genuinely sinister. He had the strong feeling it was, in some shiftless way, unsafe. And he had no choice but to go back there, if he was to gain the means to alter the awful domestic situation it was presently in his power to do nothing at all about.

Tom Curtis craved a friendly face and a bit of human warmth after his glacial encounter with the mother of his child. He decided he'd walk along the bank under Kingston Bridge and on the half mile or so to the Riverside Café. Customers would be few this early on such a rainy morning. He liked the café's proprietor and as he walked he hoped that he'd be the one doing the serving behind the counter, whistling as he always did when he worked.

After a cup of coffee, he'd walk on to Surbiton and take the fast train to Waterloo. It was a good idea to avoid Kingston Station, where he'd often stood with Charlotte on their way to her ballet class or Forest Club meetings, trips going back to the days when she still thought trains had the names he'd had to make up for her as they waited for theirs on the platform. He hadn't known until after the split the previous autumn that memories could bring pleasure and pain simultaneously.

John was there behind his counter with a greeting quite out of keeping with the grey, lightless morning. Curtis had often brought Charlotte to the café in the past, but John would be too tactful to mention his daughter unless he did. He was a man who fished and did a bit of bird watching during his downtime, and had a deep love and respect for nature. He wasn't pompous or precious about it; it was there in his smile when he saw a heron or kingfisher out over the water. He was fascinated by the mechanics and science of Curtis's craft and by the impact it could have on the character of the land.

Curtis was his only customer. The café's glass door and

walls were steamed with condensation, adding to the sense of seclusion in the building. Outside, the promenade was empty of pedestrians. Beyond the opaque glass the river swam brown and swollen with the rain that had been falling without pause since early the previous evening.

Bespoke cakes iced by hand were on display under Perspex domes. Most of the juices in their refrigerated cabinet racks were organic. The coffee was fairtrade. John knew his clientele.

'Working on anything much, Tom?'

And so Curtis told him about Pembrokeshire. He didn't name his employer, was vague about the location and only hinted at the scale of the project, but described something of the wilderness bordered by the sea which he had briefly explored and would work on there.

'I think I've only been to Wales once, to Anglesey as a kid,' John said. 'I was about seven. Don't remember it at all.'

'It's not much like England. It's remote, all a bit strange. It has its own character.'

John laughed. 'I don't know. One Butlins camp's much the same as another. Same climate, anyway. I remember it rained.'

'This place is completely wild. I think there might be some folklore attached to the region, or to particular spots there. I haven't gone into it. Not yet, anyway. I've only been on the job four days. But it's intriguing.'

John fixed himself a cappuccino and joined Curtis at his table. He picked two lumps of brown sugar from a small bowl heaped with them and stirred. He said, 'Couldn't help you with any of that. But I know a man who might be able to.'

Curtis smiled. John wasn't a creature of the Internet age. He was unaware that anyone with a laptop and broadband could access information about virtually anything just by tapping a couple of key words into Google. He wasn't stupid. He was just old school when it came to arcane knowledge. He was the sort who got on the butcher's bike he rode, pedalled off to a reference library and looked up his facts about fish and fowl in a book.

'Chap who comes in here mid-afternoon most weekdays,' he said, 'semi-retired professor. He does a bit of lecturing at

Kingston University and he's from here originally, but he was at Oxford when he worked full-time. He was chair of something.'

'Really? Chair of what?'

'Blowed if I can remember.'

'It might be geology, John. It might be astro-physics.'

'It's something to do with history, because he knows about paganism and Celtic myths, all that stuff.'

'How do you know he does?'

'You know how I know. I talk to my customers. I was talking to him only yesterday about Stonehenge.'

'Know much about Stonehenge?'

'I didn't. I do now. He certainly does.' John stood. 'Andrew Carrington,' he said.

'Professor Carrington to you,' Curtis said. He drained his cup.

'I've got his card behind the counter, Tom. Give him a ring.'

'I can't cold-call an elderly academic and then interrogate him because I'm curious about some remote Welsh wilderness.'

'Yes, you can. He likes talking. When I see him this afternoon, I'll tell him to expect you to call.'

It was how John operated. He made connections. To him, the world was a genial, intimate place without much decorum beyond a please and a thank you when you ordered your food at the counter. It had made his café a very popular place with its regular clientele.

Curtis tucked the card into his wallet, thinking it was an authority in family law he really needed to be recommended and not some elderly bloke inclined to bang on about Neolithic Britain. He hefted the bag, which was canvas and wet and quite heavy with the weight of the stacks of notes it held, secure in their rubber bands. He'd bank the money in Surbiton on his way to the station. It was just after half nine in the morning and the shops and offices on Victoria Street would be open for business now.

Two hours later he was about to leave his flat in Lambeth, having packed everything he thought he might need. Now he felt strong enough to read the letter from his daughter folded in his pocket. He took it, tore open the envelope and went and sat on his bed to read it.

Dear Daddy,

I hope you are happy and not sad like the last time I saw you when you cried but I had to write this letter, Daddy, because I am worried about you. I am worried because of the dream I keep having when you are being chased by the spooky trees and they don't catch you because you escape down the very steep hill to the beach.

The beach is not safe in the dream. It is dark on the pebbles and the sky is dark and there is a monster living there.

Do you remember last summer when we were all still living in the same house and Mummy went to China for a job and you took me to the seaside on our holidays? The beach there was full of pretty shells and we paddled and you made sandcastles and I trampled them down.

There was nothing scary. Except for the big crabs in buckets on the pier, which were a bit scary but not very.

In my dream, Daddy, everything is scary. The sea is red and has a disease and monsters live on the beach. And the trees are spooky and alive and they have crunchy voices like leaves when your feet swish through them but they say actual words.

Please, please stay away from the place in my dream, Daddy. Please promise me that you will.

With All My Love,
Charlotte

Dora Straub wasn't in Hamburg. She was on the Isle of Wight, booked into the Hamboro Hotel in Ventnor by a successful British film actor with a house in Bonchurch Village.

Dora thought Bonchurch very English in a Rupert Brooke sort of way. The film actor thought so too. He had endured a deprived English childhood on a slum estate in Manchester, and his charming old house with its spacious grounds in a twee village on Wight was his reward to himself for overcoming the setbacks of his impoverished youth.

Dora was there because of his oak trees. There were eight of them in his garden and they had been planted by the original occupant, a sea captain employed by the East India Company in the middle of the eighteenth century, not long after he'd had the house built.

One of the trees had been attacked by a fungal parasite. The actor's regular gardener had not seen anything like it before. He had not known whether the tree could be saved. He had not known about the risk of this fungus spreading to the oaks neighbouring the afflicted tree. He had said they needed a specialist and so they approached her.

The outcome was a happy one. They had summoned her in time. The fungus was virulent and spread rapidly but oaks were strong trees – stubborn survivors – and she had been able to eradicate the parasite without doing fatal damage to the host.

'How did you hear about me?'

'Robert, my gardener, read the profile piece in the *National Trust* magazine. After you did that work at Hampton Court?'

'Your gardener has a good memory for names.'

'More for faces, I'd have thought,' he said. 'There can't be many tree experts who look like you do.'

She left the compliment unremarked upon.

She was packed and ready to leave. She had the actor's gratitude and his cheque tucked into her wallet. But it was only ten in the morning and her flight from Portsmouth back to Hamburg didn't leave until eight that evening.

The actor had lent her a bicycle. He'd said that she should see Blackgang Chine. It was part of a coastal walk called the Tennyson Trail. In the event, she cycled the length of the coast road, past the Chine to her left and then Brightstone Forest to her right, all the way to Freshwater Bay, where she stopped at a beach-side café, bought a Diet Pepsi and smoked a cigarette, sipping her drink while she pondered the proposal she had received by email two days earlier from Tom Curtis.

Dora wanted to fuck Tom Curtis. She'd wanted to do that since first meeting him, four years earlier, when they'd worked together restoring an ancient apple orchard on the island of Jersey. The apples had been of a unique variety. The job had been successful. The orchard, after their intervention, flourished. But she hadn't fucked Tom because he had been in a relationship and, though she'd made it quite clear she wanted to, he'd made it equally clear that he didn't fool around.

Since then, she knew he had fooled around. And he'd been caught. And as a consequence, he was no longer in a relationship. He was single and available and even if that had not been the case, she thought the job he'd described in his email intriguing enough to become a part of. It was lucrative. It was ambitious and it was vastly bigger than anything she'd done before.

The climb up the coast road was steep to the cliffs before the descent into the bay, and hard pedalling had left Dora thirsty. She drank another Diet Pepsi and smoked a second cigarette then wandered down to the beach, thinking that the bike the actor had lent her would be perfectly safe in such a quaint little seaside spot, left unlocked against the painted railings outside the café.

She strolled, enjoying the spring sunshine, a solitary figure, slim and athletic-looking in shorts and a cotton sweater, alone because the season had not begun and there were no holidaymakers to crowd the beach as there would be when July and August came. She enjoyed the smell of the sea and the sound the shingle made crunching under her feet. She picked up a pebble absently and paused by the clear water filling a rock pool a few feet from where the waves broke.

She could arrange a sabbatical. She had just completed a paper and its publication would give her academic reputation fresh impetus even in her absence from the university. They encouraged her fieldwork and the project Curtis had described was prestigious in its scale and had impressive environmental integrity. She could monitor her students' work. Computers facilitated distance learning.

A crab danced across the rock bed of the pool. It looked weightless, its segmented limbs delicate and its shell still translucent with immaturity. Dora remembered the pebble in her hand. She opened her hand and looked at it. It was shiny and veined green against dark grey, about the size of a squash ball.

She held it poised above the pool, dropped it and watched it strike the crab squarely, then saw its shell crack and, as the water settled after the splash, saw the creature's blood rise through it, trailing and viscous.

Other crabs emerged all at once from under their ledges and leaves of sea cabbage, scenting the wound. And they tumbled through the water in their hurry to devour their damaged brother.

Or sister, Dora mused, watching the feeding frenzy with a slight smile. Did crabs have a gender? She wasn't sure. She was sure, now, that they were cannibalistic, but she'd suspected that already.

She turned her back on the rock pool and took her iPhone out of the pocket of her shorts. She would text her acceptance of the job Tom Curtis had offered her. She was quite tempted to phone him, for the pleasure of hearing his voice, knowing now that it belonged to a man ready to be courted and seduced. But that was a treat she would wait for. Anticipation was part of the thrill. And anyway, texting her decision was the modern way of doing things.

Sarah Bourne went to fetch Charlotte from her sleepover at eleven o'clock. She drove the two-mile distance in the rain. Her meeting with Tom had left her feeling more bruised and melancholy than she would have predicted. She had promised herself that she would never use Charlie as a pawn in any sort of game. She had promised him that she wouldn't, either. She was still able to convince herself that she hadn't done so, that her behaviour was reasonable, but it was an argument with flaws she was quite painfully aware of.

She had thought herself immune from pain. The theoretical possibility that bad things could happen – a terminal illness, a fatal car accident – was something she'd lived with in the same way everyone did. But she had taken care of her health and cherished her daughter, and built a successful career that had given her a degree of financial independence that meant nothing she couldn't handle was going to turn up as a nasty surprise unless she was really very unlucky indeed.

She'd been content with her lot – with their lot – until the phone call of the previous September arrived like a wrecking ball out of the blue.

Tom's affair was over by then. Spite prompted the call from the girl he had slept with and then, in her words, abandoned.

She wanted him punished. She calculated, correctly, that she could do the greatest harm to him by informing the woman he shared his life with in some detail about the specifics of the betrayal.

Sarah paused with her finger on the bell button outside the house in which her daughter had stayed the night. Charlie would be happy and oblivious, playing with Alice, her best friend from school. Alice's mother Jenny might be baking them fairy cakes. She shuddered at the memory of her autumnal caller; at the shrill insistence of the girl's voice and the relentless, unwelcome detail it had documented over the phone.

Jenny opened the door, one of those bright, attractive mums who were all Cath Kidston and Jo Malone, seemingly carefree and really very Kingston indeed. And the smile Sarah gave her seemed painted on as she thought about the suffering her broken heart was forcing her to inflict on Tom. Though 'forcing' was wrong, she knew, because it implied a lack of choice. And she was doing what she was doing quite deliberately.

She went inside. Charlie and Alice were in the dining room, drawing pictures on pads with coloured crayons at the large table there, under a window through which the rainy garden provided a grey spring light.

'Did you post my letter to Daddy?' Her daughter said this without looking up from what she was doing.

'I did post it, darling,' she said, thinking that it was her first lie of the day and, like most lies, would probably lead to more later.

'When will he get it?'

'Very soon, I should think.'

'Will he read it straight away?'

'I should think so, darling, if he knows it came from you.'

'Good.'

'Have you had a lovely time?'

'Yes.'

Charlie still hadn't looked at her mother. Sarah walked across to see what it was that was claiming her daughter's attention. Charlie could draw. She had drawn an armour-clad figure holding the dripping head of some decapitated beast. The beast was ugly and its eyes wore a pale, lifeless gaze.

'Lovely,' she said. She looked at Jenny, who was standing next to her with her head tilted and her eyes wide, staring as she was at the image on the pad.

'Nothing to do with me,' Jenny said. 'They went nowhere near the computer. They watched *Madagascar Three* before bed.'

'What's that you've drawn, darling?'

'Just a knight in shining armour.'

'What's he holding?'

'That's the monster. One of the monsters.'

'The knight looks like your dad.'

'A bit,' Charlie said.

Sarah studied the picture more closely. There was a cowled background figure she noticed, vaguely drawn. 'Who's the person in the hood?'

'She's not a person, mummy. She's the lady.'

'You can't see her very clearly.'

'She doesn't want to be seen at all.'

Sarah laughed. The laughter sounded fraudulent, even to her own ears. To Jenny, she said, 'My daughter has a lurid imagination.' She didn't know why she said it. She didn't for a moment believe it to be true.

For the second time, he read the piece in the day's *Telegraph* about the splitting into two of the ice field close to the peak of Mount Kilimanjaro. The split had been made inevitable by shrinkage. Global warming was to blame, evidently.

Andrew Carrington grimaced and swallowed beer. It would all be OK in the end, with this climate change thing, wouldn't it? They would build a few more of those useless wind turbines that blighted the English countryside in the simplistic belief that green energy could somehow tip the balance.

He folded the newspaper into four on his table. He grunted and shifted on his hip, fishing for change, and felt a flare of arthritis burn brightly through the joint. Sod it, he thought, he'd have another pint. It was not yet midday but they opened for a reason at eleven, and after a couple he'd nap and feel better when he took his four o'clock constitutional down to the promenade and a light bite of something at the Riverside Café.

He had no lectures to give and no seminars to take, and the day stretched forlorn and emptily before him. To make matters worse it was raining steadily from a sky that was uniformly grey. Would sunnier weather lift his mood? He thought it might. But the business with the Kilimanjaro ice field was depressing. It was a portent. It signified something serious that the world would blithely ignore. It would take more than a clear sky to raise his spirits today.

He decided against another pint. Instead he stood stiffly, nodded a farewell to the landlord and reached for his raincoat from the row of hooks by the door. He placed his hat on his head and went outside, nostalgic suddenly for his own past when pubs meant Oxford snugs where a man could converse with knowledgeable colleagues and fill a leisurely pipe and enjoy smoking it without breaking a ridiculous law.

Through the rain, on the other side of the road, he recognized one of his students hurrying along in a parka, a watch-cap pulled down to protect his elaborately-razored hair from the rain.

One of his ridiculous students, he thought, nostalgic again, this time for the old days when higher education wasn't a universal right imposed by the government to massage down youth unemployment figures. As recently as the eighties you had to be clever to qualify for a university place. The dullard over the road was living proof that this was no longer the case.

Professor Carrington limped and laboured up Kingston Hill towards his home. He wondered whether the trap he had set in the garden would present him with a captive. If he was lucky it would deliver a song bird. He hoped for something small and exquisite, something brightly feathered and febrile with anxious life. Twice now, squirrels had forced their inquisitive way into his clever mesh labyrinth. One had been young and manageable. But the other had been mature and strong and he had been obliged to free it.

He reached his home and unlatched the back gate. A finch resolved itself from a bright blue flutter into a living creature as he progressed through his dripping avenue of cypress trees towards the rear of his garden. The bird had evidently exhausted itself in its efforts to escape confinement. It did not attempt to take flight on his approach. Its wings vibrated only feebly in what he assumed was a reflex conditioned by fear.

He did not approach the captive straight away. Instead he went to the small shed concealed by bushes in the far corner of the garden, opened its door and went inside, closing the door behind him. A copper dish had been placed on a table in there. There were candles in ornate holders to either side of the dish and Carrington took a brass cigarette lighter from his pocket and lit the wicks of both with a few muttered phrases nobody listening would have been able to make out.

The dish contained tufts of hair, nail-parings and dried semen. These human traces had all been derived from his own body. He went out again, careful that the gust of damp air from outside did not extinguish his candles. He leant into his trap and gathered the bird in a manner made confident by frequent practice, folding its wings firmly in the grip of his left fist.

He went back into the shed, took a pair of secateurs from a hook on the wall, snipped off the head of the bird and muttered some more words as he squeezed the blood from its convulsing body on to the heaped detritus of the dish.

The blood was very bright. He supposed it was thus because the bird was young, its fresh blood dripping on to the seedy relics of his own care-worn existence. He belched and smelled beer drift sourly on his breath. He took the bird's head from where it had dropped on to the table in a smear of gore and placed it in the dish. Its eyes wore a startled look in death.

He had not yet removed his hat. Nor had he taken off his coat. Now he did so, hanging both on the hook from which he had taken the secateurs. He opened a drawer under the table and took out a bulb of lighter fluid, pinched off the teat and sprinkled the fluid over the stuff in the dish. He bowed his head and said a few more words, then used one of the candles to ignite what he had prepared. It flared into brief and pungent life. Feathers crackled and the bird's eyes hissed and popped.

You honoured the old gods. It was all very simple. Events like that taking place on the high slopes of Kilimanjaro, calamitous events, did not happen by accident. They were both a punishment and an admonition. Mankind had grown arrogant and careless and would likely pay the heaviest possible price.

Yes, you honoured the old gods. They had known that in the ancient world. Even when the sum of human knowledge had been compiled in the library at Alexandria, when the answers to every possible question had been within the reach of the scholars there, they had remembered in ancient times the oldest and most universal rule: if you wish to survive and prosper, you honour the gods. They demand it.

His sacrifice was a tiny gesture in the scheme of things. But the ritual was enacted every seven days and he never neglected to perform it with due deference and solemnity. He celebrated and, most importantly, he believed.

Modern piety concerned itself with the happy-clappy Christian God of the New Testament. If people believed at all, they tended to believe in the touchy-feely compassion and kindness of Christ.

The older gods were not so accommodating. They bore grudges. They had long memories. They were unforgiving and gleeful in their mischief. They were vain and spiteful and merciless, and it was Andrew Carrington's considered judgement that you ignored them at your peril. It was an article of faith he kept to himself. But it was one he was convinced, during the course of his academic life, had been conclusively proven to him.

She was lying next to him in her narrow student bed and she was smoking. It was her first cigarette of the morning, but the air in the confined space of her college room seemed still hazy and grey from those she'd smoked the previous night. He had enjoyed their evening out. He had enjoyed the sex, when it eventually came. She was good at it and enthusiastic too. It had been work, but he was someone who took pride in doing his job thoroughly.

Things were somewhat different the morning after the night before. Left to his own devices, he'd have been literally up and running by now, pounding the pavement with a heart-rate monitor strapped to his chest. Instead he was lying next to his pale, slightly sinewy and really rather pretty one-night-stand while she smoked and he wondered why the university didn't insist on proper smoke alarms. He ran his tongue around his teeth, doing a dental autopsy of stale booze.

'Will I see you again?'

She shrugged her slight shoulders and tapped ash into the ashtray on the bedside table next to her. She didn't look at him. 'If you want.'

'You're not involved with anyone?'

'Answered that question last night, Paul. More than once, actually.'

He wasn't actually called Paul. His name was David Baxter; he was twenty-seven years old and a private detective. But he had a youthful face and a body he took scrupulous care of. To her he was Paul, a graphics student from Richmond, and that was all she was going to get.

'Really fucked you up, didn't he? That guy you were involved with?'

'I don't like that phrase – makes it all sound like some sort of business arrangement. It wasn't. Not for me, anyway. I fell for him. He turned out to be the wrong guy to fall for, but that's how it was.'

'Was it the age difference?'

'I don't really want to talk about it. Not to a stranger.'

'Thanks.'

'Sorry. You know what I mean.'

'I don't think I do, Isobel.'

She sighed, puckered her pretty mouth around the filter of her cigarette and dragged harshly on it, exhaling in an explosion of pale grey against the grey haze she'd already created. She said, 'It was nothing to do with age. He led me on. He used me. He was living with someone and they had a daughter. It was happy families.'

'It couldn't have been. He wouldn't have slept with you if it was.'

She chuckled. The sound was un-amused. 'Whatever. He used me and then dumped me. But I got my own back. All

came as a complete shock to that smug bitch he was living
with.'

Paul, who was really David, had painstakingly researched
his case before his encounter with Isobel. He knew that Tom
Curtis and Sarah Bourne had lived as good as man and wife.
They'd had a daughter, Charlotte, seven years prior to their
splitting up last autumn. The girl lying next to him had
engineered the break-up.

That much was clear cut. But nothing else was. He considered himself a fair judge of character, but couldn't really
understand why Curtis had strayed. He'd followed Sarah a
few times when she'd taken her daughter and later picked her
up from school. She was an exceptionally good-looking
woman. She was successful and sophisticated, with an elan
the girl lying next to him would never possess. Why had
Curtis risked losing that? What had prompted the betrayal?

Maybe it was as simple as the sex. Isobel Jenks was young
and fit and hot in the sack. Variety was the spice of life and
some men thought only with their dicks in moments of impulse
or weakness. His profession reminded him of that almost on
a daily basis.

'He taught a course?'

'It was a summer school thing, a residency in ecology in a
protected area of Scottish woodland. He lectured in the morning
and there was fieldwork in the afternoon. It was all really idyllic
– picnics in the gloaming, country pubs with babbling brooks
outside them and folk music inside when it got dark. All that
stuff was going on. He was nice and good-looking and I thought
he was lonely.'

'Really?'

'That was his thing, the loneliness. That was how he hit on
me, though obviously I didn't realize that at the time.' She
lifted herself from the waist and screwed the butt of her
cigarette into the ashtray beside her, exposing the pink nipple
of one of her small breasts as the duvet ruched down. Baxter
felt a pang of arousal in his groin.

'Why are you so interested?'

'I'm interested in you.' It wasn't a total lie.

'Holiday romance,' she said. 'To him, anyway, though I

only realized that in hindsight. I thought it was the real deal.
I thought Tom Curtis was the real deal. More fool me, eh?'

'He never contacted you, even after you phoned his wife?'

'She wasn't his wife.'

'As good as, by the sound of things.'

'If she'd been his wife, he'd have been an adulterer.'

'No argument there.'

'Why are you interested in this stuff?'

'I've already said, Isobel. I'm interested in you.'

'No, by the way. I've never heard from him again and don't
expect to.'

His brief had been to check out Tom Curtis, which he'd
done pretty thoroughly. He'd already filed a detailed report.
Curtis was one of the best in the world at what he did. He
had an international reputation that would probably justify the
term renowned. But it was an esoteric line of employment and
it had not made him rich or even comfortably well-off.

In career terms, his former partner and the mother of his
child was much more successful. She was one of the busiest
and best paid make-up artists in the world. Her working life
comprised fashion shoots and movie junkets and seriously
well-paid advertising campaigns. Her exclusive contract with
the cosmetics company she promoted alone brought in sixty
grand a year.

They had met at art school. They had both been on the
painting course. Baxter had invented a pretext for visiting
Charlotte's school and had seen her illustrations on her class-
room wall and so knew that she had inherited the talent to
draw from one or both of her parents.

There was no man in Sarah Bourne's life. She balanced work
and motherhood successfully. She drove a nice car and wore
fashionable clothes. She exercised at the gym a lot and generally took care of her appearance. Baxter had concluded that
this was more to do with image than vanity. She had no choice
but to be an advert for what she did. People would judge her
skills on her appearance. It was a prejudice that went with the
territory. She seemed comfortable enough with it.

Curtis struck him as more enigmatic. He clearly doted on
the daughter he was not currently permitted to see. He took

work that was nomadic by its nature. He gave guest lectures and ran courses like the one that had facilitated his disastrous liaison with Isobel Jenks. But his engagement with the world seemed a bit half-hearted. There was something remote about him, as though he was almost a figure out of his time.

That was a fanciful way of looking at it. But Baxter trusted his ability to read character and had been unable to pull Tom Curtis, despite this, into the clear sort of focus in which people could be properly scrutinized. It was a puzzle. He was a puzzle.

Probably it was just his profession. Forests were still and silent places – weren't they? – built by nature for seclusion. There was a sense in which they harboured shade and secrecy. Even a copse of trees was cover, a place of concealment. There was little older or more steadfast in nature than a tree.

The way people went about their work gave you clues as to their characters. Some men were aggressive deal makers. Some were methodical. Some were showy and spectacular in their office dress and accoutrements or habitually fast at the wheel of their company cars.

The physical nature of what Tom Curtis did had endowed him with an enviable physique. Otherwise his work offered few clues about him. But then planting trees seemed less like a job to Baxter than some sort of ancient, arduous ritual.

In the bed next to him, Isobel said something he only half-heard.

'What?'

'I said he should have been more grateful.'

'Why?'

'The first time we went to bed? He didn't exactly seduce me over a candlelit dinner.'

'Go on.'

She sat up, squirming free of the duvet, her breasts pertly revealed, her skin sallow and her shoulders slight. He could see the dark roots in the smoke-bleared light showing against the scalp under her bleached crop.

'I couldn't sleep, one night. I went for a walk in the woods. It wasn't dangerous. It never goes fully dark in the Scottish highlands in summer. You might come across a fox or an owl, but there's nothing there that preys on humans.

'I came across Curtis, naked, seated cross-legged in a clearing on the forest floor. His eyes were open but he must have been dreaming, must have sleep-walked his way there. He was listening intently. Had that attitude, anyway – kept nodding his head. Except that nothing was being said to him because there was no one there to say it.'

'What did you do?'

'I sort of hauled him to his feet and guided him back. He came to, kind of, on the route back to the huts we were staying in.'

'Why did you think he should be grateful?'

'It was high summer, like I said. But it was so bloody cold at the spot where I found him I could see my breath. There was hoar frost on the ground. He wasn't wearing any clothes. I think if I hadn't found him there he'd have died there of hypothermia.'

'And so you seduced him, after you wrapped him in a blanket and made him a mug of cocoa.'

'No. I didn't. We got into bed and he fucked me. He fucked me like a man possessed. Since you seem so interested, that was how it began.'

FOUR

Saul Abercrombie sat and stared at the stained-glass depiction above him from the interior of the church at Raven Dip. It was overcast outside, still relatively early on a day that had broken dankly. He had trailed a path through dew on the quad on the route there. But for the noise of the engine, he had travelled in silence.

He sat on a shooting stick, its point precisely wedged at a spot where stone flags intersected on the floor, his increasingly skinny butt secure in its small saddle. He had a picnic blanket wrapped around his shoulders against the chill. The church interior was always cold, even when the sun shone outside and bathed the building in light and warmth, as it seemed unlikely to do today.

The shooting stick was a memento of sorts, a relic from the short season of trying to blast clay pigeons from the sky of a decade earlier. It had been one of the many pursuits he had tried and failed to enjoy successfully in the company of his dead wife. There had been power boating and an attempt at riding to hounds most notable for what he still thought of as the fancy dress. There had been a box for the ballet at Covent Garden.

The blanket was a happier reminder. They had enjoyed picnicking together. He had owned for a while a mill house in Cambridgeshire and he had chilled wine from a net moored for the purpose on the bank where the River Cam wound its way through the property. They had eaten and drunk and listened to an old solid state Roberts radio tuned to a station that stuck rigidly to its playlist of soul classics. Sly and the Family Stone had provided their soundtrack, Marvin Gaye and Roberta Flack and the Isley Brothers.

'What's goin' on?' Saul crooned to himself. He pulled the blanket around him, staring still at the stained-glass image. It was a good question. It was one he would be obliged to answer in part, but only in part, when Tom Curtis returned to them later in the day. He had promised. He had given his word of honour to the man entrusted to deliver on his forest dream. 'Brother, brother, brother,' he said, now, to nobody in the empty church.

How often had he and Susan done that? How many times had they sipped river-chilled Chablis, listening to Marvin while the Cam gurgled by and the evening gathered securely around them? In his mind they had done it in an endless cycle of idyllic summer nights. In actuality, they had probably done it on no more than half-a-dozen precious occasions.

Those picnics had made his wife happy. But making her happy had been a long way behind making money in his list of priorities and most of the time she had spent at the mill house had been endured by her alone, he being on trips and their only child away at boarding school.

His business life had been one long litany of money-shots, no-brainers, done deals and fire sales and ball-breakers. He'd been so fluent in the language of boardroom machismo he'd forgotten how to communicate in any other way. Profit subsumed everything. Claret on the carpet, suppliers manacled by contract clauses, partners in enterprise permanently yoked to a junior role. Everywhere he looked he was looking only for the bottom line of a balance sheet.

It had taken the cancer to stop that.

First had come the ominous suspicion that something was wrong with his throat. He'd had trouble swallowing. His tongue had felt numb. His mouth no longer told him accurately whether a drink was hot or cold. The timbre of his voice changed. It roughened. There was a sense in which his speech came to feel somehow blurred. And he was tired. For the first time in his life, he felt bone-weary and the weariness was constant.

He'd had an operation almost as soon as the diagnosis was confirmed, in New York eleven months ago. That had been kept secret from everyone. No one knew; not Francesca and certainly no one who worked for him. It was an absence of only a couple of days from his email and Twitter accounts. His retreats, his stints in rehab and his trips to remote places were so much a feature of his life that no one thought to become suspicious.

The surgery was a success. They got the whole of the growth out of him, every cancerous cell. Six months later came the all-clear. And then in February the symptoms started to re-establish themselves and he was soberly told that this time surgery was not an option. There was nowhere left to cut. Another invasive procedure would kill him. Chemo was a balance between the time it bought you and the havoc it wreaked on the quality of your remaining life. His prognosis was bleak, his case hopeless and his prospects terminal.

Saul swallowed with effort, gathered his blanket around him and thought about the picture he looked at – the narrative of it, the guy in the steel suit who had come out on top in the rumble with the creature his broadsword had decapitated. Recently decapitated, the gore still dripped from the creature's severed neck. The blow hadn't been delivered in death to secure a trophy. It had been the fatal last act of the fight.

How accurate was the depiction? Saul thought that in all the important particulars it was probably truthful enough. The guy wouldn't have been dressed like that, though. The guy detailed in stained glass looked like one of Arthur's Round Table dudes in a picture by Millais or Holman-Hunt. Saul was familiar with the style because he owned a bunch of those paintings himself. The courtly medieval world of the Pre-Raphaelite school was romantic and seductive. In this particular instance, chronology made it no more than a glamorous lie.

Warriors had dressed like the stained-glass dude in the time of the window's creation and the artisan who made it had figured on rendering what he knew from life. The real event had taken place 300 years earlier, and though the human protagonist had certainly been of noble birth and martial inclination, he would have been dressed differently. Saul figured animal skins and jewelled broaches and probably more facial hair than on a self-respecting member of the Grateful Dead.

No chivalric code to observe, that far back in history. No notion of courtly love. That came later with the French, their

manners and their madrigals and wimpled damsels prone to
bouts of distress. This guy had been different from all that.
No grail quest to distract him from his mission. That was for
damn sure.

Armed differently too, probably, Saul figured. He thought
a round wooden shield and maybe a double-bladed battleaxe
rather than a sword. The guy would have been expert in the
use of arms, lethal in combat and colossally strong. He'd
have been completely determined. And he'd have been quite
unbelievably fucking courageous.

He'd been hand-picked, obviously. But the guy had known
what he was up against, hadn't he? He'd have heard the stories
from the cradle. He'd been an inhabitant of a different universe,
one in which the few certainties were absolute and much was
quite simply unknowable. You steered clear of the edge of the
world and you kept the darkness at bay unless it was deemed
your duty, as it had been his, to deliberately venture into it.

Duty was probably wrong. Calling was more like it and the
word he would have used in his lost language would probably
most have resembled destiny among modern English words
in meaning.

Brother, brother, brother, Saul mused. His phone beeped in
his pocket. Probably Sam trying to find out where he was and
what he was up to. Sam hadn't had his Saul fix that morning
and it was his employer's belief that he had become as addicted
to the presence of his boss as he'd once been to cocaine.

What's Wrong With This Picture? That was nothing to do
with Marvin or Aretha or even the Dead, was it? It was the
title of an album by Van the Man. It wasn't a Van Morrison
classic up there with *Astral Weeks* or *Moondance*; it was a
run-of-the-mill collection, a motley assemblage of songs and
was not what had prompted Saul Abercrombie, still staring at
stained glass, to ask the rhetorical question anyway.

What had prompted it was the resemblance between the
warrior in the depiction embedded up there in the wall and
his tree man, Tom Curtis. It wasn't just passing. You wouldn't
really do it justice by describing it as strong. Uncanny was
what it was and because he didn't really believe in coincidence,
despite the warmth of his picnic blanket and the intimate

summer memories it evoked, he shivered and felt goose-flesh momentarily coarsen his skin.

Curtis was Welsh. The guy rendered up there in stained glass hadn't been. He'd come from the West of England, from Cornwall, which had been a Celtic kingdom once with its own tongue. But he'd been an English speaker, or so the place names in what was now the Abercrombie domain suggested.

He'd come in answer to a magician's plea and the land had been his reward for what he'd accomplished once he got there. What spells and brews concocted in cauldrons had failed to do he'd done with his sword or, more likely, Saul reminded himself, the whetted edge of his battleaxe. That was the legend. That was what Curtis would be told. But he wouldn't be told the whole of it.

Saul chuckled, a choked sound from his afflicted throat in the stony acoustics of the space surrounding him. He had amused himself, momentarily, with the thought of how Curtis would react if he told him the whole of it. He knew himself to be desperate. He thought that if he confided all he hoped for from what he intended to have done there, his tree man would consider him not just desperate but clinically insane.

Pete Mariner raised the unsteady hand containing his glass in a wobbly toast to good fortune. The stuff filling the glass was cider made exclusively from apples gathered from an orchard on Jersey that owed its continuing existence to the expertise of his friends and sometimes colleagues, Tom Curtis and Dora Straub.

It was only eleven o'clock in the morning. But Pete had woken far from sober at ten after the herculean bender of the previous day and had needed to defer the inevitable hangover because, just then, he didn't think he possessed the fortitude to face it.

He would sober up. He would have to, wouldn't he? He had a living to earn and a job in prospect that was a professional challenge to equal anything he'd ever accomplished in his entire adult life. The respect of Tom Curtis – the approval of Tom Curtis – was a quality intrinsic to his own self-respect when it came to what he earned his living doing.

And there was Dora. Ah, yes, there was Dora, Pete thought, gagging as his system rebelled against the toxic assault of mature cider drunk so early in the day, and he was obliged to swallow back puke just to show it who was boss.

He was in love with Dora. He thought that he might even be hopelessly in love with her, but that seemed to be an unduly pessimistic analysis as drunk as he was. He was tipsily buoyant, so he wouldn't have it that the love was hopeless until the cold light of sobriety forced him to confront that stark prospect.

Right now, he thought his prospects really rather fine. The deal Tom had offered him was generous. The job sounded not just challenging but in some almost mythic capacity, fabulous. It would present him with the close proximity of Dora in a way no one could possibly interpret as creepy or perverse. And events would have the opportunity to take whatever course they would consequently. What could possibly go wrong?

Pete took another celebratory chug of cider. This time the swallow reflex didn't work its previous magic and he barfed about eight hours' worth of stale booze out over his living-room carpet. He thought he heard it fizz as it settled into the worn pile, but realized that was probably just his ears singing with relieved pressure after lightening his body's poisonous load.

He knew his limitations. He knew them really well because he had tested them so often. The problem was that he had no respect for them. And they, frankly, had no respect for him.

It took him an hour with a towel, a bucket of hot water and the best part of a bottle of Dettol to clear up the mess and, when he'd done so, he could still smell a faint sour residue under the disinfectant.

But the energy and focus required by this distasteful task sobered him somewhat, as did confronting the pretty squalid nature of his domestic crime. There was the lad-mag lifestyle of carefree hedonism he was a good decade and a half too old for. And there was the slippery slope that led to a bed on a public ward and a sign around your neck saying Nil by Mouth.

It was just after noon when he slid back into bed. His bed had not even grown completely cold from its earlier occupation. He closed his eyes and mercifully the dark world doing so invited did not spin giddily. Just for an instant he imagined what it would be like to have Dora Straub, slender and perfumed, stretched out on the mattress next to him.

It wouldn't do at all. His breath stank of stale booze. His tooth enamel felt dry under his furry tongue from the acid in the puke. He knew he was sweating liquor from every over-worked pore. But he had time, thankfully, before the real encounter with Dora came, and when it did he would be bright-eyed and spruced-up and entirely sober.

Pete remembered the dream, then. More accurately, he remembered remembering the dream before, the way you did when they were recurrent, or you just imagined they were in the haunting manner dreams had because they were so elusive and insubstantial in their basic character.

In the dream he was being pursued. The pursuit was deadly and, when he remembered the substance of the dream, he remembered with surprise that he always endured it in a state of sleeping terror.

He had been pursued on a couple of occasions through forest. That had happened to him in life. The first time had been on the edge of the African veldt when he had become briefly the prey of a leopard. But this leopard had been a bit timid and half-hearted, and had lost interest in a confrontation in a clearing when it had seen the size of its prospective kill and factored in the work necessary.

The second occasion was more serious. He'd been working for a Russian billionaire restoring a depleted forest of conifers around his dacha eighty miles north of Moscow. Pete had been clearing dead and dying trees with a chainsaw one chilly April morning. But the noise was insistent and the weather wasn't chilly enough, because his industry woke a brown bear from hibernation and the bear came-to very grumpily.

Pete fled, literally, for his life. He could hear the bear gaining on him, careening through undergrowth, the growl of its breath and its paws scampering on the ground getting louder all the time. He could almost feel the heat of its breath on his neck as he ran and it closed the distance.

He scaled a tree. He reckoned later he climbed it faster than he'd ever climbed anything in his life. Inspired by fear, fuelled by raw adrenaline, he stopped forty feet up only because he ran out of branches and stood gripping the tree's swaying, resin-sticky summit in the embrace of both his trembling arms.

The bear shook the base of the tree. But it didn't climb up there after him. It was a large and intelligent creature and, even drowsy and irritated as it was, must have known that the branches of the tree would not support its weight.

With his feet scissored high up on the swaying trunk, Pete fumbled his short-wave radio out from his jeans pocket; it squelched into life and he summoned help in his feeble Russian. A guy riding shotgun in a Range Rover scared the bear away with a few blasts skywards from his pump-action twelve-bore and they all laughed about it good-naturedly afterwards for days.

This dream of pursuit he was having now wasn't like that, though. It wasn't anti-climactic, like his encounter with the leopard on the veldt. It didn't have the Carry-On comic quality of his encounter in a Russian pine forest with an irritated bear. It was far more ominous than that. It was somehow vastly more despairing in the mood it inflicted. Escape from it seemed a hopeless enterprise.

There was terror. But it was not of the galvanic sort that gives a fugitive his nimble energy. It was an enveloping sort of terror. It consumed the will and made flight a sluggish and futile notion.

And there was the pursuer. Pete could not see his pursuer in this dream he vaguely remembered and even more vaguely suspected he might have had before and might be having, come to that, quite regularly. It wasn't human. It wasn't even warm-blooded. It was cold-eyed and reptilian and it was sickeningly quick, possessed of a savagery that didn't seem to be of the modern world. It seemed ancient. It was primeval.

He settled, his mind void, his abused body giving vent to a fart and a belch almost simultaneously, thinking of nothing, pursued by nothing he dreamed of, followed, if by anything, only by the fate or destiny of which Pete Mariner did not yet have any compelling cause to think might actually be his.

*   *   *

The instinct was strong in him to do something decisive. He was frustrated that Saul wasn't picking up his calls. It was a boss's privilege. More than that, it was his right, since he answered to no one but himself and, without him, the machine of which they were all a part stopped running and fell to pieces, becoming so many useless component parts.

But Sam Freemantle was frustrated all the same and felt that he should do something resolute and perhaps even defining while he still had the opportunity to impress, before Curtis the charismatic tree guy returned to take centre stage in the personal dynamics and greater goings-on at the estate.

It was a drama, wasn't it? Life was a drama and events had conspired to make Tom Curtis the star of this particular show. What he had to do, now, was contrive some drama of his own to occupy the spotlight and remind Saul Abercrombie that he remained a principal player and a force in the unfolding story to be reckoned with and respected. Or at least, he thought, taken into account.

He was more comfortable with his machine metaphor than the more fanciful one concerning the stage. He was happier thinking himself the vital cog without which everything would very likely clunk to a premature halt. He was strong and functioned smoothly but his importance was totally over-looked. Consequently, the mechanism was out of kilter. The delicate balance needed redressing.

Metaphors apart, it wasn't personal. He respected Curtis and even, on their short acquaintance, found he quite liked him. He envied the man the obvious attraction Francesca Abercrombie felt for him. That was only natural. She was an alluring woman and Curtis had gained her interest without any apparent effort or intent to do so at all. Of course that was frustrating, but it wasn't the man's fault and he was clearly an expert at what he did professionally, taking Saul's scheme and all of its preconditions very seriously indeed.

He looked at his watch. It was just after midday. Curtis was expected back at about teatime. Francesca was presumably tied up doing what Francesca habitually did in her studio. Saul was exercising his vexing right to invisibility. He would be somewhere, obviously. But he wouldn't be located until he wanted to be. Freemantle thought he might be up at Puller's Reach, staring at the yew tree they'd broken the ground with by that creepy, whistling cairn of moss-stained stones.

He was in the armoury. He wanted one of the sixteen bores, the single-barrelled pump-action, that brutal artillery piece of a gun that would blast its way through a barn door. Or a thorn bush, he thought with a grin. The gun was only for entertainment really, though. The real damage would be done by the twenty litres of petrol in the jerry can he had stored already in the rear of his Land Rover.

The weather was dry, had been for days. It was overcast and though there'd been that recent bank of fog, the ground was solid and the thorn bush at Gibbet Mourning would burn like tinder, wouldn't it?

He had woken on his plan. He had thought to clear it with Saul, but Saul wasn't answering his cell phone. And there was no need really to clear it with the boss. The bush had to go at some point over the coming days and weeks. It was an ugly obstruction. He was Saul's to-do guy on the ground. He was entitled to use his initiative in the execution of his job.

And to some extent, this was personal. He'd felt a bit impotent, to be truthful, witnessing the bush and its baleful antics in the presence of Tom Curtis. When it bristled as Curtis watched it, he thought it seemed a squalid affront that he should already have dealt with decisively. Its thorny defiance should not have been there for Curtis to see. It should have been a patch of scorched earth which was what, by teatime, he'd resolved over breakfast it would be.

He locked the armoury and walked up the basement stairs and through the house, carrying the gun loosely in the grip of his left hand where its weight and solidity felt good. It smelled slightly of walnut polish and the thin oil he used to lubricate its action. The shells were looped in a leather ammo belt over his right shoulder and they smelled of their brass plugs and packed gunpowder. He put the ordnance on the passenger seat of his vehicle, aware of the grey light of the day, aware that he always felt more alive in possession of a weapon.

He turned the key in the ignition and put the engine into gear, humming to himself. He was slightly surprised when he recognized the melody. It was an old soul classic, the Marvin Gaye tune, 'What's Goin' On'. He'd never greatly cared for black music. He was more of a power ballad man, a Heart and Boston and Michael Bolton sort of person. Probably he'd become familiar with the song when sharing a cell. There'd been plenty of soul brothers behind bars, back in the day. Anyway, at that moment it seemed the appropriate choice.

The bush seemed bigger than he remembered when he got close enough to clearly make out its coiled and tangled detail. The word 'bush' didn't really do this obscene growth justice, he didn't think. It had a significant mass and density and its overall size was so considerable it was almost alarming. Had it spread? He thought it might have in the couple of days since he'd last seen it and that would make sense. Spring was the time of growth in nature, wasn't it?

It was higher than he was, rising to about eight feet at its centre and it had to be forty feet across. Feathers fluttered across some of the surface thorns in a tableau of avian death he'd seen before but never fully understood. He'd always thought birds had a kind of sonar enabling them to avoid obstacles. They had night vision and most species had superb eyesight. Yet there they were, every time, a cross-section of winged wildlife impaled and forlornly dead, the breeze maintaining the illusion of life still in their teased spreads of wings.

He had to admit, however grudgingly, that the sheer complexity of the bush was impressive. Its limbs were so thickly and intricately stretched and coiled. Even still – and it had not yet stirred – it had the look of a hellish nest of barbed serpents about it.

At least, it did from a distance. Get closer and the limbs stopped looking snake-like and took on that anthropomorphic quality that had so dismayed Curtis at dusk a couple of days earlier. As Freemantle approached, the shotgun loaded, the reassuring weight of it held evenly between both hands, the limbs of the bush, under their horny protrusions, began to look busy with sinew and muscle like something that might have evolved monstrously and complicatedly from man.

He was twenty feet away when it began to twitch and move. One whorl in a particularly thick limb at the centre seemed to blink open and gaze blankly at him before closing slyly again as the bush shivered and rattled and spat.

It was enough for Freemantle. It was more than fucking enough. He raised the gun chambering a cartridge and triggered a shot that exploded into the thorn labyrinth with a thud and then a tearing screech of destruction. Round after pulverizing round he fired, until the weapon was empty of ammunition, the barrel hot and the smell of cordite and freshly bled sap a stinking cocktail in his nostrils.

He grunted, shouldered the gun and turned to go back for the jerry can of fuel he'd brought there to eradicate that baleful growth forever. He heard something slither and grind across the ground after him and, when he turned, surprised, tendrils, fibrous and as strong as steel cable, wound around his ankles and waist and hauled him juddering and suddenly bleeding and torn, surprised, into the barbed heart of it.

'The knight in the stained-glass window was called Gregory,' Abercrombie said. 'In the Icelandic sagas he is sometimes referred to as Gregory of Avalon, slayer of dragons. So it's fair to say his fame spread throughout Northern Europe and maybe even beyond. He was born in Tintagel. And of course, it was King Arthur he served.'

'And now you're going to tell me he came here answering a plea from Merlin,' Curtis said.

'The more remote the time, the less daylight there is between fact and fiction,' Abercrombie said. 'That's the way it is with legends. That's how myths perpetuate and grow.'

'That's the way they're peddled,' Francesca said.

'But let's stick to what's verifiable. If he spoke the old Cornish tongue, he also spoke English. The place names here attest to that. This domain was his reward. He came on a quest to rid the region of something blighting it and he succeeded.'

Curtis said, 'What was the nature of the blight?'

'It wasn't vegetable or mineral,' Abercrombie said. 'So you tell me, brother, by simple process of elimination, what does that leave?'

'The thing he's cut the head off in the lead window at your little church?'

'That's an idealized representation,' Francesca said. 'He wouldn't have been dressed that way. He'd probably have more resembled a Viking warrior to our eyes.'

'I'm less concerned with his wardrobe than the creature he's just killed,' Curtis said. 'Are you two honestly telling me you believe in monsters?'

'It was a thousand years ago,' Francesca said. 'Are you prepared to completely rule out the possibility?'

Curtis said, 'You don't subject a fairy tale to carbon dating.'

'It isn't a fairy tale,' Abercrombie said. 'And there was more than one of them.'

'So they were a gang,' Curtis said. 'Or you're suggesting a tribe?'

Francesca cleared her throat. She said, 'They were a species. They were probably of the same family.'

'There's a cave,' Abercrombie said. 'Or there's supposed to be. It was their lair. In the story it extended for a long way, maybe over a mile inland. The mouth lay in the cliffs. It was approached by sea. That was how Gregory did it, according to the story.'

Curtis said, 'Past tense? Has this cave disappeared?'

'We've been unable to locate it,' Abercrombie said. 'That's a hell of a stretch of coast. There are reefs, rocks invisible just beneath the surface, rip-tides and all kinds of hazardous shit. Plus, finding it hasn't been a priority.'

Francesca looked directly at Curtis. She said, 'Do you think there really could be a cave?'

'Geologically, yes, I do,' he said. 'It's plausible. If it was there then, there's no reason to suppose it won't be there now. It isn't geology I have a problem believing in.'

'I'm only telling you this stuff because you asked to be told it,' Abercrombie said. 'This location has a history.'

'Tell me more about these creatures Gregory confronted.'

'They were amphibious. They were large and in character they were leech-like.'

'They sound charming.'

'Even less charming was the individual they served and guarded. She was a powerful sorceress.'

'Morgana le Fay,' Curtis said. 'So it really was Merlin who sent for Gregory.'

'She isn't named in the story,' Francesca said. 'It's made plain by the chronicler that her name is known to him but he won't use it. Naming her invited ill-fortune, apparently.'

'She derived her power from these creatures, so Gregory killed them,' Curtis said.

'No, Tree Man, not quite. They protected her. But she derived her power from the forest. The forest was cleared to denude her of influence. That's the story. That's the whole shebang.'

'Where are Gregory's descendants?'

'The last of his bloodline perished during the Black Death. They were wiped out by plague. They aren't even buried here, we don't think. There's that tiny church at Raven Dip but there's no family vault.'

Curtis nodded. His mind was on the letter he'd read that morning from his daughter. He was tired. It was later than he wanted it to be. It was eight thirty in the evening and dusk was descending on the terrace. The beer was cold, his host avuncular, Francesca luminescent and beautiful in the last of the light.

But he'd spent the first part of the morning within touching distance of Charlotte and hadn't seen her, let alone hugged her or spoken to her. He'd been delayed by a traffic accident on the tedious drive back. He'd unpacked irascible and weary after a day that felt long, eventful, frustrating and ultimately wasted. There was an awful lot to accomplish.

'Where's Freemantle?'

'Off on some errand,' Abercrombie said.

'He's decided his shotguns don't pack enough power,' Francesca said, fiddling with her wristwatch. 'He's gone to fetch an anti-tank missile.'

'Don't need to shop for those, honey,' her father said. 'These days you can order those on eBay.'

'Where is he?' Curtis asked again.

Abercrombie shrugged. 'Wherever he is, he took a Land Rover. He tried to call me several times this morning, but I wasn't picking up. He's probably gone to get supplies of something. He's a grown-up. Be cool. He'll be back soon enough.'

'Once it's mission accomplished,' Francesca said.

'You don't like him.'

'Human nature,' Francesca said. 'We can't all like everyone.'

'What's bugging you, Tree Man?'

'I met with Charlotte's mother this morning. It didn't go encouragingly.'

'You tried to bribe her.'

'You're very astute.'

'Didn't need to be to work out that one, brother. What's your next move?'

Curtis sipped beer. 'I'm going to plant a forest,' he said. 'I'm going to concentrate fully on that not inconsiderable task.'

Francesca said, 'And risk bringing our sorceress back?'

'She won't be ours,' Abercrombie said. 'She'll likely be her own woman.'

'It's a chance I'll take,' Curtis said. He looked out at the darkening land, at the sun descending in the western sky over to his left, thinking about the dank things that grow in the permanent gloom of the leaf canopy, unhindered by light and warmth.

Francesca left them not long after that. Saul and Tom talked logistics. They discussed where the accommodation block for the workforce would be built. Freemantle had arranged for some ex-Royal Engineers to arrive in the morning with the materials needed to build a landing strip for cargo planes and a concrete helipad where choppers could put down. They talked about the excavation machines Curtis had already ordered from a specialist plant-hire firm in Düsseldorf.

They would arrive in Fishguard harbour aboard a convoy of ships the following day. There were three of them; they were vast and would be manned by a team of nine drivers working eight-hour shifts in tandem. Much of their work would be floodlit. Once started, the job would not stop until the moment it reached completion.

They talked about the first tree shipments and Curtis briefed Abercrombie on the characters of his principal lieutenants, Dora Straub and Pete Mariner. He seemed more intrigued by the former than the latter, which Curtis thought understandable.

Everything had been thought of, from the small lab they would need to ensure none of their trees were contaminated to the banks of portable latrines the on-site workforce would require. Curtis had done all of this stuff before, just never on such a gigantic scale.

'They won't all be of a piece, Saul.'

'What do you mean by that?'

'A mature forest is a constant cycle of decline and death and regeneration. Each species of tree possesses a lifespan.'

'I know that.'

'We'll be planting everything from fully mature oaks to silver-birch saplings. It won't be neat and uniform, like a plantation of farmed conifers.'

'But it will look real?'

'It will, inevitably, because it will be real, totally authentic, exactly as in nature.'

'Cool. I got the right guy when I got you, Tree Man. I know I did. I should congratulate myself.'

Eventually, Saul Abercrombie tired. There was still no sign of Sam Freemantle. He smiled, rose stiffly and nodded a goodnight. Curtis smiled back and looked at the pale suds in the bottom of his beer glass on the table they'd shared, then glanced up at the dark vista before him, thinking of the violent, epic upheaval to which this quiet wilderness would be subjected over the coming days, weeks and months.

He didn't feel regretful about it. He didn't even feel ambivalent. There was something unlovely about the acreage Abercrombie owned, a baleful quality beyond its vastness. It was a place where things seemed to lurk and hide and to have qualities other than those they ought rightfully to possess.

That was true of the cairn of stones at Puller's Reach. It was true of the iron sign signalling the route to nowhere at Loxley's Cross. It was true of the church at Raven Dip, where the interior felt as soullessly cold as the stone of its ancient walls and flagged floor. It was truest of all perhaps at Gibbet Mourning, where that fibrous, cantankerous cluster of thorns had stretched and swollen to such monstrous dimensions. This was a blighted place, and churning it up and transforming it could only improve its character.

Mature trees were stately and serene. Nothing in nature possessed their quiet, stoic dignity. They were beautiful and benevolent. The forest would be grand and varied, and its woodland wildlife would thrive unhindered through the decades and even the centuries to come. It would be a place, despite its great size, of peace and reflection.

He thought about Gregory of Avalon. Had there ever been such a person, a slayer of dragons, deliberately seeking the mouth to the cave where the monsters dwelt on his approach from the sea? And he remembered the thing he had sensed on the shore below him in the mist as he clung to tussocks of grass at the edge of the cliff. He remembered the flop on the shingle of its blind progress and the assaulting stink of it in his nostrils.

A wildlife issue, he'd told Saul Abercrombie an hour or so afterwards.

The beast of Bodmin Moor, Abercrombie had joked, which he'd known full well it wasn't.

They'd told him everything and nothing tonight. Except he didn't think they'd told him everything they knew and he knew they'd told him nothing he could quite believe in. He looked at his wristwatch and saw that the time was a quarter past eleven. It was curious that Sam Freemantle was coming back so late. A pint enjoyed in a village pub en route, maybe. He was a grown man and entitled. Curtis reached for his own beer glass, which he would rinse in the kitchen before retiring to his room and a peaceful sleep.

Francesca had admitted that she didn't like Sam. Not in so many words, but the meaning had been plain. Did it also mean by implication that she liked him? It was flattering if she did, but no more than that. Whatever his motive in offering it, Curtis thought Freemantle's advice over any dalliance with the boss's daughter basically sound. Anyway, he had no appetite for romance.

David Baxter rose early and did his daily search for Tom Curtis as soon as his laptop had powered up. His assignment had been completed formally the previous day when he'd written up his report on Isobel Jenks and her version of events concerning the affair she'd had with Curtis and its fall-out.

He'd emailed that as a Word document to his employer. The fee for the job had cleared in his account. But curiosity informed much of what he did and he was still curious to know what it was that connected a tree expert so closely to Abercrombie Industries that Saul Abercrombie had felt the need to have the man so thoroughly investigated.

He got his answer after an hour of Internet probing. Three machines were en route from the docks at Hamburg to the Welsh port of Fishguard. They were gigantic contraptions, excavators generally used for the laying of pipelines deep under the earth when security or environmental concerns deemed the need for their concealment. They were so large that a separate cargo vessel had been chartered to carry each of them.

The name on the bills of lading was that of Tom Curtis. And Curtis had been busy elsewhere outside of Europe. He'd been active in North America and Canada where he'd been quoted prices for deciduous trees. The quotes looked competitive to Baxter's untrained eye. You could get quite a lot of tree for your dollar. Even more surprising were the quantities. Curtis was inquiring about hundreds of thousands of tons of live lumber.

Baxter was quite good at putting two and two together. But as the scale of the project began to become clear to him, he was also slightly incredulous. It was a mad scheme, a megalomaniac's folly. It was also a sensational story waiting to be written because he was damn sure he hadn't read a word about it so far in a single newspaper.

He had a contact in the newsroom of the *Mirror*. It was a relationship he was careful to nurture. Will Davies was a good reporter with a journalist's belligerent instinct for protecting his sources. Baxter could do Davies a favour confident that the tip-off would never be sourced back to him. Confident also that Davies would one day reciprocate.

He used his pay-as-you-go phone to call Davies and outlined

what he'd discovered. He gave him the human-interest stuff he'd learned about Curtis too.

'Just colour, Will, but worth knowing, I reckon. It's not redundant information.'

'There's no such thing, mate,' Davies said.

'Watch out for a bloke called Freemantle if you do any door-stepping down in Pembrokeshire. He did five years for armed robbery and has a coke habit I don't reckon is quite as far behind him as his boss would like to believe.'

'Do you have a contact number for Isobel Jenks?'

'I do, as it goes. You're going to talk to her?'

'Pursue every angle, mate. This is a biggie. I owe you large if it's got the legs I think it has.'

It was funny, Baxter reflected, when he ended the call. Two privately educated middle-class men obliged by fashion to communicate like the bastard offspring of extras from an episode of *The Sweeney*. Such were the paradoxes of the modern world. He shut down his computer, put on his kit, strapped on his heart-rate monitor and ran around Richmond Park for an hour.

Twice, he thought he saw Isobel Jenks. The first time her pale and sinewy little body and bleached crop receded into a ripple of reeds atop a pond so he didn't need to convince himself it was a trick of light and shade. And preoccupation, he thought. Some tricks were played in the mind.

The second sighting was more disturbing. She resolved herself out of a smudge as he approached a tree uphill, leaning against the trunk and smoking in a parka with the hood up, framing her pert features as she stared hard at him. He paused to wipe a stinging droplet of sweat from his eye and when he looked again, still a hundred feet away, she had vanished.

He was a student to her from Richmond. She couldn't be stalking him, could she? He had given her no address at which to reach him and she'd have been going on a false identity. Had it been her, she would have confronted him, wouldn't she? What was the point of seeking someone out and then being too timid to communicate? She hadn't exactly struck him as shy.

He had showered and changed by the time he noticed that

he'd had a call while he was out on the pay-as-you-go. No message had been left but he recognized the number. It was Will Davies' cellular.

'Mate,' he said.

'How close were you to Isobel Jenks, Dave?'

Neither tone nor tense struck Baxter as right. He swallowed. His skin felt cold and tingled. The phone shook slightly, responding to a sudden tremor in his grip. 'I wasn't,' he said. 'I wasn't close to her at all. Why?'

'She topped herself last night. Hanged herself by a bootlace from a hook in her college room. She left a note, the contents not divulged, obviously.'

'You don't know what it said?'

'Not officially, no. Someone would have had to tell me and that would have been a breach of protocol because it's privileged information.'

'So what did she say?'

'Something to the effect that her work was accomplished, Dave. She said she had finished what she'd been meant to.'

'You're going to follow this up?'

'Just putting you in the picture, mate. The forest is the story. It's fucking huge. And so's Saul Abercrombie. There's a rumour about Abercrombie's health, something filed by a stringer in New York in September of last year I need to try to verify.'

'Good luck with it, Will. Keep me in the picture.'

'That's a given, buddy.'

Baxter walked from his sitting room, where he'd picked up the call, into his study, where he sat at his desk before his closed laptop and stared out of the window he faced. The view was neutral. Semi-detached houses confronted him across a tree-lined street sparse of traffic once the commute to the office and the school run were done.

She hadn't hanged herself. Hanging was carried out by skilled executioners like Albert Pierrepoint, the last man paid to do the job in Britain. They were professionals who knew how to tie a proper noose. They calibrated the drop necessary to have their bodyweight cleanly break the neck of their subject and kill them pretty much instantaneously.

The wait for the moment standing over the trap door was an ordeal, the fitting of the rope and the canvas hood over the head while you waited further ordeals. Traditional hangings had generally been the punishment for a capital crime, after all. But in the moment of execution, hanging correctly accomplished was a relatively merciful way to kill someone.

When prisoners who couldn't stomach confinement hanged themselves from the bars of their cells with strips of bed linen or rolled towels, it was totally different. Their deaths did not involve a broken neck. It was slower because they suffocated or strangled themselves into extinction.

That's what Isobel Jenks had done. She'd done it from a coat hook with a bootlace. He'd seen the boots he assumed the lace had come from – Doc Martens – placed at the end of her bed. They'd been recently polished.

Baxter shook his head. It was a shock because it made no sense to him. Choking away your own life was not a cry for help. It was a slow and certain death demonstrating only contempt for your existence. Isobel hadn't struck him as someone self-destructive or even really lacking in self-esteem. On the contrary, she'd been possessed of the cocky self-regard that had prompted her indignant call to Sarah Bourne after what she considered to be Tom Curtis's betrayal of her.

He could still taste her; taste the memory of her and the scent of her too, sweating slightly and toiling under him as they shared a farewell fuck slightly less than twenty-four hours earlier. He would need to make a voluntary statement to the police. They'd likely find traces of his semen still inside her at the autopsy. They'd be carrying that out now, wouldn't they?

He shook his head and smiled a pained smile to himself. It was a mystery. He had seen no sign and yet he made a living from being intuitive. Should he see her again, he would try to have the presence of mind to ask her about why she had done it. He thought that he might see her again. He couldn't rule it out. He was pretty certain now that it had been the dead Isobel he had seen staring at him in Richmond Park that morning.

FIVE

Andrew Carrington learned about the girl's death because he was copied into the group email warning faculty staff members not to talk to the press about her character or speculate on the reason for her suicide. There was to be a meeting concerning this unfortunate event at eleven thirty that morning. Since he hadn't taught her, his attendance wasn't mandatory. But the email implied that everyone who'd had contact with her should try to be there. He had given a second opinion on an essay she had written about woodland clearance in Scotland; about the economic consequences and the ecological damage inflicted.

He'd thought the essay rather good. She'd had a clear gift for analysis and a forthright prose style. She had also shown a bias for unspoiled country that was more ideological than the soupy romanticism that compelled students to decorate their walls with Arthur Rackham posters depicting elves and faeries cavorting under ferns and toadstools.

Woodland clearance wasn't strictly his field. But over the past term he'd marked a number of history essays and appraised an English Literature student's thesis on the fiction of Tolkien. Budget shortfalls meant that academics these days were in the business of multi-tasking just like people in the wider world.

Practically, the fact that he was copied into the message meant that they weren't thinking of dispensing with him any time soon. The girl's death was obviously sad but this was reassuring. The work the university put his way was part-time but essential to his lifestyle. He could not manage on his Oxford College pension and the trickle of royalties from his books without imposing strict economies on himself. So at the appointed time he walked into the seminar room in which the meeting was to be held with a jaunty step and an uncharacteristically generous smile.

Her course had been land economy. Her course tutor had

been Simone Butler. And though the vice-chancellor was one of the seven faculty members Carrington joined in the room, it was Professor Butler who chaired the meeting.

To Carrington, she was Simone: a severely handsome woman in her early forties he rather admired because she had a first-rate intellect and didn't make a song and dance about her lesbianism. As always, she was impeccably dressed in a black designer suit. She leant against a desk with her arms folded across her chest and they sat in a semi-circle before her.

She first explained that the meeting was both informal and confidential and because it was off the record no minutes would be taken. Having established its parameters, she began the discussion.

Isobel Jenks had apparently hanged herself the previous night. A cleaner had discovered the body early that morning. She had knocked on the door and then used a master key to enter the room when she got no response because she had smelled cigarette smoke and suspected the source of the smoke to be inside Isobel's room. In the event the smoke was stale and its occupant already stiff with rigor mortis, suspended by a bootlace from a hook screwed into her wall.

The note she'd left was vague and cryptic rather than clear on why she'd taken her own life in such a bleak and lonely manner. But the police and their forensic team had concluded straight away that the death was not suspicious. No one but its victim had been involved in it.

She'd taken a call from the journalist Will Davies earlier that morning. He'd asked questions about an affair Isobel had apparently been involved in late the previous summer with an arboreal expert called Tom Curtis.

Simone had rightly said that Curtis was not a member of the university's academic staff and further stressed that he never had been. But she had been obliged to admit that he had run a forestry summer school organized by her faculty and that Isobel had been one of the students who travelled to Scotland to take part in it.

Carrington had never heard of Curtis, but he could see where this was going. The university had a duty of care to its students.

Isobel had been much more young woman than little girl. But this Curtis chap might turn out to be one of those serial womanizers and if that were the case, hiring him and paying him out of college funds could look bad, irresponsible and possibly even negligent.

The vice-chancellor, grey-headed, distinguished-looking, the safe pair of hands for which he was handsomely paid linked in his lap, spoke up. He said, 'What were your reasons, Simone, for choosing this chap Curtis?'

'He's the best,' she said. 'He came highly recommended by Dora Straub at Hamburg. She's worked with him on a number of projects. She described him as highly qualified and completely reliable.'

'How did he strike you?'

After a pause, Simone said, 'Picturesque. Physically he looks like something out of a Burne-Jones painting.'

'Did you tell the journalist that?'

'Of course I didn't. But to some extent it goes with the territory. In the same way that rock stars look like rock stars and eco-warriors have piercings and dreadlocks, tree people tend to look like Tom Curtis does.'

The vice-chancellor said, 'It's extremely unfortunate.'

'He lived locally, about two miles from here. That was convenient when it came to the meetings held for setting up last summer's event. Also, bluntly, he didn't strike me as the sort of philandering idiot who would shit on his own doorstep.'

'But he did,' the vice-chancellor said, 'heftily.'

Simone looked at him neutrally and then looked around the room. For a moment, she caught Carrington's eye. She said, 'I called this meeting to warn everyone present to be on their guard against indiscretion. Personally, I think this unlikely to be followed up. The death of Isobel Jenks is of course extremely unfortunate, tragic for the girl and for her family, the waste of a young life with great potential. But I got the feeling Will Davies won't take it further.'

The vice-chancellor said, 'Why?'

'Well, partly because the affair between Curtis and Isobel Jenks fizzled out six months ago. In tabloid terms, it's ancient history. Mostly because to splash on that would be to obscure the bigger picture. And the bigger picture is vast. Tom Curtis is working on a megalomaniac scheme dreamed up by the billionaire Saul Abercrombie. That's the real story and Davies knows it is. Everything else, including poor Isobel, is a side-bar at best.'

'Or worst,' the vice-chancellor said. 'What is this Abercrombie scheme?'

'He's going to restore an ancient forest reaching deep inland from a stretch of Pembrokeshire coastline. He plans it to be huge, dense and deciduous, and for this rich man's folly he's made Tom Curtis project manager.'

Carrington said, 'Restore, Simone? As in, recreate? The forest was there originally?'

'Apparently, Andrew, yes, it was.'

'Do you know where in Pembrokeshire?'

'Davies mentioned a place called Raven Dip. Also some-where I think he called Loxley's Cross. It sounded like it'll stretch over half the county.'

Carrington was too numbed by what he'd just heard and by its appalling implications to comment further. The rest of the meeting did not really register at all with him. It might have gone on for a little longer. Eventually it ended, because it must have done for him to have left it. But the specifics of what he was doing did not really return to him until, at a quarter to two that afternoon, he found himself at a table on the promenade outside the Riverside Café, a cup of coffee in front of him, his fingers absently toying with the cellophane wrapping on the complimentary Italian biscuit accompanying his drink.

He saw the river, which he was facing. He became aware of the brightly painted green and red tables to his right and left, vivid colours in early afternoon sunshine within the scope of his peripheral vision. There were a couple of other customers seated as he was, outside the café. It felt quite warm. You might even describe it as pleasantly so. To his rear he could hear John, the Riverside's proprietor, whistling mellifluously as he performed some necessary task.

The whistling got louder. A shadow loomed to his rear. And

then there was a scrape of metal as chair legs were pulled out and John was seated across from him, backed by blue water and the orange clay path of the far bank, an expression of concern on a face that had always struck Carrington as not just friendly, but kind.

'You all right, Prof?'

'Of course the water isn't blue at all, is it? That's just the reflection of a blue sky in sunlight. It's essentially a happy bit of visual trickery.'

'Andy, it's me, John. Are you all right?'

'Very clever, putting him in the way of temptation like that. The affair with the girl sullies his virtue. It weakens him in the conflict. The old rules and customs endure. The chivalric code had yet to be written but its values were understood and the bitch knows best of anyone how to undermine an opponent.'

'Who are you talking about?'

'Curtis. Who else would I be talking about?'

'Tom Curtis? He's called you?'

'Of course he hasn't. I've never spoken to him in my life. Until today I'd never heard of him. Why would he call me?'

'I gave him your card.'

'Well, Curtis hasn't called me. But I fear I must call him.'

'That's a hell of a coincidence.'

Carrington blinked at John. What was he talking about, coincidence? It was nothing of the sort. It was nothing as innocent or banal as simple chance. Fate was what it was. Predestination was what it was. 'I might have to go there,' he said. Suddenly he felt weary, every day of his age weighing on him and terror clutching coldly at his heart.

'He's in Wales,' John said. 'I think he's from there originally. He's a Welshman.'

'He's a Celt, from Cornwall,' Carrington said.

'I'm sure he said he's Welsh.'

'He might be,' Carrington said, 'but there's Cornish Celt in his DNA. It was where his ancestors came from. It was where one of them came from, anyway, the important one, a thousand years ago.'

John looked at him like he was speaking Ancient Greek.

Or Demotic Greek, it was all Greek to John, who was a good and industrious man but no linguist and no student of mythology either.

'I knew it,' Carrington said, 'when I saw that the ice field had split high on Kilimanjaro a few days ago.'

'Knew what?'

'That it was a portent. I knew it signified something, some shift or acceleration in matters. I knew it symbolized something serious. It was a warning to anyone alert to such things. I didn't dream it was warning of something as calamitous as this.'

'You're talking in riddles, Prof,' John said. 'You've lost me completely.'

'Pray they stay riddles,' Carrington said. 'I've an awful feeling they won't.'

The day began badly. The press were on to what they were doing. A reporter called the head office of Abercrombie Industries at mid-morning. He wanted confirmation concerning the scale of the project they had begun. He wanted clarification concerning the state of Saul Abercrombie's health. He had the name of the project manager and a contact number already for Tom Curtis, he explained. He had not used it only because he wanted to observe the niceties and allow Abercrombie to cooperate with the splash they planned for the paper's next edition.

It was the private opinion of Curtis that going public had never been their choice really to make. A battalion of ex-Royal Engineers had arrived with their fleet of cement and tarmac-laying lorries at first light that morning to construct the runway and helipad. In an hour or so, a firm that specialized in pre-fabricated building would be hammering together the accommodation block for a workforce so substantial it might constitute a private army. The excavators were expected at Fishguard harbour later in the day.

There wouldn't just be wide loads to consider when they were hauled on to the giant flatbeds hired to transport them. They would close roads. They required police escorts and that meant lights and sirens and for ordinary motorists, delays the

RAC and AA had already needed to be briefed about. Jesus, the diggers were more gigantic machines than anything Curtis had seen outside of an episode of *Thunderbirds* or a *Star Wars* movie. You didn't hide plant like that. You couldn't, and it aroused curiosity in people. They wanted to know what it was for.

You couldn't keep industry on this scale a secret. Curtis thought it pretty miraculous that they had kept it quiet for as long as they had and paradoxical that so flamboyant a man as Abercrombie normally was should have wanted it kept quiet at all. It was ambitious. It was actually quite breathtaking in the epic extent of its ambition. And its ecological credentials were unimpeachable. What was wrong with going public on the project?

It was his illness, of course. Close scrutiny of Saul Abercrombie threatened to reveal his cancer and the fact that the end of his life was approaching quite rapidly. What would that do to the Abercrombie Industries share price? The myth of his invincibility would take not just a dent but a mortal blow. Literally a mortal blow, Curtis thought.

They were on the quad bikes. He'd been in his room, working on his phone and laptop, looking forward to the scheduled arrival later in the day of Pete and Dora, though not necessarily in that order. He'd already greeted the ex-military guys laying the airstrip, having had to because there was still no sign of Freemantle on the estate and Francesca had knocked on his door and asked him to do it. He'd obliged happily enough.

Saul had also knocked on his door, half an hour ago, his helmet strapped to his head but no sign of his steampunk goggles today. Curtis took this as an indication of his less than playful mood, a judgement proven when his employer said, 'Have you been gossiping to the press?'

'No, I haven't. I banked twenty grand of your money yesterday.'

'Your money, Tree Man, I gave it to you.'

'My point being that I wouldn't have done that and disobeyed your instructions concerning my job conditions. I'd consider it theft.'

'Yeah, well, it would be theft. And you wouldn't be the first person to regret ripping me off.'

'Except that I've not spoken to any reporter. You've got the wrong culprit, if there even is a culprit.'

'Someone tipped this guy off. He knows about the cancer.'

The cancer, not *my* cancer, Curtis observed. He said, 'Is there any sign of Freemantle?'

'That's another thing. Where's my to-do guy on the day when I need him like I've never fucking needed him before? Talk about lousy timing.'

'Could he have gone to the press?'

That question made Saul Abercrombie laugh. It seemed to lighten his mood slightly. 'If he did that, he'd be going public on his own past. And believe me, brother, Sam has enough of a past to have a very good reason to keep quiet.'

'What do you mean?'

'I mean he didn't acquire his skills-set in quite the manner you seem to have assumed.'

'Where are you going?'

'It's where we're going. We're going to look for any sign of Sam.'

'The construction guys are due and they'll need to be told where to build the compound.'

'There are security people at the gates to greet them. Fran can show them where to build. It's not like they're restricted choice-wise.'

'I've earmarked a spot along the eastern perimeter. It's good for road access, drains well, doesn't impede the digging and puts five miles of privacy between you and the workers and their galley, canteen and bunk houses.'

'And latrines,' Abercrombie said.

Curtis shrugged. What could he say? It was a labour-intensive business. It needed muscle as well as machinery. He'd liaised with the recruitment company he always used. The people would start to arrive as soon as their accommodation was completed.

'Show Fran the spot on the map and then grab a quad, brother,' Abercrombie said to him. 'We've got some searching to do.'

They found Freemantle's Land Rover after two hours of looking. They had known it was not going to be near the landward boundary of the estate because the security guards now manning the perimeter would have spotted the vehicle and called the sighting in.

They first went to Raven Dip and then to Loxley's Cross. There was no real logic to this except that the Dip was just that, a depression that could hide the presence of someone there. And the Cross was somewhere that led to places and so seemed marginally less barren than the wastes of grassland around them distinguished by no name at all.

The Land Rover was the same green as the ground and so naturally camouflaged. Against the background of the thorn bush it couldn't be seen at all until you were almost upon it, Curtis realized, wondering why Freemantle had parked it quite so close to the great thorn tangle dominating the ground.

He thought he had his answer when they looked in the back of the vehicle and saw the red jerry can strapped upright in a bracket there. When he freed and hefted it, he discovered it was full. Freemantle had come here to do some damage to the bush, maybe to scorch it out of existence. So where was he and why hadn't he accomplished this relatively straight-forward task?

'Over here,' Abercrombie said, still astride his quad bike, gesturing at the ground. Curtis walked across. He saw a shotgun lying in a tangle of grass. It was a pump-action, heavy calibre, probably a sixteen-bore and had been beautifully maintained up to the moment of its abandonment. There was a polished lustre to the walnut stock and the metal glimmered without tarnish in the spring light.

There were several spent cartridges littering the ground in the vicinity of the gun. Curtis was no firearms expert, but judging from where they lay, they had been expelled during one long, sustained burst of fire. He looked up at the sky. Had Freemantle been firing at a bird?

There were estate managers who would down a sea eagle without any qualms if they thought they could get away with it. But they tended to be the jealous protectors of livestock or game birds on land where organized shoots represented the day-to-day business of the place. Freemantle had no farm beasts to care for or stock of pheasants to protect from a predator. And there were more than twenty spent cartridges when he counted them. He reckoned on Freemantle being a better marksman than that, aiming at something big and low in flight.

Maybe he'd been shooting at the bush itself, he thought, looking at the intense, writhed tangle of thorns, with its feathery blossoming of dead sparrows and finches. *Up with the larks*, he thought, remembering Freemantle's joke on the phone the first time they had spoken.

It was insane to think that. It was also impossible. The shotgun would have done some serious damage at such close range aimed at the thorn bush. It would have been a target impossible to miss and yet here it was, squatting and massive, dense and quite intact, still and somehow poised in a way that made him feel disgustedly that he ought to take the can of fuel and finish the job Freemantle hadn't had the opportunity to start.

He couldn't do that. He couldn't even pick the shotgun or the spent cartridge cases up off the ground. This could be a crime scene. 'Should we call the police?'

'No,' Abercrombie said. 'Sam's a guy who can take care of himself. I don't want filth on any land with my name on its title deeds. I couldn't handle that, brother.'

Curtis remembered then the picture of the arrest back in the seventies in Red Lion Square. Saul had been dragged away from the demo by officers with truncheons and riot shields. He'd seen the Old Bailey from the defendant's perspective before spending six months behind bars in Brixton gaol. Maybe the scars of that experience had been slow to heal. Maybe they hadn't healed at all.

'Freemantle came here to torch the thorn bush,' he said. 'It's something we discussed on the night you got him to bring me here, when I said I was curious to see the place called Gibbet Mourning. My thinking is that he could have been followed here and then confronted.'

Abercrombie said, 'Followed by whom?'

'You're a wealthy man, Saul. This is an isolated spot. Could be anyone from a poacher to an investigative journalist, but my money would be on something like a Balkan kidnap gang. Eastern criminals are coming to Britain because they think the pickings are easy. What if you're an abduction target and they needed to deal with Sam before nabbing you?'

'You sound like an opinion piece in the *Daily Mail*.'

'And you're not naïve. Think about it.'

'Sam would have hit two or three of them, taken them out,' Abercrombie said. 'We'd be looking at corpses. At the least, we'd be looking at casualties. Look around you. There isn't even the residue of a fire fight. There's no blood, no muscle or bone tissue, no clothing fragments, not even any spent ammo apart from the stuff a single gun discharged and Sam was holding that one.'

'He fired it at something.'

But Abercrombie merely shrugged.

Curtis was quiet for a moment. He did Abercrombie's bidding and looked around. The wind was slight, but the thorn bush stirred in it. Its branches brushed and cracked like the sly loosening of stiff, inhuman limbs.

'You won't even think about the police?'

Again, Abercrombie said, 'Sam's a big boy. He can take care of himself.'

'There's another reason.'

'Yes, Tree Man, there is. Not everyone takes my enlightened approach to the rehabilitation of offenders.'

'What does that mean?'

'Sam Freemantle did five years for armed robbery. He did the crime, brother, and boy, did he do the time. But it means he couldn't get a gun license, not now and not ever. There's some serious hardware in the basement of the house and not one item of it is held legally.'

'That's just fucking stupid.'

'I know. I know it is,' Abercrombie said, climbing carefully out of his saddle and stooping stiffly to retrieve the weapon from the ground. 'But I really didn't figure, Tree Man, on mysterious shit like this.'

His mobile rang then and Curtis answered it. It was Francesca. He glanced back at the bush, behind him, because he sensed some movement there that was furtive and unnatural, deliberate, mindful somehow rather than determined only by the strength of the breeze. When he looked, though, it was still. It was crafty, wasn't it? He had almost caught it out but it had been too cunning for him. It was a ridiculous train of thought but one that made him shiver as he said goodbye to his caller.

'Dora has arrived,' he said. 'She's taking a shower before unpacking and Francesca is having a late salad lunch prepared for her. She wants to know whether we'll be joining them for their meal. It'll be served in about an hour.'

'Call her back and tell her yes,' Abercrombie said. He was retrieving spent shotgun cartridges from the ground and putting them into his jacket pockets. What he was doing, Curtis thought, was removing evidence.

'An hour gives us time to stop off at Puller's Reach before we head back. I want to check on my yew tree.'

'Your yew tree will be fine.'

'I know. But I want to see it. That reporter's nosing around is a hassle I don't need and I'm worried too about Sam. I need cheering up, brother. I need to have my spirits lifted if I'm to meet the lovely Dora in any kind of disposition to act like a proper host.'

'You're her employer.'

'I've seen her picture. I intend to flirt with her, if she's as captivating as she looks. Call it the privilege of a dying man, but I feel entitled.'

Curtis laughed. He had to.

Abercrombie let go of a long breath and came across and punched him playfully on the chest. 'A man takes his compensations where he can,' he said.

Pete Mariner was lost. There were euphemisms such as side-tracked and diverted. But they were bullshit, really, he thought, taking out his phone and trying the SatNav app for the umpteenth time. But the SatNav didn't know where the fuck he was and, frankly, neither did Pete.

He'd opted to bike the distance to the Abercrombie estate in Pembrokeshire. He'd decided on this because he looked pretty good in motorcycle leathers and it was a dashing way to travel that might possibly make an impression on Dora. He didn't think he had ever succeeded in making an impression on Dora before. Now was definitely the time. Arriving astride his 1200cc beast of a bike, with its gleaming chrome and throaty purr, was definitely the way.

He had headed west and hit the coast because the weather was benign and if you were going to endure the discomfort of a bike, you might as well enjoy the benefits. Coastal roads tended to wind entertainingly in both the vertical and horizontal planes. They were not heavily used like trunk roads were. They offered exhilarating views. There was the bracing salt breeze and since Abercrombie's domain stretched to the edge of the sea, how far wrong could he go?

The problem was that he had run out of road. His tyres were now on packed sand. To his right there was a ragged expanse of grass that looked like the rough of a golf links, except that it stretched as far as he could see. To his left, a hundred metres away, was the water. Waves were breaking gently against the shore. In that direction, westward, eventually was Ireland. If he kept on travelling north, he had to reach his destination. He figured on the basis of the mileage he'd done that he couldn't be more than a dozen miles away from it.

He rode slowly in second gear, watchful for anything that could chew his expensive tyres and so strand him punctured on a remote stretch of coastline. He had his phone and it had plenty of battery life but the need to be located and rescued didn't form any part of his plans. Dora would be unimpressed by that particular dilemma.

Women like Dora never needed to be rescued. It was a plight she would rightly consider ridiculous. She wouldn't even find it funny. She had many attributes, but a sense of humour wasn't prominent among them. So he rode deliberately and studied the sand and shingle route before him, not really noticing the contour of the land rising to his right until it was a cliff wall about eighty feet high.

When he did notice this change in the topography, he braked and scrutinized the cliff face. It was the solid granite rampart

Tom Curtis had described to him. If he wasn't yet on Abercrombie's land, he was surely close to it. The cliffs were getting higher. In places Tom had remarked that they rose to 200 feet. He whistled, getting a sense for the first time of the vastness and remoteness of the area they were going to be altering so fundamentally in character.

Before him, about 800 metres distant, was a headland. He couldn't see beyond that. He began to feel a little uneasy about running out of beach. He didn't know to what height or even at what time of day the tide came in. He didn't know whether it extended to the cliffs themselves and if it did, to what depth. He didn't want to subject his beloved bike to a salt-water soaking that would ruin its engine. Its twin panniers were packed with his precious stuff. Most importantly, he didn't want to drown.

Pete decided that he would see what was beyond the headland. He would make a decision then as to whether to press on or return the way he'd come. There was no way he could get the bike up the cliffs. His best strategy might be to double-back to the grassland a few miles to his rear and then ride inland parallel to where he was riding now. That way he'd eventually find the perimeter fence Tom had described and he could follow that until it led him to a gate.

The headland was just a promontory. Beyond it more cliffs stretched in a ragged northerly sweep. Such was the isolation of the place that it was easy for Pete to imagine himself the only person in this pale, still world. He couldn't really hear anything. The rumble of his bike's engine was more vibration than sound inside his cushioned, full-face helmet.

He switched off his ignition and swung out the bike's stand with a booted foot. He took off his helmet and rested it on the saddle. He did this because he had seen something he hadn't expected to in the granite contours of the cliff. It was a cave mouth, and he thought he would take a look at the cave interior because it would offer clues as to when and to what height the tide encroached.

The entrance was a black and empty arch shape in an oblique facet of rock. It was about eight feet high and about six across and the angle of the rock meant that it could only really be seen when you faced it directly. Move even a few metres to the south or north of it and the opening became invisible.

Caves were dangerous places. That was true even when they weren't sited at the foot of cliffs in remote locations at the edge of the sea. It was extremely foolish to explore a cave alone, without the right equipment, unprepared and without having informed anyone about your intentions.

He wouldn't explore very far. He'd look for rock pools and seaweed. If he found beach detritus like driftwood and boat debris, he'd scarper back the way he'd come as quickly as he dared ride having learned all he needed to about the tide's treacherous reach.

The cave maintained the dimensions of its entrance as he walked into it. It might have narrowed slightly, but he didn't have to crouch. He could stand upright. The walls were smooth and parallel, but the route into the rock was not straight. After about eighty metres the cave veered quite sharply to the left and then swung to the right, its shape effectively blocking off the light from the entrance and casting Pete suddenly, as he rounded the second of the two curves, into total darkness.

The only light source he had was the torch app on his phone. He switched that on and played the beam around the space he was in, painting light on to stone. The beam did not illuminate very much of whatever space lay in front of him. It was quiet, profoundly silent in a way that made him retrospectively aware of the noises he had not noticed on the shore a minute earlier: the breaking of shallow waves, the cries of seagulls flying above, the light ruffle of the breeze at the edge of the sea.

Then he heard something. It sounded like a splash and it came from a distance further inside the cave he could not accurately have judged. He listened for it to repeat and it did. It wasn't a splash at all but a sort of wet thud, like something soft and fleshy slapping heavily against stone.

He swallowed. He thought it was probably a seal. He listened and heard it again and though he didn't know how far away it was, thought that it sounded quite significantly closer. And he could smell it now. A faint odour of fishy decay was drifting out of the darkness towards him. It smelled cold and dead but the dead aspect was contradicted when he heard whatever was making the noise thump forward again towards him.

And then it thumped again. The intervals between the damp whump of its impact on the cave floor were getting shorter. It sounded much heavier than a man. It sounded clumsy and huge. It was hurrying, whatever it was, in its urgency to get to him.

Pete retreated. Once beyond the dog-leg, when he could see the cave entrance in daylight again, he jogged and then sprinted for the opening. He was on his bike and had it running and was off back the way he'd come before he'd bothered to secure the chin-strap of his helmet. Beach churned under his bike's tread with no thought now for the preservation of his tyres. Under his leathers and long-johns, his skin crawled with goose-flesh as his trembling hand wrenched back the throttle to further increase his speed.

He no longer thought it had been a seal. It had been bigger than that, hadn't it? But it hadn't been a walrus either. It had been some creature with the stink of decomposition about it and he had the feeling it had been trying to approach him as quietly as it could. Its haste had betrayed it. It had wanted to get at him pretty badly and had given itself away.

Such speculation made no sense. He'd see things more rationally, he knew, when he reached the house on Abercrombie's estate, met the man himself and saw Tom and Dora again in surroundings that were convivial and civilized and safe, and where he could steel himself with something fortifying from a well-stocked drinks cabinet.

He'd been badly spooked. He vaguely remembered a dream of a pursuit he'd been having. He tried to concentrate on the ground running rapidly beneath his wheels because sand and pebbles weren't tarmac and the bike was heavy and the panniers loaded in a way that made it more difficult than it usually was to handle. But he was all the way back to the grass that reminded him of a golf links and had swung inland across it eastward before he felt properly safe again.

Abercrombie and Curtis didn't get to see Saul's yew tree at the time they'd decided to do so. Curtis was on the point of calling back Francesca when he got a call from the security team at the western gate to tell him Pete Mariner had arrived there aboard his motorcycle. Gibbet Mourning was roughly equidistant between Puller's Reach and the gate. They decided they'd ride there instead and then escort Pete back to the house.

Curtis called Francesca and told her that there'd be three of them joining her and Dora for their late salad lunch. He looked up at the sky and around as he ended the call. It was shaping up into a lovely spring afternoon and he was looking forward to seeing his old colleagues and friends.

'We can all take a trip to the Reach and see the yew after lunch,' Abercrombie said. 'Your people can get a feel for what we're doing here. It's only one tree, but it's a potent tree at a potent spot.'

Curtis nodded. He remembered the cairn of whistling stones, the enigmatic figure he'd seen watching him from the cliff top, the sounds he'd heard there in the blind limbo of the fog bank. The Reach was a potent spot, all right.

Gibbet Mourning was another, he thought, looking at the squat shape of the great thorn bush and then at Freemantle's Land Rover, parked there like an open secret, taunting them. Abercrombie's pockets were stuffed with his spent cartridges. The illegally held gun was hidden under a tarpaulin now in the back of the vehicle. They'd have to retrieve and garage it in time. But there was no rush. It wasn't as though it was going anywhere.

Pete seemed subdued to Curtis. He seemed a bit taciturn, which wasn't like him at all. He thought it might be to do with the magnitude of the task. A set of map coordinates didn't really prepare you for the sheer expanse and emptiness of the area of Wales they were going to transform back into dense woodland.

It was a task when you were actually there that seemed rather to defeat the imagination. He thought that would only change when the diggers arrived and the land turned black in swathes and the smell of loam permeated the air. In a sense this was the calm before the storm, but so pervasive was the calm that the storm was hard to visualise. It was coming, though, and soon. And it would be turbulent and mighty.

Even the sight of Dora didn't animate Pete much and Curtis privately believed that Pete had carried a torch for his German sometimes-colleague since they'd first met five or six years earlier. Dora was good-looking and, unusually for someone who worked outdoors, seemed always to manifest the sort of worldly sophistication he associated more with nightclubs and casinos than with any rural pursuit.

She always seemed somehow polished, to him. She was good enough at the theory to hold down a professorship. But she really didn't mind getting down and dirty in the field, either. It was one of the things Curtis thought most attractive about her. She was one of those rare women to whom mud didn't do anything to diminish the glamour.

She was dressed in jeans and a denim shirt and when he hugged her in greeting and kissed her on the cheek he smelled in her loosely worn hair her familiar scents of Shalimar perfume and tobacco. And it occurred to him that had he intended to cheat on the partner he'd loved, he would have cheated with Dora rather than with any other woman. She'd been a temptation he'd resisted. Then to his own bewilderment, he'd cheated anyway with a callow and charmless girl.

In the event, he didn't join them for lunch. That was fine – the meal was an opportunity for his boss and Francesca to get acquainted with his two trusted lieutenants and for Pete and Dora to try to get the measure of the man they were all ultimately being paid to satisfy.

Curtis had to go and check out what the ex-army logistics and mechanics boys were doing with the helipad and the airstrip they were improvising. Though the amount of material they'd bought along in their trucks suggested the results would be anything other than improvisational.

He had to check out too the progress being made with the living quarters being erected at a spot close to the estate's eastern apex. It was a reminder of the vastness of the place that these substantial projects could be going on at two locations on it and, unless you knew, you could sit on Abercrombie's sun terrace and really believe you had the tranquil wilderness stretching before you entirely to yourself.

These jobs were weather dependant and they were working

to a schedule that was more than just tight. He'd worked with both teams before and knew that they were good. They'd have called him if they'd been confronted by snags or setbacks or with routine questions and they hadn't. They'd been thoroughly briefed, they were specialists and they were getting on with it without any attendant drama. But he still had to verify their progress. It was his job.

He spent an hour with Stanhope, the former Royal Engineers Captain who'd built a thriving civilian business with ex-forces comrades constructing everything from tennis courts to pontoon bridges in the wake of large-scale floods. He asked Stanhope whether it would be possible to get some ex-army ordnance – specifically a couple of military-grade flame throwers and the petroleum jelly to fuel them with.

'Shouldn't be a problem, but they're pretty heavy-duty, Tom. You sure you can't manage with the civilian kit?'

The civilian kit had a throw of about twelve feet and was fuelled by propane. It was used mostly to clear canebrakes. 'No,' Curtis said. 'I want the serious hardware for the job I have in mind.'

He ate a sandwich and shared tea from a flask with Carew, the Irish ganger supervising the building of the accommodation block. Leaving Carew with a handshake, he had a moment when he realized guiltily that he was revelling in the freedom Sam Freemantle's absence had given him. He was pretty sure Freemantle would have deliberately cramped his style. Still could, should he come back. In the meantime he was getting on with things.

And so it was close to six o'clock by the time he returned to the house and observed without surprise that the quartet he'd left behind had by that time enjoyed a drink together.

They weren't exactly pissed. They'd had one, possibly two drinks apiece. Doing so hadn't noticeably affected Dora, but Francesca gave him a smile on his return that he thought Freemantle would have scowled on seeing. Abercrombie's cheeks wore a slight flush and his eyes had brightened. He'd retrieved his steampunk goggles from wherever. They were hanging around his neck. Curtis thought it a measure of his increasing frailty that a man who'd been such a hedonist in the past could be so affected in the present by a couple of glasses of beer.

Pete's demeanour was most altered by the booze. He'd loosened up. He'd changed out of his bike leathers and boots into a track top and a pair of khaki shorts. He'd brushed out his long blond hair, which the crash helmet had flattened on his journey there. He was relaxed and smiling and Curtis thought he'd probably been treated to a couple of outrageous anecdotes from Abercrombie's rock 'n' roll repertoire. Or maybe Dora had put him at his ease. She was sensitive to mood and with Pete knew from experience which buttons to push.

'Took your time, Tree Man,' Abercrombie said. 'Everything simpatico?'

'Both teams are slightly ahead of schedule. They've both got shifts working through the night. The airstrip boys should be done by midday tomorrow and the accommodation block will be up and running by tomorrow night. That's plumbing, wiring, generator, the lot. They're good.'

'You get what you pay for,' Abercrombie said. Then he said, 'Your people are very curious to see my yew.'

Curtis wondered at the veracity of this remark. Bus men and holidays came immediately to mind. How excited could seasoned arboreal pros like Dora and Pete be to see a solitary yew?

He just nodded. He wanted to see it himself. Moreover, he wanted to see how his people reacted to the atmosphere of Puller's Reach.

They all went and they went on the quads. And the surprise announced itself to the sharp eyes of Tom Curtis a good two miles short of their destination as they travelled over the undulating ground. He didn't comment. A comment wouldn't have been heard over the noise of five competing engines. He glanced at Abercrombie to see if there was some reaction in his expression, but behind the goggles it was impossible to tell.

There wasn't one yew tree. There were two, the second slightly smaller than the one Curtis had planted. It stood parallel with the first to the edge of the cliff with about five feet of space between them. The earth around the base of its trunk was undisturbed. It looked as though it had emerged from the ground a couple of decades earlier and matured and thickened through the seasons.

'Sam Freemantle must have planted it,' Abercrombie said.

Curtis, who knew that the inviolate ground contradicted this theory, said nothing in reply. He could think of no natural explanation for what he was looking at. It was as though the yew he'd planted had been rapidly and exactly cloned and subject to growth so accelerated it would qualify as miraculous. Or uncanny.

To her father, glancing across to Curtis, Francesca said, 'I reckon it's that Balkan kidnap gang that's stalking you, Dad. They're probably bored. The devil makes work, and so on.'

So Abercrombie had told her about the earlier conversation they'd had on discovering Freemantle's Land Rover. Of course he had. She was here because he was dying and he kept nothing from his daughter.

'Well, they look like they belong, that's for damn sure,' Pete said.

Curtis looked at him and then for Dora, who had wandered away from the group and stood forty feet away, examining the Puller's Reach cairn on her haunches.

'Amen,' said Abercrombie, slapping Pete on the back, raising his goggles to rest on his forehead, clearly pleased rather than freaked out by what he was looking at. He was a businessman. Production in his latest enterprise had just doubled and the increase in output had come at no extra cost.

Curtis studied Pete's expression. It was slightly dazed, as though something had shocked him, unless he'd just had a couple more than the one or two beers the rest of them had cracked. He'd ridden his quad OK, but then he was an experienced motor cyclist and the terrain gave him plenty of room to steer a stray line or have the odd wobble.

He walked across to Dora. He said, 'There's only supposed to be one yew. Only one was planted. Nothing else has gone into the ground.'

'Well, something's come out of it,' she said. She was fingering the stones of the cairn, stroking their moss and lichen-stained surfaces with delicate fingertips. 'I've seen these before, in parts of Saxony and the Polish forests,' she said.

'What do they mean?'

'It's what they symbolize, Tom. It's what they warn of.' She stood and looked around and then held him directly with her eyes. They were dark brown, almost black, difficult to read. 'They signify places of enchantment,' she said. She brushed moss from her fingertips off against the fabric of her jeans where it was taut against her thighs.

He turned and walked past Francesca on his way to talk to Pete, who was staring down over the cliff face at the beach with a slight grin of bemusement. He smiled at her in passing. He didn't realize how perfunctory the smile must have appeared until Francesca whispered after him, 'She's beautiful.'

'What?'

'More a question of who than of what, Tom. Dora is beautiful. And she's lovely, which might prove to be what my dad would call a bitch.'

'I don't know what you mean.'

'I think you do. But go and talk to Pete. He looks like he needs you to.'

'I've known Dora Straub for years. Her professional credentials are impeccable.'

'God, you're so pompous in your project manager hat.'

'How much did you lot have to drink?'

'Go and talk to Pete, before he falls off the bloody edge of where he's standing.'

He went and stood next to Pete, able to smell the beer on his breath, aware that somehow Pete had managed to sink a couple more than the others had.

'Still no word on Charlotte?'

'Nothing you'd call encouraging.'

Pete gestured at the beach. 'There's something fucking odd about this place. Something's not right, Tom.'

'I've been here a while. I thought it was just me.'

'Nope, things aren't right here. They're sort of out of kilter, if you know what I mean. This is a weird location, strange vibes.'

'I need this job. It'll make our reputations.'

'You and Dora already have reputations.'

'I don't have a pot to piss in, is the truth of it. I was with Eddie Stanhope earlier, who drives a Bentley. Then I had tea with Patsy Carew, who has a villa on the Algarve. I've never made any real money, Pete. This job's my shot.'

Pete turned and looked at him. 'Going to court over your girl?'

'Yes, unless Sarah has a sudden change of heart.'

Pete belched. 'Then this job's got you by the balls, Tom.'

SIX

Andrew Carrington had spent hundreds of hours in the Ashmolean Museum in Oxford. He had researched there, written there and curated exhibitions there that had proven very popular with both the public and the press critics who reviewed such events. He had never stolen anything from the museum, though, and had never dreamed that he would. But he was about to do it now and couldn't help but muse on how very strange it felt to be on the verge of committing a crime serious enough not only to ruin his professional name but to put him behind bars for a couple of years.

The artefacts he was after were not on public display. That was a blessing. It made the theft an easier proposition practically. And it meant that it would take longer for the theft to be discovered and for the police to be alerted and begin their dogged and meticulous process of recovery.

The theft would be discovered, that was inevitable. It might remain undetected for a few weeks or even months, but eventually someone would realize that something irreplaceable had gone. A process of elimination would point the finger of blame inexorably at him. He had the feeling, though, that by that time it wouldn't matter very much and if it did, by then he wouldn't really care.

The pieces he intended to steal were part of the Mandrake Hoard. It had been stumbled upon by an amateur treasure hunter armed with outrageous luck and a metal detector. He had made his find in the Cheviot Hills. This particular hill had not been a hill at all, but a burial mound. His treasure trove proved to be the possessions of a Saxon chieftain or possibly even a king. Carrington had helped to inventory and catalogue the hoard once lottery money had been used to pay for it at auction.

Most of the hoard was on display. It was the most spectacular collection of precious Saxon metalwork since the haul discovered at Sutton Hoo. The chieftain had been buried in his armour, with his sword and shield, and they were intact and with his helmet represented the finest examples of Saxon weaponry ever found in Britain.

The two items Carrington coveted were not on display because they did not really fit in. They were Celtic artefacts and they dated from a period a century before the other stuff the tomb had contained. They were, frankly, anomalous, a chronological and racial contradiction that had proved to be nothing more than a headache for scholars during the two baffled decades since the find.

They were a pendant and an amulet. They were heavily scrolled and fashioned from gold. The pendant had at its centre a flawless emerald. They were handsome pieces and despite their anomalous nature, they were priceless. But Carrington was not stealing them for their black market value. He was doing so because he was confident he had worked out what they were for. He thought he would have need of them should fate conspire to take him to Pembrokeshire.

The elements of the theft that made it so easy for him were also those that would make it obvious he was the thief. He was a Friend of the Museum, with a special swipe card giving him access to secure areas to which the public were not permitted to go. He did not have to endure the public indignity of having his bag searched on the security desk when he left. He could visit the museum at hours when it was not open at all to the general public. All of which was very convenient.

He saw three or four people he knew and was obliged to acknowledge on his way to the room where the pendant and amulet were tagged and shelved. The room was heavily locked and the heat and humidity of its interior were controlled. He didn't know how frequently the items it contained were dusted. Even dusting them would be a specialist job and the climate control might make it completely unnecessary. If it was done, that was how long he had before they were on to him.

He barely looked at the two items before lifting them from the shelf and putting them in the bag. He was surprised handling them, as he always was, by their weight. They were gold and their purity was absolute. But he thought their weight owed as much to their significance as objects as to the density of the metal from which they had been fashioned.

A cosmological chart had been one of the items recovered in the Mandrake Hoard. It was engraved in bronze and it had been theorized that the noble occupant of the grave had been a distinguished traveller in his life, a man who had explored in sea-faring voyages well beyond the shores of his native country.

Carrington did not share this belief. He thought the chart signified activities much darker and more interesting than using the stars as a navigational aid. The objects now in his briefcase were the proof of that. A Saxon king had not commissioned their creation. But they had somehow come into his ownership and he had appreciated their properties, hadn't he? He'd had sufficient regard for them that he'd had the pendant and the amulet buried with him.

Carrington endured a bad moment on his way out of the museum. An ex-colleague stopped him and insisted on discussing a matter over which they had disagreed for thirty years.

The rotund figure confronting him was Harold Flowers, a St Margaret's medieval history don with an irritatingly amateurish sideline in mythology. He'd written something absurd speculating that Nazi militarism had been influenced by the cult of Odin. Then he'd compounded his sin by having this rubbish published in a respected journal. Carrington had dismissed it witheringly in an essay of his own. Now here the idiot was, wanting not so much to prolong as to exhume their original argument.

He felt he had no alternative but to capitulate. There was a place for academic pride and scholarly integrity, but it wasn't with a briefcase full of stolen loot bulging heavily under one's arm. He admitted to Flowers that he'd been mistaken. He accepted defeat totally and with good humour, he said. The argument for what Flowers had claimed was over-whelming. He congratulated his opponent with magnanimity and a smile. It almost made him physically sick to have to do it, but it was what the circumstances demanded.

He made for the exit cursing his luck. He thought that should he ever see Flowers again it would likely be as a performer in the witness box at his own committal proceedings.

It was just after seven in the evening. If he hurried he could be on the seven-thirty London train and back in Kingston by half nine. He'd deposit the contents of the briefcase in the strong box in his study and with luck he'd be in the pub by ten. Food did not really figure in his plans for the evening, but then he was fairly indifferent to food. A drink was a different thing entirely and Carrington felt he'd have earned a pint or two by the time he got to the pub tonight.

David Baxter was fairly sure he was being haunted. It wasn't the stereotypical stuff, the creaking doors and phantom thumps on stairs with no one walking up or down them. There were no cold spots in his flat and he couldn't claim to have witnessed a poltergeist cabaret of kitchen implements pitched as missiles by an antic spirit.

It was subtler than that. It was almost sly in its calculation. He'd been unnerved and irritated by it and after enduring almost a full day of it, he really wanted it to stop. He certainly wanted it to stop before night fell.

His flat occupied a quiet spot on a residential road in Richmond. It was an old stable conversion and he was extremely proud of it. His study had a wood-burning stove and his galley kitchen glittered with chrome and high-tensile steel. There was a Naim hi-fi system worth several thousand pounds. He'd been to their Salisbury showroom to audition in their listening suite before selecting and paying for it with his platinum Amex card.

It was the hi-fi system that was giving him the trouble. It had been doing so all day. He would leave his sitting room, where its components were mounted on their custom-finished hardwood shelves and the lights on each would glow, indicating they were innocently poised on standby. He would return and music would be playing. It was always the same tune and the system signalled that the source component producing the sound was his CD player.

It was a Dusty Springfield song. He knew that because he had heard her distinctive voice often on car journeys when he tuned into Radio Two. The song playing each time he came back into his sitting room was easing out of his speakers softly, at low volume. The song was, 'I Only Want to be With You'.

Baxter didn't own any Dusty Springfield CDs. Open the disc drawer and it would be empty and the song would sigh to a halt only to have begun again if he left the room and then re-entered it.

Anyway, it didn't exactly sound like Dusty Springfield. It sounded a bit like Annie Lennox, who had recorded the song with her first band, the Tourists. It didn't sound exactly like her either, though. It sounded like an amalgam of the two of them and the instrumentation was subtly off-key. How the song actually sounded was less real than recalled by someone's slightly inaccurate memory.

He didn't think it would be happening if he wasn't there. If he was working on a case, busy following someone or checking out their company profile in the Public Records office, he reckoned his hi-fi system would remain content to be switched off in his absence. It was more than tedious, it was genuinely unnerving. And after only a few hours, his haunting had taught him something he hadn't really known about himself: that he lacked physical courage. He was well organized and very intuitive and disciplined. But he really did not want to be confronted by the ghost of Isobel Jenks and he knew that it was her spirit responsible for the trick with the music and, because he knew how vindictive she had been in life, he suspected this was only the start of things.

He didn't want to open a wardrobe and reveal her hanging from a hook with a vacant leer across her dead face. He didn't want her staring into his eyes from over his shoulder when he studied his reflection in the shaving mirror. Soon it would be dark and if her pale face smudged one of his windows looming from outside he thought that he might actually scream.

The smoke was the reason he suspected he might see her. He'd been aware of it really since the morning. He'd had his second conversation with Will Davies, the one in which the reporter had broken the news to him about the fact and manner of Isobel's death, half an hour after he'd seen her in the park, by which time she was probably on an autopsy table. He had broken the connection. And he had smelled cigarette smoke in his flat.

Baxter didn't smoke and he never had. It was a smell to which he was consequently sensitive. He was also house-proud and the idea that his furniture and towels might start to reek of fag smoke was a distasteful one.

He checked the windows, but the odour wasn't drifting in through any of them. He opened them all to try to air the place. There was a light spring breeze that failed to do the job. The smoke scent lingered and grew stronger. By late afternoon, it had started to mingle with a scent by Calvin Klein he remembered, from his one-night-stand with her, that Isobel Jenks had worn in life.

By then he'd become familiar with the lyrics of the song Dusty/Annie persisted in singing on his sitting-room stereo.

Shortly before dusk fell he decided he'd go out for a drive. His BMW was his pride and joy. It was a rare sports coupe model he'd bought on eBay from a collector in Germany. It had a three-litre engine and would do close to 200 miles an hour at the top speed he'd never come close to reaching in it. The insurance premium was high but Baxter had been driving since he was eighteen, had an unblemished licence and could comfortably afford it.

He'd nicknamed his car the Beast. He thought there were people who might snigger at that, but every time he got behind the wheel of the Beast and keyed its ignition, he felt his self-esteem bolstered. He always climbed out of his car after a drive feeling several inches taller.

He settled into the contoured leather driving seat and backed it out of his garage. He put his side lights on because it wasn't fully dark. He thought that he might drive around the M25 for a while. Five lanes of rush-hour traffic wasn't everyone's idea of fun, but it was everyone's idea of normality and David Baxter badly needed that.

He might come back to his flat tonight and he might not, he thought. His wallet was in the hip pocket of his jeans. He thought that if he didn't fancy coming back he could spend the night in a Travelodge without drama just by taking the exit from the motorway for Kingston or Wimbledon. Both had branches of the budget hotel chain and they were clean and comfortable and they didn't have ghosts.

He could come back in the morning at nine a.m., when his Polish cleaning lady Jana was due. Jana was in her mid-twenties and ever-cheerful, and he didn't think his hi-fi would get up to its delinquent tricks with Jana humming about the place with her polish and her dusters.

He drove in the outside lane of the motorway, when he reached it, at a steady seventy-five miles an hour because the traffic was light and because he'd read reliably in the *Daily Mail* that the overhead speed cameras had not been loaded with film for at least a couple of years.

He'd decided on the Kingston Travelodge. He could expense the modest cost. Later in the evening, they would have first editions of tomorrow's newspapers. He could read a hard copy of the *Mirror,* see what sort of a splash they'd made of the story his tip-off had given Will Davies.

He didn't expect anything about the enigmatic Tom Curtis much beyond a name-check. It would be all about the mad scale of Saul Abercrombie's scheme. They'd run the archive shot of his arrest at the Red Lion Square demo back in the seventies. They'd do a run-down of his business career. There'd be an attempt at clarification on the state of his health. He didn't expect a quote from the man himself.

They might have a graphic of the proposed forest and its impact on the Welsh countryside. There'd be stats on acreage and tree numbers and infra-structural upheaval and the cost. He could read the story on his iPhone, but it would have much more impact on the printed page.

Reminded of Tom Curtis, he wondered resentfully why Isobel Jenks had chosen to bother him. Perhaps it was because she had already damaged Curtis as much as she needed to. He had discarded her callously. She had then, by turn, taken from him the woman he loved but had betrayed and the daughter he loved without reservation.

Baxter was confident she had been unaware, in life, of the deception involved in his own brief and admittedly cynical relationship with her. She was an unforgiving sort of character.

But how could she be aware in death of what she'd not known when living?

What had she meant by saying her work was accomplished? She hadn't completed her university course and been awarded her degree yet she'd been a diligent and bright student. The only thing Baxter thought she'd accomplished had been done obliquely, when she'd called Sarah Bourne and told her about her affair with Curtis.

Six months on and the repercussions from that call had compelled Curtis to take the job in Wales. In ordinary circumstances a man as fastidious as he was would probably have turned down something so grandiose. But he needed the money to fight for the right through the courts to see his daughter. He'd taken it on out of desperation. And he'd committed to the job only a few days before Isobel killed herself. But she couldn't have meant that, could she?

Baxter's car stereo blurted suddenly into life. His hands trembled slightly on the wheel and settled. He recognized the song. Over the course of the day, it had grown very familiar. He smelled the leathery cockpit of his car fill with the scent of the Calvin Klein fragrance she'd worn. He had the name of it now. It was called Eternity. And his nostrils filled with cigarette smoke, freshly exhaled from the seat next to him.

He only glanced at her. He only looked at her for a fraction of a second. She did not look good in the bleached halogen light of the night motorway. She was dead-eyed and grinning, her face a foot away from his, the impression from the bootlace black and livid encircling the soft tissue of her neck. The steering wheel convulsed in his grip.

He was aware of the crump and jolt as his nearside tyre burst and his wheel rim hit the rise of the central reservation, but the impact of the bridge pillar he collided with was head-on and at the speed he was doing, David Baxter felt nothing at all as his car impacted with its flat concrete mass.

It was past her bedtime and she knew it and she knew that her mother knew it too, Sarah thought, watching Charlie as she sketched on her drawing pad in her pyjamas. Sometimes she was guilty of keeping her daughter up just for the company.

Sometimes she was guilty of doing it to try to compensate for
the things that made Charlie a sadder and more reflective child
than she ought to have been at seven.

'What are you drawing, darling?'

'It's the angry man.'

Angry didn't sound ideal, but man was better than monster,
she supposed. Sarah had been almost concerned enough about
her daughter's dreams and the violent images inspired by them
to seek professional help.

Charlie seemed calmer though than over recent weeks.
She'd been much more relaxed since the delivery of the letter
to her father a couple of days earlier. Sarah hadn't read its
contents because she felt that would have been a betrayal of
her daughter's trust. But she guessed from Charlie's relief
after it had been delivered that it had some connection to
the dreams.

She could ask. She could do it now. But she didn't think it
a good idea to raise the subject of the father Charlie pined for
just before her daughter went to bed. She wanted Charlie's
room to be a happy, cosy place and for sleep to come easily
to her without tears and melancholy.

She'd text Tom to ask him whether he intended to respond
to the letter. She'd do it after Charlie went up. If she did that
he'd be confident that she'd be given the reply and that it
wouldn't be intercepted and torn up by her spiteful mother.

Was she spiteful? She thought that she probably was. Hurt
was what she definitely was. Mother and daughter both bore
the wounds of Tom's betrayal. But whatever he'd done, he
loved his daughter and, encouraged, would find the time to
write her something kind she could place under her pillow
and re-read whenever she needed to be reminded of him in a
positive way. It was what you did with children. You nurtured
them.

There had been something about the Abercrombie project
on the evening news. The story was being broken as an exclusive in the following day's edition of the *Mirror*, but journalists
gossiped and as soon as a teaser appeared on the paper's
website, there were speculative stories on the Sky and ITN
bulletins. They were sketchy and sensational, but they claimed

the project was unprecedented in its scale and ambition and its ecological credentials.

It was ironic that Tom should succeed on such a stage now after years of obscurity and under-achievement. Sarah was confident he would succeed. She might be still hurting, but she still knew that he was brilliant at what he did for a living. The forest would flourish. Saul Abercrombie would realize a rich man's majestic folly.

'Can I look at the picture of the angry man?'

'It isn't quite finished.'

No, young lady, Sarah thought, with a smile at the use of the classic staying-up-that-bit-later ploy. 'You won't finish it tonight, darling. It's way past your bedtime already.'

Charlotte sighed and paused. She said, 'It's almost finished. You can look if you really want to.'

The angry man looked like he was covered in tree bark. There were whorls and runnels in his skin. When she looked closer she saw that they were rents in his flesh, as though he'd been wounded everywhere and the wounds had not been stitched or bandaged but allowed to begin to heal grotesquely.

'He's very ugly, sweetheart, never mind angry. What's he so angry about?'

'I don't know. The words he says in the dream make no sense. He talks nonsense. I think he might be mad. He's lost. Maybe he's angry about being lost.'

'Is he scary?'

'Everyone in the dreams is scary except my dad.'

'Who is scariest?'

'I think the lady who doesn't want to be drawn. I haven't seen her face, Mummy. I wouldn't like to.'

'Is your dad in danger in the dream?'

'Yes. That's why I had to write the letter, to warn him. But I've warned him now and my daddy is quite brave and clever, you know.'

'Of course he is, Charlie. Now go up and brush your teeth.'

'Will you come and snuggle me in?'

'Ten minutes.'

When Charlie had gone up, Sarah switched on her desktop and went to the BBC website to see if there was anything further on there about the Pembrokeshire project. As she scrolled down a local story caught her eye. There'd been a motoring fatality on the M25 not far short of the Kingston exit. There was a picture of a car flattened against a bridge pillar.

She winced, looking at the picture, which she assumed had been taken on a smart phone by a passenger in a vehicle driving past the scene. These modern devices, with their auto-focus and mega-pixilation, were the bane of her industry, because of the flaws they exposed whenever they were pointed at a celebrity face.

But they had a worse role to play in the way they intruded into personal tragedy, ensuring that nothing ever really remained private anymore. The car wreckage was a ragged concertina of chrome and glass and fawn bodywork and seat upholstery, and there was a vivid crimson splash against the concrete where the accident victim had collided with it after crashing through his windscreen.

The only consolation was that the twenty-seven-year-old at the wheel had been the only person travelling in the car. It wouldn't be much of a comfort to his grieving family, but it was something.

There was a head and shoulders shot of the dead man. He was young and nice-looking in a studious sort of way, and Sarah thought there was something vaguely familiar about him.

There was nothing really new about Pembrokeshire. There was speculation about the budget and a bit about some diggers awaiting customs clearance in the port of Fishguard. But anyone could conclude that the roots of mature trees would require quite a bit of planting space. And excavating machines, whatever their dimensions, were not the sort of thing Sarah really got excited reading about.

She switched on the radio. She liked Smooth Radio – easy listening without the obvious clichés, a serene contrast to the frenetic MTV based stuff she was always obliged to endure on shoots. She poured herself a glass of wine. Dusty Springfield was singing the last few bars of, 'I Only Want to be With You'. Or it might have been the version by the Tourists. The presenter was fading it out and it was too indistinct and brief a snatch of song to tell. It was followed by Marvin Gaye singing, 'What's Goin' On?'

Humming along, she walked over to the table carrying her wine glass and sat and turned Charlotte's sketch pad around so that she could make a clear study of The Angry Man. She grimaced. He was shaven-headed and heavily muscled, sitting despondently beside a cairn of stones and he looked like he'd been flayed.

She had the sense that these images were being presented to her daughter whole. They had nothing to do with her imagination or her interests. They were as skilfully done as they were because Charlie had inherited the gift for drawing that both of her parents possessed. But she executed them as though it was some ponderous responsibility.

For Sarah, the proof of this lay in the bottom corner of the page, to the right of the cairn, where Charlie, bored, had sketched her father's smiling face. It was careless and cartoonish and didn't belong with the grim exactitude of the main image represented there. That she'd done out of a kind of duty. This she'd done purely for fun.

She looked at her watch. Eight minutes had elapsed since Charlotte had climbed the stairs. She was supposed to brush her teeth for two. She'd be in bed. Sarah would go up now and snuggle her in. Her daughter might already be asleep, but Sarah was a woman who liked always to keep her promises.

Saul Abercrombie was in the basement communications room reading about his forest project in various on-line media and Francesca had retired to bed when Pete told Dora and Curtis about his experience earlier in the day on the shore. He seemed relieved to get it off his chest. Curtis concluded it was what had been bothering him since the moment they'd met him at the western gate.

'I don't know if it was on Abercrombie's land or it wasn't,' he said. 'If it wasn't, it couldn't have been far from being.'

'The cave's on the estate, all right,' Curtis said. 'It's quite famous. You might say it's almost mythic. I don't think there can be two of them.'

They were on the terrace. Night had long since fallen and they had a busy day ahead of them and a full day just behind them, but none of them had felt like turning in and, old friends as well as colleagues, they'd had some catching up to do with one another.

'I was scared,' Pete said. 'I don't mind admitting it. I could try to butch it out and say otherwise and that's a temptation now, full of Dutch courage as I am, but being scared seemed like sound instinct at the time. Running away struck me as nothing more than common sense.'

'You're a wuss,' Dora said, reaching from her side of the table they shared and ruffling his hair. 'It was probably an unwanted dog, a stray that's made the cave its home.'

'It wasn't. No dog on earth smells like that. It was too bloody big to be a dog.'

'It could have been a dog with distemper – one of the larger breeds. Maybe a Rottweiler, something like that. There's a mundane explanation, whatever it was,' she said.

Curtis said nothing. He thought that Pete's story fitted very neatly with what he'd heard from Saul and Francesca when they'd told him the legend of Gregory, slayer of dragons, the knight summoned from Cornwall to dispose of monsters hereabouts. On the other hand he didn't know of any living creature that could endure for a thousand years. A tree could do it, an oak at a push, a sequoia comfortably. But not a mammal or reptile and besides, Gregory had done what he'd been sent to do and killed all the monsters.

He didn't think there was anyone living who thought this location was weirder than he did. Freemantle might have; he'd known it for substantially longer and knew it much better. But Curtis had come to the conclusion that Freemantle was unlikely still to be alive. Maybe his old gangland contacts had caught up with him over something unresolved. If he was alive, he would have returned.

His thinking pretty much echoed Francesca's on that. He thought nothing mattered so much to Sam Freemantle as did the approval and attention of his boss. He'd said he'd take a bullet for Saul and the claim hadn't struck Curtis at the time as hollow rhetoric. He'd failed to return because he'd been unable to. Death was a conclusive limiter of choice.

But Curtis had decided to keep quiet about the weirdness. If Pete and Dora discovered it for themselves, experienced and spoke about it, then that was a kind of vindication. He'd know then that he wasn't just being over-imaginative in a place sufficiently desolate to provoke the senses into irrationality.

There was another reason, more compelling than the first. His persistent belief in this was a major reason the weirdness hadn't deterred him from first staying and then returning and then resolving that nothing would scare him into running away.

He sincerely believed that once the great diggers churned the earth and they began to root trees firmly and in earnest, the character of the land would be transformed. If it wasn't benign now, it would become so. He'd bloody well see to it.

He'd build a land if not quite fit for Center Parcs, then fit for a family day out in the forest. There'd be picnics and ramblers and maybe a bit of orienteering and hard-core mountain biking over dedicated forest trails. A sanctuary for red squirrels wasn't out of the question. Looking out from where he sat, knowing that Puller's Reach and Raven Dip and worst of all Gibbet Mourning were out there in the darkness, it all still seemed pretty improbable. But he was determined to achieve it.

'Why don't we take a look tomorrow?' Dora said.

'Because there won't be time,' Curtis said. 'There are a hundred and fifty men and women arriving the day after tomorrow. They need to be shown to their quarters and fed and inducted and briefed. Shortly after they arrive, the first serious tree tonnage will start to come in. That's road and rail and air and it's a twenty-four-seven operation. You know all this. We don't have time for Famous Five adventures.'

'There are only three of us,' Pete said.

'Five if we include Saul and Francesca,' Dora said. 'And you've just confirmed we have free time tomorrow, Tom.'

Curtis said, 'When the diggers arrive.'

'With teams to drive them,' she said. 'You only have to show them where.'

Curtis shook his head. Dora was a wilful woman. He knew from experience that it was sometimes hard to deflect her from what she wanted. That said, he was proof it could be done.

'Won't Saul want to explore this cave? Or has he done so already?'

'No, he hasn't. He's never located it. It's never been explored in modern times. It's mostly been a detail in a story from folklore. He could have looked for it, I suppose. He's owned the land here for a decade. But it's never been a priority. I don't think he has any great relish for potholing.'

'Sensible man,' Pete said, 'neither do I.'

'I think it would excite his curiosity,' Dora said.

And Curtis knew that she intended to tell him about it, regardless of the consequences. Abercrombie must have kept his promise to flirt with Dora while he was busy with Eddie Stanhope and Patsy Carew. They'd established some sort of a relationship and Dora wanted to contribute something to it beyond batting her eyelashes and blushing at his compliments. Maybe she was also intrigued by the idea of the cave. She was an adventurous woman. She wasn't frightened of Rottweiler dogs.

'I'll tell you what I know about it,' Curtis said. 'I'll tell you what Saul and Francesca told me. It can be your bedtime story, folks, because I reckon on turning in, fairly shortly.'

'I love a bedtime story,' Dora said, smiling.

'Will there be time afterwards for questions?' Pete said.

It was close to midnight when Curtis reached his room, closed the door softly behind him and began unbuttoning his shirt with a yawn that made his jaw stretch and crack. He was about to ease it off his shoulders when he felt his mobile vibrate in his breast pocket. This late, he thought it might be Sarah, to tell him Charlotte had been stricken by some child ailment. Estranged and distanced as he was, he dreaded that. But it was Saul Abercrombie.

'Yes?'

'I'm in the comms room. I need to speak with you, Tree Man. It won't wait. Find your way down here.'

His first thought on entering was that the comms room would have done a nuclear submarine or an intelligence services monitoring station proud. It was bristling with hardware and everything was bleeping or pulsing and bright and shiny and state of the art. His second thought was that Abercrombie looked, for the first time, like a man without much time left to live. It had been a long and strenuous day for him. He'd probably drawn the same gloomy conclusion Curtis had about Freemantle and was grieving the loss of his to-do guy.

'I just spoke with the journalist, Will Davies, the dude breaking the story about our project here tomorrow. He informed me of the death of a guy who did some very recent work for me. The death isn't suspicious. The work concerned you.'

'You'd better explain.'

Abercrombie took a breath and paused. He was seated half in shadow, intermittently lit by flickering displays on some of the machinery that enabled him to keep in touch with a far-flung business empire from a remote location in rural Wales. Curtis felt his mobile vibrate in his pocket with an incoming text.

'Saul? I said you'd better explain.'

'This project is life and death to me, Tom. It's the last and most significant act of my life. It can't go wrong. I had you checked out. You know I had a private detective scrutinize your life to make absolutely sure you were my man. A guy named David Baxter. He was a perfectionist, or he was a completest, maybe.'

'Meaning what?'

'He went too far. He went further than I wanted him to.'

'How far was that?'

'Isobel Jenks.'

'Jesus.'

'Isobel Jenks is dead, Tom. She killed herself yesterday. Nothing to do with Baxter, that's just a ghoulish coincidence. Will Davies might call you, so I had to tell you. And I want to apologize for the intrusion into your private life.'

'A completely unnecessary intrusion.'

'I didn't know that until Baxter confirmed it. There's our paradox, brother. I couldn't gamble on good faith, not with the stakes as high as they are here. I had to betray your trust to prove to myself you're a man worthy of mine.'

'Neatly put.'

'I'm sorry. Will you resign? Will you quit on me?'

'The late Mr Baxter will have provided you with the answer to that one, Saul. You know I won't quit. Pride's a luxury I can't afford.'

'Rock and a hard place, brother. Tough, for a man of principle.'

Curtis was tempted to ask Abercrombie what the fuck did he know about principle? But it was very late at night for futile point scoring. 'Pete Mariner found your cave, by the way. Totally by chance. He was lost on his way here. Dora's all for exploring it tomorrow.'

'I'm sure Fran will be too,' Abercrombie said. 'I'm sorry about Isobel Jenks, if you still felt anything for her, I mean.'

'I never did,' Curtis said. 'I barely remember what happened with her.'

He remembered the text he'd received a few minutes earlier when he got back to his room. He discovered that there were two unread. The first was from Stanhope. A chopper was making an inaugural landing on the helipad just before first light the following day as a formal test of its fitness for purpose. There would be a crate in its payload bay. The contents of the crate were two-mil spec flame throwers equipped with two full tanks of fuel apiece.

The second text was from Sarah. It was a reminder to write a reply to the letter Charlotte had written him.

He decided he would write it there and then. He could compose a letter on his laptop and send it as an email attachment. Sarah could print it off for Charlotte in the morning. But she had taken the time and trouble to put pen to paper and then find an envelope and a stamp. It was quite a series of tasks for a seven-year-old to accomplish. It was the least he could do to do the same in return.

Eddie Stanhope's crew would be packing up and leaving at noon the following day. He'd give the letter to Stanhope when he went to pick up the flame throwers and ask him to post it. Military types were reliable in obliging with a favour of that nature. Soldiers above all people appreciated the importance of mail.

He finally fell asleep musing drowsily over the contents of Charlotte's letter. Her warning had been grave and uncannily accurate in some of the specifics of the Abercrombie domain. But there were no monsters to pursue him, were there? It would be proven when they explored the monsters' lair on their Famous Five adventure. That was if Saul was up to it, which he hadn't looked, to Curtis. They'd find no monsters, though. Gregory of Avalon had slain them all a thousand years ago.

Francesca awoke at four a.m. slightly hung-over but completely sober. She'd turned in at ten and generally got six or seven hours of uninterrupted sleep. So she'd had six, which was probably about right, given how uncharacteristically early she'd gone to bed. But retiring early had stranded her in the small hours with no real prospect of further slumber. The house was completely quiet. No one was yet coming out to play. For a while, at least, she was totally on her own.

She'd made a fool of herself at Puller's Reach with Tom Curtis. She hadn't realized how attracted she was to him until the competition arrived in the alluring shape of Dora Straub. She'd felt dismayed at Dora's arrival, seeing the lithe, dark-eyed German woman with the sculpted cheekbones and the shining hair pull up at the house in her Jeep. She'd chided herself silently for being shallow and frivolous and then over-compensated by being awfully English and nice.

And then she'd had too much to drink with Pete and Dora and her father and come out with the stupid remarks to Curtis that she'd made on the edge of the cliff.

There was some mitigation. There was the booze, obviously. There was her father's increasing frailty, which his reduced tolerance to drink had made poignantly obvious. That had upset her. There was the cumulative tedium of having lived in isolation on the estate for the weeks she had since her father's prognosis, with only Freemantle, the steroid-fed lap-dog, for light relief. And the weirdness with the yew tree had thrown her. It had provoked her puerile joke about Balkan kidnappers, but it had actually been unnerving.

Despite these excuses, she felt foolish and humiliated. It

was premature and immature to have the crush she had on a
man she'd only spent a few hours with. It made her wonder
whether he had this effect generally on women. It made her
wonder whether he the sort of cynical opportunist who took
advantage of that if he did.

She groaned, sat up in bed and groped carefully for the
glass of water she habitually filled before turning in. It wasn't
there. Her bedside table held no glass. She'd been too tipsy
to remember it. And the further problem was her intuition
insisting that Curtis wasn't that type at all. He'd been happily
monogamous, before his one ill-judged foray into infidelity.

She was thirsty. She was regretful. She was embarrassed
and Francesca was also by this point quite wide awake. She
pulled back the covers, swung her legs out and planted her
feet on her bedroom floor. She got up and went to her window,
pulled back the curtains and saw fog pressed up as dense and
pale grey as something solid against the panes.

She felt distrustful of fog. Not ordinarily, but here, on her
father's Welsh domain, she was uneasy about it. She had only
experienced it once before and she had nursed the suspicion
then that it was less a benign natural phenomenon than it was
present to achieve something specific. Its purpose had been to
disorientate and frighten Tom Curtis, to make him wary about
the history and character of the land he had been engaged to
transform into something other than what it was.

She saw that one of the panes was streaked. Moisture had
dribbled down four parallel vertical lines that looked as though
a human hand had trailed them on the glass and left them
there. She recoiled and stepped back a couple of paces into
the body of her room. She stumbled on the edge of a rug and
very nearly screamed doing so.

Members of the Balkan kidnap gang Curtis had feared were
out there, really out there, surrounding the house, ready to
break in and take her sick father away in a kidnap effort that
would surely kill him in his debilitated state. It was an ordeal
he didn't possess the strength to survive. For the first time she
felt the novel sensation of missing Sam Freemantle's bois-
terous, swaggering presence.

But it couldn't be a gang. Even in the fog they would have

tripped the security lights. Freemantle had placed those and had done so with an ex-con's expert appreciation of the manner in which crimes involving breaches of security were carried out. The lights couldn't be disabled from outside the house. Men creeping about out there in numbers would certainly have triggered them.

She couldn't wake the others. Not on the strength of a trickle of condensation and a fraught imagination, she couldn't. It was said there was safety in numbers and it was a temptation to rouse them. Curtis and Pete were powerfully built men. Teutonic Dora didn't seem the sort to panic at the threat of danger; quite the opposite, in fact. But if there was nothing out there – and the absence of the lights suggested there wasn't anything – she was the one who would look like she'd panicked.

She decided she would go and fetch a pistol from the armoury. Freemantle had insisted she learn how to use one a week earlier. Any number of tedious drills had followed. She'd proven to be an excellent shot. He'd made her try three or four models and asked her to choose the one which felt happiest in her hand.

Francesca didn't like guns. She had an English attitude towards them. She thought guns and happiness mutually exclusive. But they were useful tools in dire circumstances and she wasn't going to shoot anyone accidentally. The Glock was the pistol she had felt most comfortable with. It had a good balance, a fast action and it held seventeen nine-millimetre rounds. Hand guns were not particularly accurate weapons. But close-up, the Glock was as accurate as they got.

She was on her way back to her room, her feet finding the familiar route along the corridor in darkness, when a figure loomed from her left and blundered heavily into her. She tightened her grip on the pistol, stepped back and steadied herself, raised it between both hands and slipped off the safety catch as she did so, pointing it at the hulking silhouette.

'Sorry.'

It was Pete. She recognized his voice. There was enough light to see a pale suggestion of blond hair framing his face.

'Is that a gun?'

'Why are you up?'

'Went to the kitchen for something cold to drink from the fridge, dehydrated from all the beer. Sorry.'

'It's OK.' She had almost shot him and not accidentally.

'Why have you got a gun, Francesca?'

'I think there's someone outside the house in the fog. They shouldn't be there. Can you shoot?'

He yawned and scratched himself. 'I can, actually. Coniferous job in Russia, oligarch billionaire, bears in the woods, long story. But yes, I can shoot.'

She took him down to the armoury. He selected and loaded a .22 Remington bolt action using only the dim light above one of the rifle racks so that they wouldn't be blind when they got outside. Not that they'd see very much if the fog was as thick as it had looked from inside her bedroom window.

She noticed that Pete Mariner slept in track pants and a singlet. His biceps bunched powerfully when he checked the Remington's action and the singlet was taut across his pectoral muscles. She was glad to have found him awake and relieved not to have killed him. He was reassuring, a comforting presence.

He put the rifle over his shoulder and glanced around and yawned again. 'Your dad runs a private army?'

'Come on.'

They exited the rear of the house, the route Francesca habitually used to make her way to her studio. Her bedroom window was set in the wall to their right, when they rounded the corner, eighty or ninety metres away, closer to the front of the building. The fog was dense and palpable, almost sulphurous to breathe, like some element delivered them from a remote and darker time.

She felt there was something there, observing them. She had an inkling of something still and watchful but it had alerted her senses and raised and coarsened her skin in gooseflesh in a way that nothing merely human ever had.

Pete must have sensed it too. He put out an instinctive arm and pushed her to his own rear protectively. Practically, it was a slight she could live with. He was twice her size and she noticed he moved silently across the grey, damp ground beneath them.

Ahead of them, there was a bark of sound. It was as anguished as a death rattle and as inhuman as the shrill of wind through reeds. It pronounced her name. It struggled with the consonants. But it was unmistakeably her name that reverberated through the folds of mist.

Pete raised his rifle. He chambered a round. He swung the barrel from left to right in a long, chest-height lateral sweep. He swung it back again, alert to sound, seeking a solid target in all the groping blindness before them. She observed that the weapon was rock steady in his grip.

'There's nothing there,' he said, eventually.

'There was, though.'

'Yes, there was. It spoke your name. But whatever it was is gone now.'

SEVEN

They took a Land Rover to the spot where Eddie Stanhope's boys had built the airstrip and helipad. The five of them breakfasted together first and it was decided that they'd explore Pete's cave once Curtis, with Pete's help, had finally eradicated the thorn bush at Gibbet Mourning. When they'd completed that bit of unfinished business, Pete could return in the vehicle they were taking out and Curtis could return the one Freemantle had left there.

Curtis got the impression over his wholemeal toast and Marmite that Abercrombie never really expected to see his estate manager again. It was a mysterious and possibly ominous state of affairs but in an ironic way quite fitting. Soon there would be no estate for him to manage. There would instead be a huge forest for which his skill-set was not required.

After they'd told Francesca about the cave, she told them about the nocturnal interlude she'd shared with Pete. Dora stressed Pete's terror in his brief exploration of the cavern in the cliff face. She played the story for laughs and got them from everyone, except Francesca. When Francesca related her story, she seemed determined to portray Pete as someone possessed of a cool and laconic courage.

'He's schizophrenic,' Curtis said, who thought that Pete might be on the way to making a conquest.

'The mark on the glass was a freaky incidence of condensation,' Abercrombie said. 'Not even that freaky, when you consider how often people claim to see the face of Christ in a soiled dishcloth or on a potato chip. The noise you heard was some nocturnal creature you disturbed. This is a wilderness, remember? We're the interlopers here, not the other way around.'

The fog had thinned slightly by the time they set off for the rendezvous with Stanhope. Curtis called him first just to make sure that the conditions on the ground allowed for the scheduled chopper flight. He was told they did. He remembered his letter to Charlotte, which was buttoned into his jacket pocket.

Curtis drove. He released the handbrake and depressed the clutch and eased the transmission into gear. After a minute, he said, 'The thing is, I never know where I stand, do I, Pete? I mean which Pete's sitting beside me? Is it the trembling, cowardly Pete, or Pete the dashing hero? From one minute to the next, how the hell am I supposed to know?'

'Very bloody funny, not. Did you notice Saul this morning?'

'Of course I did. He's our boss.'

'I mean did you notice how he looked? He looked terrible.'

'Don't try to change the subject. Where did last night's alpha male stuff come from? Was it just showing off?'

'I had back-up. And I had a rifle in my hands.'

'Get you, Annie Oakley.'

'That would be a more fitting name for Fran. She was packing the pistol. And it's probably escaped your notice, Tom, but she's female.'

'So it's Fran, is it?'

Pete shrugged tightly, staring straight ahead at the featureless view through the windscreen.

'I'm only kidding, mate. I haven't had a chance to do much of that over the last few weeks. It's really good to have you here.'

Pete didn't reply for a moment. Then he said, 'I'd say it's really good to be here, Tom. But I've got my doubts and they're getting more serious all the time.'

'What do you think that was, in the fog?'

'I haven't got a fucking clue. But I can tell you she didn't imagine it. Whatever it was, it was out there. Fingers trailed that mark left on her bedroom window. I'm not saying they were human fingers, but that mark was left by a hand.'

In his breast pocket, Curtis felt his mobile start to vibrate. He asked Pete to take the call. There was zero chance of being caught doing it, but out of ingrained habit, he never used his cellular when he drove.

'He's driving,' Pete said into the phone, flatly. He listened for a while. Eventually he said, 'I'll tell him. Goodbye.'

'There's little about you more heart-warmingly impressive than your phone manner,' Curtis said. 'Who was it?'

'Some bloke called Carrington, sounded about a hundred and fifty years old. Said it was important you looked up the story of the Crawley family and what happened to them. They lived at Loxley's Cross in Victorian times. He probably knew them personally. Why are you so cheerful this morning?'

'Because of what we're going to do when we get what it is we're picking up from Eddie Stanhope,' Curtis said.

'A bit of routine clearance has got you this excited? Since when have you been a pyromaniac?'

'It isn't routine clearance,' Curtis said. 'It's personal. Andrew Carrington, right?'

'Professor Andrew Carrington, yeah, and the family were the Crawleys. He said the info's in the public domain. He said you can get it doing an Internet search.'

'And this is important, now, more than a century after the events?'

'Vital, was the word he used,' Pete said.

Curtis shook his head. The big diggers were due imminently. Trees were scheduled to start arriving by road and rail and air. A workforce so substantial it required its own quartermaster to keep it stocked in food rations and soap and toilet rolls was about to take up residence in a purpose-built village and begin the serious toil of planting.

The air would be alive with the judder of heavy machines and the calls and commands of labouring men and women. They would churn and sweat and upheave and transform. And he was supposed to find the time to research a Victorian family who had once lived on a part of Abercrombie's land.

He supposed he could do it, if he remembered to. He had found the time to write to Charlotte. That had been important. But he was prepared to waste that very afternoon with what he now thought of as Dora Straub's Cavern Club.

They were there. Under the fog, with its landing lights and neatly painted navigation signage, the smooth expanse of the strip looked so immaculate and out of place it seemed altogether surreal.

*   *   *

Dora felt slightly resentful that Pete had been Tom's default choice as deputy in the thorn bush assignment. It was a routine task and it was physical in nature but she was hardly what the British called a shrinking violet. She was strong and capable and confident handling equipment and machinery. And she hadn't had a chance to have Tom to herself for a moment since her arrival.

It was true that she had a more cerebral, even spiritual approach to the whole subject of forestry than Pete Mariner did. Her great-grandfather had been a fairly high-ranking member of the Nazi military elite. He had hunted deer and wild boar with Goering. He had shared Goering's semi-mystical faith in the cultural and folkloric power of woodland. The Aryan paganism they had begun to explore back then had set great store by woodland traditions and beliefs.

She didn't discuss this family influence on her thinking. She knew it would be stupid and even self-destructive to do so. It would cost her the position she valued at the university. Professionally, it might lead to her being ostracized. But it was there, undeniable and ineradicable in her bloodline and subconscious mind.

None of this interest in and empathy for the spiritual aspect of the forest affected her ability to carry out practical tasks. She thought Tom had chosen Pete, influenced by Pete's gung-ho reaction to the intruder Francesca had imagined was outside her room. It was easy, to her mind, to put on a bold display of courage when you not only carried a loaded gun but knew your protagonist was illusory. Faced by what he regarded as real danger, in the cave in the cliff face, Pete had simply fled.

She'd wanted to at least see the great bush at Gibbet Mourning Tom had described before its destruction. It had sounded to her like an intriguing hybrid. She suspected someone had bred and planted it there for a purpose. That purpose would now go undiscovered and she was a woman who liked to get to the bottom of botanical and biological mysteries.

The fog was thinning. Francesca was painting in her studio. Saul had departed for his comms room after breakfast saying he needed to deal with what he called the fallout from the newspaper story about the project they were here to facilitate. A delegation was threatening to turn up at the gates: a mixed interest group of naturalists, ramblers, local politicians, curious neighbours and even an environmental historian. Dora hadn't been aware that such an academic specialism even existed.

She could sit smoking on the terrace, which was all she had done since breakfast finished. She could stare out at the limited view allowed by that light blanket of grey. Or she could do something worthwhile in the time before their planned exploration of the cave.

She decided that she would take a quad and go and look again at the cairn of stones at Puller's Reach. She wanted to examine the second yew tree, the one Tom was insistent had not been planted there deliberately. Amid the tipsy showboating of the previous evening's visit, she had not really examined that mystery as thoroughly as she felt she should have.

She wanted too to get a real, authentic feel for the land. She had not thought the British Isles possessed the space for a wilderness like that which Abercrombie owned, bordering the sea on a vast western flank and reaching and stretching for miles inland. But then this was her first visit to Wales. She tended to work on the delicate and the carefully nurtured, like the recent job on Wight or the job on Jersey when she had first met her two companions here. This was a desolate place, a task of historic magnitude.

It was also an ancient place. Yews had seemed fitting species in their lonely spot at the edge of the sea. The cairn had hinted at a dark and secretive past. She would enjoy Puller's Reach on her own. She felt in no danger, at no risk whatsoever of physical harm here. It was an empathetic location. And Dora was a woman who revelled in her own company.

They stood beside the helipad with Stanhope and a couple of his boys and when they heard the rotors judder overhead, the boys went to either side of the pad and triggered flares. The flames burst into orange incandescence and the aircraft descended in a shit-storm of downdraft that Curtis thought might dispel the mist further. With the whump and vibration of the rotor blades and smoke from the flares blowing acridly about the place, it was difficult to tell.

There were protective suits and masks along with the flame throwers when they unloaded and unpacked the crate. The suits were flame and heat retardant and of the slightly cumbersome one-size-fits-all variety. Curtis and Pete Mariner climbed into them.

There were asbestos-lined gauntlets too, but these were a relatively snug fit, necessary because the manipulation of the petroleum jets was a delicate business. It required no real skill or even much experience. Basically you pointed and triggered. But it needed to be done precisely because of the throw of the flames and the ferocity of the temperature involved. It wouldn't do to be careless in what they were about to attempt. Fire maimed and destroyed and nothing could survive the heat this kind of hardware was built to generate.

They tossed their helmets into the back of the Land Rover, where the flame throwers had already been carefully placed. Curtis congratulated Stanhope on the work his outfit had accomplished. They were actually finishing ahead of schedule. He took out the letter he'd addressed to his daughter and asked if Stanhope could post it, a request met with an immediate promise to do so at the first opportunity. They shook hands, Curtis got back behind the wheel, and he and Pete were off on their way to Gibbet Mourning.

Had it not been for the fog, he perhaps wouldn't have noticed. But the fog was persistent and still dense in some clinging banks and drifts, and so he had fed the coordinates into the GPS on his smart phone.

The thorn bush was not where it was supposed to be. It no longer squatted balefully at the spot Freemantle had told Curtis was Gibbet Mourning. Nothing, from within the Land Rover, distinguished that location from any other.

When they got out of the vehicle, they saw signs of where it had been. There was a scatter of feathers and the corpses of a hundred or more small and pitiful birds. There was the wrench from the ground of a deep and solitary root system. But the thorns, the menacing presence that had defined the

place and given it its spiteful character, were gone. All that
was left was the vague smell of chlorophyll, a taint of avian
decomposition, the pungency of torn earth.

'This is too fucking weird,' Curtis said. He'd found
Freemantle's ride. It was the vehicle that looked like it had
moved, because it was nowhere near the landmark it had halted
close to. It was equipped with wheels. It was designed to travel
to places. But it hadn't. The thorn bush had.

'There,' Pete said, lifting an arm and pointing a finger
westward.

'All I can see is grey,' Curtis said, squinting into the distance.

'It cleared for a moment. I saw something, Tom. I saw a
smudge on the horizon in that direction. What else could it
be?'

So it was they found their bush, a thousand metres westward
of where it had been when it had surrendered a shotgun and
a clutch of spent shells and no clue whatsoever as to what had
happened to Saul Abercrombie's to-do guy on the ground, the
previous day.

They strapped on their harnesses. The metal cylinders
containing the jellied petroleum were heavy. The throwers
gave off an acrid, oily odour when they tested the flames and
the blossoming of radiant heat was wince inducing, even trig-
gering a fraction of the full throw they possessed.

The two men were where they had parked their vehicle,
still a good hundred metres distant from the closest reach of
their intended target. Curtis could not have articulated a reason
for stopping so far short. It was instinctive, this caution. He'd
seen the bush shiver and bristle in the gloaming a few evenings
earlier. He'd seen Freemantle's shotgun abandoned beside it.
He couldn't help noticing, with a clutch of dismay at his
stomach, that it had grown substantially since his last encounter
with it.

'It's fucking huge,' Pete said.

It was. Its thorns from this distance had the cruel enormity
of rhinoceros horns or the beak on a giant squid. They emerged
from limbs as thick as a man's torso and they glittered blackly
against the green tangle of the bush itself. They were of a
number impossible to count.

'Let's go,' Curtis said. 'Don't get too close to it, Pete.' His voice was no more than a murmur. His eyes were locked on the bush. He reckoned it to be twenty feet high at its centre and at least eighty feet across. It looked wary and malevolent in its dense and intricate coils. Worse than that, it looked somehow poised.

They walked towards the thorn bush. They were fifteen feet away when it began to shiver and hiss audibly and Curtis saw the limb-thick tendrils closest to them begin to convulse and uncoil and reach across the ground.

'Now,' he said. Twin spurts of orange fire burst and bellowed from their flame throwers, burning and blackening everything in the ferocity of a thousand withering degrees of heat.

The bush screamed. It rose and scrabbled in a frenzy of movement, Curtis thought, like some great arachnid creature as its limbs were turned to carbon. The two men walked forward, steadily, methodically, scorching and destroying the thing writhing and shrieking in front of them.

They stopped only when it was entirely reduced to ash. Pete lifted the visor of his helmet. He was sweating, breathing heavily. Curtis could feel the heat of the thrower's hose barrel through his asbestos gloves. He could feel heat rise from the smouldering ground. There was a sweetish stench from where sap had boiled and bubbled out of the thorn limbs and then been blackened to cinder by the heat of the flames.

'It was alive,' Pete said.

'Of course it was fucking alive,' Curtis said.

'I mean it was animate,' Pete said. 'Fucking thing screamed.'

'Calm down,' Curtis said.

'I'll have a beer tonight,' Pete said. 'Reckon I've earned it.'

'You have a beer every night.'

'Tonight's is justified.'

'I'll join you,' Curtis said, 'but we've got Dora's Cavern Club excursion to come before then.'

The mist was clearing from the coastline as Dora approached Puller's Reach. A couple of times en route she glanced southwards, to where the map had told her Gibbet Mourning lay. But it was too far away for her to see the macho pyrotechnics she knew Curtis and his dopy sidekick were indulging in there. On a clear night, she might have seen a distant flicker of orange fire. On a grey day the view was opaque and diminished. Curtis had described the thorn bush though and it hadn't sounded like the sort of protagonist you'd take on in the darkness.

That was why she'd been so intrigued to see it, really. He'd made it out to be hazardous in a way that seemed to manifest deliberate malice. Plants were not malicious. Even a Venus Fly Trap took no pleasure in what it did. It was just a mindless evolutionary novelty. Giving plant-life human qualities was stupid. Thorns were sometimes described as vicious, it was true. But that was really no more than linguistic laziness. The barbed growth at Gibbet Mourning had got to Curtis, had rattled and provoked him.

Now she was doing it. The provocation hadn't been deliberate, had it? It couldn't possibly have been. But he had been angered by the ugliness of the bush, by its squat density and size and by the grisly feathered trophies it unwittingly displayed. Destroying it had become a point of principle for him. She had never known him react so emotionally to a job as he was doing to the specifics of this one.

She was there. And there were three yew trees at the spot. She only became aware of this when she dismounted from the bike. The third yew, smaller than its fellows, had been hidden from her sightline on approach. It lay directly behind the yew Curtis had planted, equidistant between that and the edge of the cliff.

She got down on her hands and knees and examined the ground around its slender trunk, tracing the surface with her fingers and palms. It was not just unbroken but unblemished. The tree emerged from grass that would pale and wither and grow brittle in the future in its shade, but for now it was still healthy and undisturbed.

She stood and backed away from the small copse the trio of yews now amounted to. She sniffed salt air and looked out over the water, which had a glazed serenity under the seepage of sunlight the clearing mist allowed. She heard a snigger of laughter, as if at nature's mysterious joke. And she realized that it wasn't laughter but a trick of sound created as the wind whistled and soughed through the stones of the Puller's Reach cairn.

She looked in that direction. And she saw that there was a figure standing still and watching her from beside the stone monument. She didn't think it was the half-human interloper who had spooked Francesca Abercrombie in the small hours. The figure was slight, attired in a dark hooded shawl. Dora couldn't see facial features – the hood concealed them. It was either an adolescent boy or it was a woman. She did not think that adolescent boys in rural Wales wore shawls.

Dora didn't sense any danger. The descent to the shore was eighty or ninety feet. The drop was sheer. A lunatic could jump her in so remote a spot and send her toppling over the edge of the cliff to her death. But she was almost certainly physically stronger than the person in the shawl and she could not now be taken unawares. She approached the cairn. She felt only the impulse of curiosity in doing so.

'Hello, Dora.'

'You know my name.'

'I know all your names.'

'Then you have me at a disadvantage.'

'Oh, the disadvantage is all mine,' the woman said. She laughed.

She sounded quite young and completely relaxed to Dora, who had still not been able to make out her features, shadowed as they were by the hood. She'd thought the fabric black from a distance. This close, she saw that it was an intensely dark shade of green.

'You'll have to explain that remark.'

'There's some question over ownership, Dora. There's a modern saying that possession is nine points of the law. Saul Abercrombie has possession, but this land will never belong to him.'

Dora didn't think the saying sounded very modern at all. She thought it probably dated from property disputes at least as long ago as early Victorian times. She said, 'You're claiming an ancestral right to this domain?'

'Historic,' the woman said.

'And you hate the idea of what we're here to do?'

'On the contrary, Dora, I love the idea of what you're here to do. It's utterly enchanting.'

'Well, it will be,' Dora said, glancing at the cairn, aware of having mentioned enchantment at that very place the evening before on first seeing it. 'You lost your historic rights? Your title deeds were stolen or confiscated?'

'We can't right past wrongs, Dora. We can't change history. No point dwelling on the past. We can only learn and try to profit from it. I think you of all people would appreciate that.'

Dora had certainly profited from history. Her family referred to her great-grandfather's war service euphemistically as his European tour. He had brought back souvenirs from Paris and Moscow, paintings her father had sold at auction for spectacular prices in the fine art boom years of the eighties, in the period just before provenance started to become a problem for German collectors.

The money had changed their lives. She had been fourteen then. They had gone from living in a fairly modest Berlin apartment building to an estate with stables and a cherry orchard on the edge of the Black Forest. It was where her interest in what she did had first been sparked and formed her personal history but this woman couldn't possibly be aware of it. Could she?

'What's your name?'

'Amelia.'

'It's a lovely name.'

'Yes, it is. By contrast Dora is an ugly name, but that matters little with you because its owner is quite beautiful.'

'Thank you. Why are you here? I mean at this spot?'

'I came to look at the yew trees.'

'They're a mystery, the way they've appeared to multiply.'

'Regeneration is what nature does.'

Dora looked back towards the trees. 'Yes, but I'm used to seeing that accomplished in less mysterious ways.'

Amelia took down her hood.

'Goodness. And you call me beautiful.'

'I want you to do something for me, Dora,' Amelia said. 'I want to ask of you a favour. It won't compromise your work here in any way, but it's important to me. And if you can help me, I'll be a good friend to you in return. Please feel free to say no. If you can find it in your heart to say yes, however, I'll be enormously grateful.'

Dora was mostly amused at the formal quality of this enigmatic little speech. But she was also intrigued. She liked adventures and she enjoyed surprises. She replied with an English phrase she'd heard but never used before. She said, 'I'm all ears.'

There was an argument before their departure over guns. Since none of them was held legally, Curtis felt they should be left under lock and key in the armoury. He reasoned that their ownership was a crime compounded by carrying them around loaded with the possible intention of using them.

Saul Abercrombie disagreed. He said that since they had the guns, they might as well take them. If the creature Pete had heard in the cave was still there, they would inevitably corner it on their approach. It might become hostile and dangerous and if it did, the guns would be necessary.

'We'll be unschooled marksmen, firing off rounds in a confined space with the real danger of blue on blue hits and the hazard of bullets ricocheting anywhere off granite walls,' Curtis said.

'Except I'm not unschooled,' Francesca said.

Dora said, 'Neither am I.'

Abercrombie looked at Pete. He said, 'Well?'

Pete looked at Curtis. 'Sorry, chief,' he said, 'I'm all for arming ourselves. I'm with Saul on this. It's just foolhardy not to, a total no-brainer.'

They travelled in two Land Rovers. Abercrombie judged the spot Pete had described to be about three miles inside the northern border of his land. When they reached terrain that looked like a giant golf links, Pete nodded, recognizing it. A few minutes after that they could smell the sea, then the shoreline came into view and they swung right along the strew of sand and pebbles parallel with the water.

They passed the cave entrance three times, backtracking laboriously, before Pete finally spotted it, crouching across the rear seats of the vehicle he was in with his head at the height it would be if he were seated astride his bike. In its oblique facet of rock, the entrance, even when visible, looked more like a shadow than an opening.

Each of them had a big Maglite torch, the sort that doubled as a club when used by police forces in America – heavily knurled metal housing long-life batteries and boasting a piercingly powerful beam.

They became silent as they progressed along the cave's length. They crept more than they walked. They were on a shallow descent, Curtis realized. After five or six hundred metres they had descended far enough underground for his ears to pop. He listened for Pete Mariner's flapping monster, but all he could hear was Saul Abercrombie's breathing, shallow and laboured. He'd looked shit that morning, as Pete had rightly observed. He really shouldn't have come.

Francesca said, 'Can anyone smell anything?'

'Only soot and petroleum from our two action heroes,' Dora said. 'They smell like a gas station forecourt on a hot day.'

'You smoke too much to possess any sense of smell,' Pete said.

'And you should have showered, both of you.'

Abercrombie said, 'All continentals, Dora, are obsessed with personal hygiene.'

To Curtis, despite his levity, Pete had sounded nervous.

Francesca said, 'I can smell something. There's a dead odour, like decomposition.'

'You're right,' Dora said, after a pause.

A dozen more metres further on, the odour had become so sharp and pervasive that Curtis thought they all must be aware of it. His feet slid on something. He crouched and looked and Francesca banged into him from behind. He was almost tipped into the puddle of slime on the cave floor in front of him. Be thankful for small mercies, he thought. At least her bloody gun didn't go off.

'Ugh. Sorry. What is that stuff?'

'It has the same viscosity as the mucus that comes off a slug. But it smells of the sea.'

'A sea slug?'

'There's about a gallon of the stuff down there.'

'Nothing's that slimy,' Pete said. He giggled. The giggle sounded nervous.

Francesca said, 'Well, clearly something is.'

Pete said, 'Dora's Rottweiler.'

Curtis rose and they pressed on.

He began to think about Gregory, the warrior from Cornwall who came here to despatch monsters millennia ago. He didn't know how much of the legend to believe. It bothered him that Francesca had described the account as a chronicle rather than a saga.

He knew enough about history to know that the former meant a true account, often written under oath, at a time when scribes believed not only in God but in the prospect of eternal damnation if they sinned. A lie of that magnitude would be a mortal sin. He would have to ask Carrington about the significance of that, should he remember to return the professor's call.

Gregory had approached this place from the sea. He had sailed there and beached his craft unwitnessed. He hadn't possessed a Maglite or a Glock pistol like the one holstered on Francesca's waist or the short-barrelled pump-action shotgun Pete had slung from its strap across his back. He'd probably carried a makeshift torch topped with burning pitch and a battleaxe thrust into his belt. Worst of all for him, though, was the fact that he'd come here entirely alone.

It would have been a hell of an ordeal. They believed in monsters then. They believed in demons and witches. Men of his class were bred for the quest, steeled psychologically for the tests they endured almost as a routine aspect of life. Heroism was an expectation that came with their noble station in life. But Curtis thought that even if you found no enemy to confront, exploring this place alone would be a fearful experience.

There was something tomb-like about the cave. It was just a corridor hewn from rock. It gave the impression of narrowing the further you travelled into it, but that was just the knowledge that every step towards its end took you deeper under the ground and further away from the light. It wasn't a tunnel, because it dead-ended eventually. He thought a catacomb must be like this.

The smell was rank and growing stronger, so strong that the urge to retch was becoming difficult to resist. Abercrombie's respiration now was a shallow rasp and Curtis realized that their boss hadn't spoken since entering the cave only because he didn't possess the necessary breath.

'We should rest for a minute,' he said.

'We should just keep going,' Pete said. 'The sooner we get to the end of this thing, the sooner we can get back out again.'

'Seems reasonable,' Dora said.

Francesca said, 'No, we should take five. Tired people make stupid mistakes.'

And Curtis thought that she had noticed how distressed the exploration had made her father and was being as tactful as was possible. There was his ego to consider. However frail, he was in overall charge.

After another moment, Abercrombie said, 'This is me done, people.'

Curtis said, 'That's a wise decision.'

'I'd love to go on, brother,' Saul said, 'but the decision's been made on my behalf. A throat like mine constricts the breathing. The further we go, the staler the air. Not a problem for you guys. For me, maybe a killer.'

'I'll stay with you, Dad. Come back with you, I mean.'

'The bogeyman doesn't scare me, honey. You go on.'

'Continue if you want to,' Curtis said to her. 'I'm happy to go back now with Saul. There's nothing down here but darkness and geology.'

'And whatever secreted that slime,' Pete said. 'And whatever's generating that stink, unless it's the same thing.'

'Which logically it would be,' Dora said.

'It must terminate fairly soon,' Curtis said, 'given how far we've already come.' He looked at Francesca.

She said, 'Everyone? Turn off your torches.'

They did. The darkness was abrupt and absolute. There was no hint of light. The only sound was their collective breathing. She said, 'Nothing lives down here. The air is rank and nothing could tolerate this total absence of light. Maybe something hides here from time to time, makes of it a refuge when it feels threatened. But this place is uninhabited. There isn't even a ghost.'

Pete switched his torch back on. Curtis would have bet money he'd be the first to do so. Women were more practical than men, weren't they? He felt pretty spooked and more uncomfortably claustrophobic than he ever had in his life. He didn't feel merely confined, but trapped. Dora and Francesca, of the five of them, were coping best.

He switched his torch back on. They all did. He said, 'You wait here with Francesca and Saul, Pete. I'll continue with Dora for another hundred metres or so. If it doesn't play out, we'll abandon. If it does, we'll take a quick look around and come back. Give us the ten minutes Saul needs to recover his breath. Then we're all out of here.'

Everyone but Saul nodded agreement. He rested on his haunches against the cave wall with his head on his knees. It occurred to Curtis that the route back was one long, steady incline. He thought that had probably occurred to all of them.

His hunch proved correct. About a hundred-and-twenty metres on, their torches revealed a gallery. It was where the cave ended. It seemed a natural feature, its walls and roof smooth, the dead stink that had accompanied them there possessed of a miasmic power here at the cave's conclusion.

They played their torch beams around. Dora's lit on an aperture about eight feet up in the wall to the left of where they stood. It wasn't much bigger than a crack, a chink of blackness at a blind angle it wasn't possible, from where they stood, to illuminate.

'Can you get me up there, Tom? I can reach it if I stand on your shoulders.'

'It's narrow. It probably leads to nowhere. You could get stuck. I don't think it's worth the risk.'

She shrugged and smiled at him. 'We've come this far,' she said.

He held on to the cave wall with both arms outstretched. She climbed up him, smooth and agile, and disappeared into the narrow opening with a kick of acceleration that ground the heel of her boot into his collarbone.

He waited nervously for a falling thump or shriek of pain signalling she'd trapped herself. A minute passed. Two minutes became three. Her feet and legs appeared and she squirmed out and down. He caught her and delivered her to the floor. She felt lithe and shapely in his arms and he inhaled the perfume physical effort had just revived on her hot skin. She smelled of fresh sweat and Shalimar.

'Led to nowhere, like you said it would,' she said. 'Could have been a storage space a thousand years ago but I'm with Francesca. No one ever lived here. It's too dark, even for monsters.'

'Let's get out,' Curtis said.

The excavators would take the rest of the day and most of the night to be unloaded from their giant trailers and properly set up for their work. A team of engineers had accompanied them in transit. Once set up, they would only ever pause to re-fuel until their task was complete.

They were parked just inside the northern gate. There, a section of fence had needed to be taken down to admit their bulk before being straight away put back up again. Curtis led the two-vehicle convoy to go and see them as soon as their party emerged from the cave mouth into light because he thought the sight of them would do Saul Abercrombie good.

Saul was in the rear Land Rover with his daughter at his side and Dora at the wheel. Curtis sat in the passenger seat of the front vehicle making and taking the calls he needed to catch up on. Pete drove. He said, 'That was a shit adventure, not very Enid Blyton at all, frankly.'

'We'll have lashings of ginger beer later,' Curtis said.

'We'll hold the ginger, eh? Just concentrate on the beer.'

'Enid's version would have given us something cute and trapped to rescue. The monster usually turns out to be a puppy. We got nothing.'

'Something left that residue on the floor. Something organic left that stink behind. I'm willing to bet it wasn't plant-life. You believe I heard something in there yesterday, Tom?'

'I came across that same odour in the fog at Puller's Reach before you and Dora arrived here. I didn't see anything. But there was something substantial at the edge of the water. I heard it. It wasn't a puppy.'

'Or even a Rottweiler,' Pete said.

It was about eight in the evening before Curtis became aware how tired and listless he felt. He knew the reason. He had spent a lot of adrenaline earlier in the day in the fire fight with the thorn bush. That was how he'd thought of it, he realized, as an opponent rather than just as an innocent obstacle. In the cave he'd been running on empty. Now he felt too depleted to do anything further concerning the demands of the job.

He'd delegated some stuff to Pete and Dora, who were busy dealing with those various tasks in the comms room. Francesca was with her father, having a drink on the terrace. Saul Abercrombie was under a rug in a wicker chair with wheels looking every day of his seventy-odd years. They'd had an early dinner, the five of them, during which the conversation could not honestly have been said to sparkle.

Curtis decided he would go to his computer and look up the Victorian family that Café John's professor said had been located at Loxley's Cross. Carrington had said the family were called the Crawleys and that it was all in the public domain.

It was something mildly diverting that would take his mind off how tired he was and maybe enable him to relax sufficiently to get the sound night's sleep he knew he needed. He kept thinking about how animated the scream made by the burning thorns had sounded. He kept thinking about the sticky residue left by whatever had secreted it in the cave. At least he wasn't thinking about Charlotte. At least he wasn't thinking about her all the time, anyway.

He soon found out that Alfred Crawley was one of those polymath Victorians with a strong interest in English folklore. He'd been left a generous legacy by his father and hadn't really needed to earn a living of his own. So he'd made a study of Morris Men and travelled to Cornwall looking for archaeological evidence of Camelot. He'd written a paper about the myth of the Green Man and why it had endured so persistently down the centuries.

He'd travelled about when single in a Romany caravan

pulled by a horse. He'd painted this prototype mobile home in a style that reminded Curtis a bit of William Morris wallpaper. He concluded from the appearance of the caravan that Crawley hadn't been a man who cared very much what other Victorians thought of him.

He'd first travelled to Wales as a young man intrigued by the legend of the sea monster said to inhabit the coastal waters off the port town of Barmouth. He'd tried to locate and catch it in a hired fishing boat, obviously with no success. From the illustrations of the monster, Curtis concluded that it had probably been an unusually large conger eel. They were territorial and could live for a very long time. It was longevity that engendered the sightings and stories inflated by fishermen over the years.

Crawley had become fascinated by the story of Gregory of Avalon and the legend of the vast wood from which the sorceress he'd vanquished had derived her power. He believed in ghosts and curses, ley lines and other magical properties to do with location; the resonant mystical power of particular places to endure through centuries.

He built a wooden house at Loxley's Cross. In the pictures Curtis sourced on the Internet, this looked like something between a traditional Swiss or Austrian ski chalet and one of those old-fashioned railway signal boxes from which gates at crossings were opened and closed manually. He fancied himself as an architect, on top of everything else. But Curtis concluded with a wry smile that architecture was something Alfred Crawley hadn't been very good at.

He'd married by this point and fathered two daughters. When the girls reached the age of six, he decided to build them a maze as a place of recreation. There were some photographs of the maze. They were aerial shots, taken from a hot air balloon.

The first pictures had been taken in the spring of 1862. They showed the maze to be an intricate geometric puzzle covering an area about the size of a cricket square on an English village green. The second pictures had been taken in the summer of the following year and when he saw them, Curtis almost gasped audibly.

In the second set of pictures, the maze covered an area about the size of two football pitches laid side-by-side. Most of its internal space was cast into deep shadow by the angle of the sun. The balloon must have taken flight at some point on a late and clear afternoon. Curtis calculated that the height of the hedgerows from which the maze was composed would be around thirty feet. It wouldn't be fun to play in confinement like that, he didn't think. It would be terrifying and, for a child, a nightmare.

The story of the Loxley's Cross maze had a tragic conclusion. Dismayed by the dimensions to which it had grown, Crawley planned to have it razed and then uprooted and the land it grew on ploughed under and left to lie fallow. The work was scheduled to be carried out in the January of 1864. But before it could be done, his girls wandered into the labyrinth he'd planted and became lost.

By this point they were in the charge of a maid called Amelia, a young local woman Crawley had taken on as a sort of housekeeper-cum-nanny. Their parents were at a dinner in Cardiff where they were booked into a hotel overnight. When they returned they could see no sign of their daughters. Eventually the girls were found, both frozen to death, in one of the false paths of dense and towering privet to which their father's leafy puzzle had led them.

Crawley had the maze destroyed as planned and demolished the house. He and his wife had left England and re-settled in Canada. They thrived in British Columbia, Rachel Crawley giving birth to a son and another daughter who both, happily, outlived their parents. They seemed to have recovered entirely from the earlier tragedy in Wales. But people had been more resilient then and child mortality far more common. Children died all the time of typhus and diphtheria. Adulthood was not the near certainty in Victorian times that it was in twenty-first-century Britain.

He searched for and eventually found a family group shot from the Loxley's Cross period that showed a slight, smiling young woman he assumed to be Amelia. She seemed familiar to him, like an actress he might have seen in a film he'd only half watched. She was certainly good-looking enough for films.

But she'd been born rather too early for stardom of the celluloid sort.

Curtis took out his wallet and found Carrington's card. He called the mobile number. Carrington picked up after a few rings. 'This is Tom Curtis.'

'Good evening. Enjoy your homework, Mr Curtis?'

'What happened to Amelia? You sound like you're in a pub.'

'That's because I'm in a pub. She disappeared. She was never seen again.'

'Can you go and stand outside?'

'With the smokers, you mean?'

'I'll be able to hear you.'

'I'll call you back in a moment, Mr Curtis.'

'Tom.'

'Very well, Tom, as you wish.'

Carrington called back about a minute and a half later. Time spent draining his pint and having a pee in the gents, Curtis thought.

'It's not the whole story, is it, this stuff in the public domain?'

'Alfred Crawley was an inveterate taker of notes and a compulsive diarist. He compiled an account of the events at Loxley's Cross. I'm sure he did. I'd stake my reputation on it. But it's never been found. If it exists, it was deliberately hidden. Had he made the whole story public, he would have been derided as a madman.'

'He doesn't seem to have bothered much about what people thought of him.'

'He would have been lampooned and ostracized and he knew it. He had a streak of exhibitionism but he was no fool. He wouldn't have wanted his wife publicly shunned. He loved her. Just because he was slightly eccentric doesn't mean he wasn't socially aware. He had good reason to keep quiet.'

'What did happen?'

'If I told you that over the phone, Tom, you'd consider me a crank.'

'Try me.'

'Has the planting begun in earnest yet?'

'No. The excavation machines are being set up as we speak. The serious work begins tomorrow.'

'If you restore the Forest of Mourning to its original state you will invite catastrophe, Tom Curtis.'

'The Forest of Mourning?'

'Its original name.'

'I didn't know that.'

'I doubt there's another human being alive who does,' Carrington said.

'I know you're not a crank, Professor, but I can't just stop this project in its tracks for no reason. If I did, Saul Abercrombie would simply fire me and get someone else to do it. He could do that tonight. The wheels have been set in motion. There's a woman here already eminently well qualified to supervise the entire job.'

'What's the name of this woman?'

'Frankly, that's none of your business.'

'Has nothing struck you as odd while you've been there, Mr Curtis?'

Everything has, Curtis thought. But he wasn't about to share that impression with a semi-retired academic with a belly full of something potent bought from a hand-drawn pump. He said, 'What would likely strike me as odd? Can you think of anything?'

'It's dangerous to restore trees to that domain. Crawley discovered it was so just by planting hedgerows for his children's maze. He paid an appalling price. Before he left, he took preventative measures.'

'He did what?'

'He planted something himself that feeds on flora.'

Curtis laughed. He was incredulous. 'Trees aren't carnivores, Professor Carrington.'

'This was a hybrid. It was highly aggressive and essentially parasitic. It was designed to choke the life out of anything that grew there above the height of grass. It would embrace a tree, smother it and starve its surrounding soil of nutrients before it ever matured from a sapling.'

'It could move around?'

'It could.'

'It was a thorn bush, wasn't it?'

'Was?'

'It was a thorn bush with magical properties.'

'That's a fanciful way of putting it, Mr Curtis. Crawley believed only in a very practical sort of magic where horticulture was concerned. His thorn bush was a precaution.'

And it had been on its way to Puller's Reach when they'd destroyed it. It had covered a thousand metres of the journey it was taking to devour the yew they had planted which it had hungrily sensed.

'We burned the bush at noon today, Professor. We destroyed all trace of it.'

'I doubt that.'

'We reduced it to carbon.'

'We'll see. Have you planted anything?'

'Yes.'

'Has anything odd occurred in the vicinity of the trees you put in the ground?'

'No.'

'You're a liar, Mr Curtis. And you're a very poor one.'

'I think this conversation's reached its natural conclusion.'

'There's nothing natural about the Forest of Mourning, as you'll discover to your cost.'

'Goodbye, Professor Carrington.'

'Do you remember the seduction in Scotland last summer? Do you recall the event that has made you such a willing pawn of your present master? You don't, do you, Mr Curtis? And there's a reason your memory of your affair with Isobel Jenks is so vague.'

Curtis broke the connection. He didn't think he'd heard the last of Andrew Carrington and he thought much of what he'd been told was probably true. But the professor had been wrong in one important particular, he was sure.

He was no scholar. He possessed no detection skills. But he felt certain that at least one other living human being was aware of the forest's original name. He suspected that Crawley's account of his time at Loxley's Cross existed and had been found. Saul Abercrombie had rediscovered it. And Saul, he was bloody sure, had devoured its every page.

EIGHT

They started along the coastline, slightly inland from the edge of the cliffs, a logical method of progression dictated by the need to keep unobstructed the route the stock of trees would take to where they were planted as the forest progressed and grew and flourished.

The machines turned vast swathes of wild grassland into soft and loamy beds for the root systems of mature trees. And the trees came. They arrived from all over Britain, from France and Germany and Italy and Spain, from America and Canada and even from India and Japan.

For Tom Curtis it was a relief to stop thinking about subjects sinister and unknowable and to concentrate fully on what he knew best. He concerned himself with the pH balance of the land; with irrigation and screening for blight and disease and the correct balance between density and the sunlight needed by each separate species for photosynthesis and the best possible chance of growth and prolonged lifespan.

He was obliged to represent Saul Abercrombie in meetings with concerned interest groups. He was obliged to liaise with individuals and organizations worried about the environmental impact and the cultural significance of what they were doing. Most people considered reforestation a good thing, he discovered, even if they were taken aback by the scale of what was to be accomplished.

Curtis could argue that it was fundamentally a job of restoration. But he thought his Welsh ancestry a priceless asset in dealing with some of the more entrenched and conservative groups: those opposed to radical change it seemed to him almost on principle.

Over three or four weeks the workforce quadrupled. The new recruits came from Welsh villages and towns, learning on the job from the core of skilled workers already present. The compound in which they were housed and fed grew correspondingly until to Curtis it resembled the sort of township that might spring up spontaneously in response to an oil strike or a gold-rush a hundred years earlier. Five miles from Abercrombie's house, eight from the nearest hamlet boasting a post office and a pub, the place developed a frontier atmosphere of nightly carousing and drinking and song.

Curtis left them to it. The work-hard, play-hard philosophy prevailed among the compound's resident population. Violence or any hint of sex crime he would have cracked down on through Pete Mariner, whose hands-on job it was to liaise with the gangers and foremen on site. But the labour force was content. They were mostly young people being well paid for exhilarating work. Every day there was cause and spectacular effect as the forest spread and strengthened and matured in character in their hands and before their eyes.

None of them had ever witnessed the like. Curtis and his two lieutenants had all worked in Britain planting native broadleaf forests. The work carried out by conventional means followed a pattern, almost a ritual.

The area determined the woodland classification decided by the National Vegetation Communities. A couple of dominant species were decided upon. On Abercrombie's Pembrokeshire domain that would probably have been lowland ash and oak.

Added to those would be an assortment of smaller tree species: birch, small-leafed lime, field maple, cherry, hornbeam aspen, sweet chestnut, rowan, whitebeam and perhaps willow. Bare root whips were planted, small saplings generally about two years old in a season running from November until March. They would be protected from deer and rabbits by plastic sheaths.

Rides would run between the planted areas, avenues about fifteen metres wide. The area around each planted tree would be kept clear of any weed or fungal growth that might drain the soil of nutrients. Birds and squirrels might seed areas spontaneously, but the whole thing would be managed and planned from inception over patient decades to mature consequence.

'I didn't think this was going to work,' Pete Mariner said, three weeks after the diggers cut their first swathes of

Abercrombie's earth. 'I'm only daring to say that now because I think I was so wrong.'

He was on the terrace at the house with Dora and Curtis and Francesca, enjoying a brandy in the aftermath of a meal the four of them had shared, Saul Abercrombie absent at a clinic in Harley Street for a procedure all of them had been warned was a secret worthy of keeping.

'I thought it would be unnatural. I thought it would look unnatural. You know, bogus, like transplanted hair on a bald man's head. Or artificial, like film set props are artificial.'

'I had my doubts,' Francesca said. 'Not about dad's commitment, or any of you and your credentials. I just thought it wouldn't possess its own character, somehow.'

Dora said, 'In what way? The trees have been perfectly cast for their role. The stock is coming from everywhere. But every species is indigenous.'

'Did you ever buy an album, Dora? Did you ever buy CDs, back in the olden days?'

'I'm thirty-seven years old. Of course I did.'

'Pop? Rock? Indie?'

'All of those.'

'And a dash of Goth,' Pete said.

'Guilty as charged.'

Francesca said, 'I thought the forest might be like one of those greatest hits compilations. I feared it might be contrived, characterless, too much of a good thing. Do you understand what I mean?'

'I know exactly what you mean,' Dora said. 'I think it's a great analogy, actually. I also think it's a scenario we're avoiding.'

'I'll drink to that,' Pete said. 'Tom?'

But Curtis didn't feel much like drinking to anything on that particular evening. He'd had a rough audit done earlier in the day on a gut feeling he'd had. A helicopter had overflown what they'd done and it had counted more trees than they had put in the ground.

The disparity was substantial. Forests were supposed to grow. But there was growth and growth and this was of a sort for which his experience provided him with no reasonable explanation.

This wasn't the yews at Puller's Reach. They had grown in number; there were seven of them at the most recent count. But 'Freemantle Theory' had been applied to them. The prevailing suspicion was that the land manager had gone rogue, was living rough somewhere and doing his own planting on the estate.

This had become a slightly callous and rather stale standing joke. But it was convenient in justifying something inexplicable. Where the Puller's Reach yew copse was small and inexplicable, however, the body of the forest was enormous. And a disparity in volume between what was planted and what was there represented chaos to Curtis and was very bad news indeed.

Their whole methodology on the Abercrombie domain was radical and crude and, if Curtis was honest, distasteful to him. Forestation was a slow and subtle process ordinarily. You colluded with nature, you did not dictate to it with huge machines and an army of labour and halogen floodlights to enable the work to continue relentlessly without pause until you reached a conclusion you were imposing on the land.

He had become conflicted. A part of him was pleased to be busy doing what his expertise enabled him to among people with whom he was familiar and for whom he had affection and respect. He was pleased too that there had been no setbacks to have to deal with. Mechanically, biologically, politically and people-wise, the project was running smoothly and to schedule.

But on a fundamental level he didn't like what they were doing. When you walked through the land they'd reforested it was cool and serene and shaded and offered no hint of how recent it was or how dramatic had been the process by which it came into existence. It felt not just established and not even old, but ancient in character. It was not, though, a happy place. If it felt authentic, it also felt gloomy and imposed a brooding mood of isolation when you crept through its dark, quiet and ever-growing immensity.

How to explain the disparity between what they'd planted and what was flourishing in the re-born Forest of Mourning? He couldn't. He decided he would not yet mention it to the others. They were buoyed up, ebullient. He would make no mention of it until he could find an explanation for it. Freemantle Theory didn't begin to do that.

'I'm going to turn in,' he said.

'Me too,' Pete said, 'Busy day tomorrow.'

'They're all busy days,' Curtis said, smiling and nodding a goodnight to the two women they were leaving behind at the table they'd shared.

'Once upon a time,' Dora said after they'd gone, 'common courtesy would have insisted they remain until we were ready to retire.'

'I like their attitude,' Francesca said. 'I can't stand the sort of man who treats every woman as a date. They see us as colleagues and nothing more. It's refreshing.'

'I think Pete sees you as more than a colleague, Francesca. At least, potentially.'

'And you'd like to go to bed with Tom. And Tom has no doubt thought about what it would be like to go to bed with you. But that isn't going to happen, I don't think.'

'Wouldn't you like to go to bed with Tom?'

Francesca hesitated before replying. She said, 'When he first came here, I could have fallen for him rather hard. Obviously he's nice to look at. He's intelligent and good-natured. And he seemed melancholy and quite a lonely man. I realized fairly quickly that the isolation isn't a pose or a seduction ploy. He's still in love with the mother of his child.'

'Hopelessly so,' Dora said. 'That relationship is extinct.'

'But genuinely so. It makes him a lost cause.'

'When did you realize this?'

'Not soon enough. Not before I'd made a fool of myself with him on the day you and Pete arrived. I drank too much and said something petulant and stupid. There'll be no repetition.'

'I think that's wise.'

'You would say that, Dora. And the reason you say it is because you don't welcome the threat of competition. But I think you're wasting your time. Like I said, he's a lost cause.'

'I know him better than you do.'

'You've known him for a lot longer,' Francesca said, smiling. 'But I'm a good judge of character.'

And Dora smiled back.

'That brings me to a question I've been meaning to ask you.'

'Ask away.'

'It's bothered me ever since our exploration of the cave. You remember we had a discussion about guns. You made the point that you were experienced with firearms.'

'I remember, yes.'

'Yet you didn't take one. Pete chose to arm himself and so did I. You didn't.'

'Maybe I just thought a Glock pistol and a Remington pump-action was insurance enough against a stranded seal.'

'You weren't frightened, were you, Dora? I was. Pete and Tom were. I'd say even my father felt a degree of trepidation when we entered that cave. You treated it like a stroll in the park.'

Dora shrugged. She lit a cigarette and inhaled. She tilted her head upwards and exhaled at the sky. Francesca thought she saw light glimmer westward where their graveyard legion of diggers and planters worked through the night. It was probably just her imagination, as they were beyond the horizon darkness made invisible, still too far away to be seen.

'I don't believe in ghouls, Francesca. Oh, I believe in monsters. I've even met a few. But they've always been of the human variety. I've never encountered a ghost or a devil and I really don't expect to.'

'Would you put my father in the monster category?'

'No, I wouldn't. I'm sure he's done some dubious things. He made himself wealthy and that doesn't happen by accident. I'm sure he's quite ruthless in business. He's been absolutely charming with me.'

'That can change in a heartbeat.'

'I don't doubt it can.'

'When the forest is completed, where we're sitting now will have been razed and consumed by it. Will you walk through it comfortably?'

'I'll take the guided tour,' Dora said.

Sarah Bourne suspected she was being followed. She'd had this suspicion before a couple of weeks earlier, but it had been vaguer then. She had been unable to think of a reason anyone might wish to track her movements. And if there was a pursuer, he was skilled at surveillance because she hadn't caught sight of anyone watching her in a way that seemed furtive or gratuitous.

This was different. She kept catching sight of the same man always roughly the same distance to her rear. He didn't look physically intimidating. He resembled neither a detective, nor a hired thug, nor an obvious pervert. What he looked like was an academic nearing retirement age. He was tweedy with leather elbow patches and wire-framed spectacles. When she caught him watching her, the look wasn't obviously salacious. It was surprised and she thought slightly sheepish.

He was there when she left the gym. It was eleven a.m. and her gym was the Virgin Leisure branch next to the Sainsbury's superstore at Surrey Basin. He could plausibly have been going to Sainsbury's, she supposed, to do his weekly shop. He hadn't been shopping already, because he had with him no bags full of stuff.

He wasn't shopping, though, was he? He didn't own a car. He didn't do weekly shops. He'd never become that comfortable with domestic organization. He shopped probably at his local newsagent where he bought everything from milk to loo roll only when he noticed he'd run out. He was a bachelor. He had a bachelor's frayed, uncared-for look. His interest in women would be an exaggeration termed 'an interest'. He wasn't interested in women. So why was he following her?

She walked up to him. 'Why are you following me?'

'Has your daughter had very bad dreams?'

'Mind your own fucking business. Why are you following me?'

'I can assure you, Ms Bourne, I am not doing it for the good of my health or because I consider it a form of entertainment.'

'Then why? What's this about?'

'It's about what Tom Curtis is engaged with in Pembrokeshire. He's in grave danger.'

'You're a crank.'

'I'm a university professor. My area of expertise is

mythology. My name is Andrew Carrington. My details are on the Kingston college website. You can check me out.'

'I don't wish to check you out. I want you to stop following me.'

'Has your daughter intimated that her father might be in danger in Wales?'

'I've already said that's none of your business.' She took her iPhone out of the pocket of her track pants. 'I'm going to call the police.'

Carrington looked around. He looked a bit desperate. He was out of his depth. He seemed sincere and, despite herself, Sarah felt a tinge of sympathy for him. Crank that he almost certainly was, he surely represented nuisance more than threat.

'Do you know the Riverside Café?'

'Of course I do. Everyone does.'

'Meet me there in an hour. Give me thirty minutes of your time. Listen to what I have to say and I promise you'll never see me again.'

'You're unwise to try to blackmail me into doing anything, Mr Carrington.'

'Please,' he said. He flapped and wheeled about and, with a tweedy shuffle, retreated in the direction of Richmond Road.

She went. She rode her bike there along the river cycle path. It was a pleasant day. The Riverside's proprietor was a former police officer. It was a safe place in broad daylight and by then she had visited the Kingston University website and checked Carrington out. Unless he had an identical twin he was exactly who and what he'd said and she was honestly a bit intrigued. She didn't like being reminded of Tom; the subject was tender still. But it was odd that Carrington had known about Charlie's dreams.

'Do you have any religious beliefs, Ms Bourne?'

'I like first names, Andrew. I think the use of them encourages transparency.'

'Very well, Sarah. Would you please address the question?'

'I was led to believe I couldn't have children. Even if I hadn't been, I'd consider my little girl a miracle. I'm sure lots of parents feel the same way. I don't really go in for mystical belief. My faith in human nature took a severe blow last autumn.'

They were seated outside. Their table was painted green. The river was intermittently blue when the sun shone between clouds so pretty they looked painted on to the sky. Carrington said, 'This is a lovely spot.'

'Why am I here?'

'The source of every villainous female myth is the same, Sarah. It's consistently the same character, right through history. The same creature who inspired the story of Eve and the fall is also the snake-headed goddess Medusa and the sorceress Morgana le Faye. It's inhabited many guises over the centuries, this creature, but it's always been as a woman.'

She doesn't want to be seen at all. 'Go on.'

'A thousand years ago an ancestor of Tom Curtis defeated and vanquished this creature. She can't be killed, but she was weakened. It's my belief she's growing strong again.'

'It all sounds very colourful.'

'I believe she entranced Tom Curtis in a Scottish forest last summer and that was why he was unfaithful to the woman he loved with a girl to whom he was physically and emotionally indifferent.'

'I'm leaving, Professor Carrington.' Sarah rose to go.

'Transparency, Sarah Bourne. Do you know that Isobel Jenks is dead?'

She sat down again, heavily. 'No.'

'She left a note saying her work was done. She didn't mean her coursework. She meant that Tom is reviving an ancient Welsh forest. I'm guessing the money is vital to him?'

'He wants to fight for access to his daughter through the courts. He thinks he needs the money to pay a lawyer.'

'Only thinks?'

'I won't fight him. I'm just hurt and angry with him. I thought we had something wonderful. He betrayed it. Why would this Eve creature want the forest restored?'

'A thousand years ago it was her kingdom. It was her domain. She ruled it, cruelly and savagely. The project Tom is supervising will enable her to do so again.'

'Through magic, I suppose?'

'It's a very dark and cunning sort of magic. And it's contagious, Sarah. Your daughter will have been dreaming of her. She has been, hasn't she?'

'Why has she?'

'The blood bond with her father is the reason. The creature will kill him to avenge what happened to her the last time her kingdom was whole. The Forest of Mourning will be a place of grief again. She'll make it a place of permanent grief.'

'I don't believe a word of this.'

'No, of course you don't, and who could blame you?' Carrington said. 'The modern world revels in disbelief. Ours is a mendacious age. Incredulity is our default setting and the creature will thrive as a consequence. Before anyone takes the danger seriously, she'll be too powerful to stop.'

'Why are you even telling me?'

'I'm telling you so that you can tell him.'

'You can tell him yourself.'

'He'd laugh in my face. As you would, if you weren't so polite.'

'I'm leaving now, Andrew. Please don't follow me again or I shall feel obliged to inform the police.'

'I'm going to Wales.'

'You're doing what?'

'I was always going to Wales. It's fate, you see. I knew that in the museum at Oxford. It was why I travelled to Oxford. I had need of the artefacts. I was always bound for Wales. I've known that really since this started.'

'Now you're talking in riddles.'

'I was accused of doing so the last time I sat here. It was as untrue then as it is today.'

'Goodbye, Andrew. Take care of yourself.'

Better care than you have been, she thought, turning and taking her bike from the rack to the left side of the café. It was strange the way clever people could ignore the basics like their utility bills and personal hygiene until the surprised moment someone cut off their electricity or complained about the smell.

It was tempting to believe him. This was not because she had a taste for mythology or craved belief in something epic and dark and paranormal. Sarah's normal was affluent and quite glamorous and would do very well for her.

She was tempted to believe because Andrew Carrington's version of events exonerated Tom. They meant that he wasn't to blame for an affair from which he had derived no pleasure. That was the bit Sarah was tempted to believe in. Belief in that was almost as good as going back to the time before his betrayal and her exposure to it in the relentless drone of Isobel Jenks' voice over the phone.

Was Isobel Jenks really dead? Carrington had suggested she'd taken her own life. He was in a position to know – he taught at the university where she'd been a student. Sarah decided she would find out for herself whether that was true and if it was, whether the dead girl had made final mention of having completed her work. She didn't pick Charlie up from school until 3.15 p.m. She had time to go home and do that before then.

She wondered how Tom was doing in his Welsh forest. She thought about his desperate urge to fund the legal battle he was committed to having to fight. For the first time since picking up the phone and hearing Isobel Jenks on the other end of it, she felt some sympathy for the father of their child.

Carrington had been right about that. Tom had committed to a scheme on the lunatic scale he had only for money. He was a man to whom money had never mattered very much. But circumstances had conspired to make him more desperate to earn it than he'd ever been in his life. The Jenks woman had been complicit in that. But when Sarah thought about it, not nearly so complicit as she herself had been.

Tom was compromising himself terribly in Wales. This Pembrokeshire scheme was the brainchild of a megalomaniac. No one had come out directly with the claim that Saul Abercrombie was terminally ill, but that was the persistent Internet rumour. Tom had become involved in the final folly of a dying man governed totally by his ego.

This project was actually monstrous. She didn't think it would unleash the Eve creature Carrington warned against. Even with the evidence of Charlie's gruesome drawings, that idea was way too medieval for her to entertain. But it was madness and would do Tom's reputation no good whatsoever.

The mauling in the thorn bush had left him changed. By the time he had the mental fortitude to look back upon it rationally, he thought of it really as the mauling *by* the thorn bush, because that's what it had been. The bush had been animate and sly and strong and quick and vicious. It had relished mutilating him. He had no doubt in what was left in his mind about that.

He thought the sight in the single eye he had left was fading quite quickly now. The other had been gouged from its socket. It had thrust a mandible down his throat and torn out half his vocal cords. His face and body were scarred in a manner that made a sort of lattice of his surviving skin.

Its jest had been in sparing him. He didn't honestly know why he wasn't dead. He thought his wounds should have killed him; that toxic shock or septicaemia or simple blood loss should have delivered permanent oblivion.

He suspected it possessed some biological predisposition to survive. It was how the shotgun damage had healed so quickly and completely after he'd blasted away at it with volley after volley of lead shot. Some cellular or chemical quality endowed it with stubborn life. It had infected him with a little of that. It had contaminated him with its thorny vigour. And so he lived too.

It was just a theory. He didn't have the knowledge of horticulture generally an expert such as Tom Curtis possessed. Neither was he stupid. And he was possessed of a set of singular skills that had so far enabled him to hide in his ruined state while he pondered on what to do next with his horribly compromised life.

He'd concealed himself by day in a hide he'd constructed in a shallow depression in the ground near Loxley's Cross. At night he'd taken to foraging in the food bins behind the galley at the compound built for the labour force restoring the forest. He was living on scraps but they were plentiful scraps and concealment was relatively easy. In his old fugitive days there had been police forces with dogs out looking for him when he'd been on the run. No one was looking for him now.

They would get to Loxley's Cross in weeks if not days with their diggers and planting. He thought the forest itself was probably big enough and dense enough by now for him to build a home in. It was a little too far distant from his food source as yet. But that was a situation altering every day as the growth stole relentlessly over what had once been the wilderness he'd managed for Saul.

He'd had a moment of weakness. He'd crept up to the house in the small hours desolately lonely and welling with self-pity and he'd spied on Francesca for an hour as she slept fitfully, watching her through the window of her room. There'd been a chink where the curtains had been carelessly pulled. His one-eyed sight had been better, then. He'd easily eluded the security lights and, of course, he'd meant her no harm. But she'd woken and roused help and he'd almost been discovered and shot by a man he did not recognize.

Fleeing that night, he'd realized that there was no going back. His status now was somewhere between a freak and an invalid. Saul would feel compassion for him and pension him off and pay for cosmetic procedures. Where he'd had the respect and trust of his boss, now there would only be pity. Francesca would wince, looking at his ruined face and scarred body. Even blind, he'd sense her doing it and it would be intolerable to him.

He'd felt in some ways like the master of this domain. Saul's increasing physical weakness and Francesca's indifference to her surroundings had encouraged that illusion. He realized now that the weapons he'd amassed in the armoury had been deadly symbols of empire building. He'd wanted to turn the house into a powerbase. The gym had been his parade ground. The comms room had been the observation tower from which his fortress could be vigilantly watched-over and defended.

Arrogance had undone him. As a consequence he'd lost his status, his looks, his health, his ambitions and his pride. He'd been angry at first at the indignity of what had been done to him. He'd been furious. He'd gone to the church at Raven Dip and sneaked inside and spat insults at God through an entire night, the oaths and blasphemies croaking out of his ruined throat so they rasped and repeated around the cold stone walls.

It did no good.

Eventually, after a fortnight had passed and the anger had subsided, he had gone back into the church and he had prayed. He had beseeched God to offer him a sign that all wasn't as hopeless as it seemed be. Suicide had always seemed the coward's way out to Sam Freemantle. Even in a remand cell awaiting his sentence for a string of armed robberies, he hadn't seriously contemplated that.

To his astonishment, the sign came. It arrived in the shape of a slim, slight woman called Amelia, who'd approached him as he sat by the cairn of stones at Puller's Reach, where the wind whispered through the leaves and branches of what he'd noticed, with surprise and failing sight, had become a copse now of yew trees.

He'd have challenged her as a trespasser only weeks earlier. He'd have drummed and harried her off Saul's land with legal threats and quite probably some rough physical treatment as he pushed her into the passenger seat of the Land Rover and drove her to the exit of the western gate. He'd have taken her photograph and given it to the security boys who'd been manning the gates since shortly after Curtis arrived. He'd probably have emailed the picture to the Pembroke Constabulary.

But he was a changed man, humbled and reduced and what he craved was human company. He listened as she told him she had inhabited a cave on the shore and that he was welcome to share her refuge and her provisions whenever he wished to.

'I come here every evening, at dusk,' she told him. Then she laughed and said, 'Of course, that's only if the coast is clear.'

Once, her joke would have irritated him, made as it was slightly at Saul's expense. But he'd been replaced in Saul's affections by a new favourite in Tom Curtis. Maintaining the integrity of the estate was no longer his responsibility. And he found Amelia's humour only mischievous and charming.

'A warm welcome awaits you,' she said. 'Your presence won't go unappreciated, Sam Freemantle.'

'How do you know my name?'

'I know everyone's name in this locality.'

'I'm no longer Sam Freemantle. Something happened to me.'

'Were you hurt helping Tom Curtis? Did this happen because of him?'

'Had he not come here, it wouldn't have happened.'

'I can make you forget your pain and disfigurement, Sam. I can make you forget them entirely.'

'Can you really?'

'I promise you, it's true.'

And so the evening came when he craved company beyond endurance and he waited by the cairn for her, gnawing on a piece of stale loaf salvaged from the compound galley bins, what was left of his sight sensitive to the diminishing light in the spring sky as it reddened to the west and dusk approached.

He supposed she was one of those shiftless alternative types. They were hallmarked by piercings and tattoos. They wore their hair in dreadlocks and travelled in convoys of camper vans. They attended the summer solstice at Stonehenge and gate-crashed the festival at Glastonbury. Once he would have avoided such people. Now he didn't care.

She came. She led him down a goat-narrow path on the cliff face he hadn't known existed. She led him along the strand of shingle with the smell of brine making mucus well in his damaged throat as the sound of the waves brought a soothing rhythm to his ears.

They walked south for quite a long time. They came upon the planting atop the cliffs above them to their left. Freemantle heard the wind change in character as it soughed through dense foliage. 'The forest,' he said, to his companion, 'the trees.'

Amelia laughed. It was a pleasant sound. 'The memory of trees,' she said.

He blinked and focused his remaining eye on her. She removed the hood she habitually wore from her head. He saw no metal puncturing her face. Her skin wasn't inked. Her hair was abundant and silky. She was really quite beautiful.

Gloom descended and the air became cooler as they entered the cave and then darkness enveloped them completely. A new

smell replaced the clean ozone smell of the sea and to Sam
it smelled dead and ancient. There was something troubling
about it and when his feet lost purchase in a pool of skittering
slime on the cave floor he groped for Amelia's hand, unsure
of himself.

She returned his grip. Her hand was small and surprisingly
strong and reassuring. She said, 'Soon, Sam, you'll have no
cause for concern.'

He heard something splash heavily in the distance ahead of
them. The sound shuddered off the cave walls. He heard a
gasp of life and arousal and there was a hurrying, rubbing
chafe as things that stank loathsomely lurched along the tunnel
in their approach.

'What's that?' he asked Amelia in the fetid darkness.

'Company,' she said. Her voice came from behind him. She
was no longer at his side. 'Goodbye, Sam.'

He barely had time to scream. And then they fell on him.

In what he thought of as more robust times, Saul Abercrombie
had been a betting man. He'd bet at the tables in Las Vegas
and Acapulco and Monte Carlo. He'd bet compulsively on
business hunches. He had an actuary's calculated under-
standing of risk. So he knew how heavily the odds were stacked
against his survival. He had a chancer's instinct and he nursed
no illusions. Without a miracle, he would die within weeks.
It was why he treated the evening prior to his departure back
for Wales as what might be the last he would ever spend in
London.

He felt better physically. He was stronger than he'd been
on the day of the cave exploration. The Harley Street man
had injected him with something as potent as it had been
expensive. It was temporary, but temporarily it was working.
He felt strong enough to stroll among the sites that had
meant so much to him in his long and colourful career in
the capital.

He walked through Bloomsbury until he came to Red Lion
Square. The square hadn't changed greatly since the day of
the demo and his arrest. It had lost a few trees to Dutch Elm
Disease. It had lost a few more to the Great Storm of 1987,

the one the weather forecasters had rather infamously failed to predict and warn people about. But essentially it looked the same, surrounded as it was by austere and elegant Georgian houses no one lived in anymore.

Abercrombie remembered the turmoil of the times, which had been political. And he remembered the turmoil in his mind, which had been to do with being young and insecure and having yet made no impression on the world. He had been a student of politics in those days at the LSE and as he stood there in the gentle rain of a London spring, he recalled a quote coined by the great German statesman Otto Von Bismark he'd come across back then.

Bismark had not been a believer in the afterlife. He'd been a Junker and a soldier and was a pragmatic man. He'd said, *the only true immortality is posthumous fame.* It was a good line and in so far as it went, it was probably correct. And Saul thought that he was famous enough for the memory of his life and his accomplishments to endure after he was gone. But he wanted the present state of affairs to continue for rather longer than nature seemed to have planned. He was content to have Bismark's dictum proven by his own demise eventually. He just wasn't ready for the moment to arrive quite yet.

He walked from Bloomsbury to Soho and to Soho Square, where he'd enjoyed his epiphany a decade earlier. Jittery with crack, damn near psychotic in the aftermath of a huge crack binge, he'd kind of come-to there one summer dawn with no idea how he'd stumbled into that particular location.

He still believed that had he become aware of his surroundings in a nightclub, or even a store or a car park, he'd have broken down completely and been committed, despite his fame and wealth. He'd been close to that, a cigarette paper's thickness away from it, truth be told.

But he'd regained something of his sensory awareness in Soho Square. The light had been soft through the leaf canopy and there'd been the smell of grass and flowers and bark and a chorus of happy birdsong. He'd hugged a tree. He'd actually hugged a sycamore tree and its gnarled surface had been real against his cheek. Its solidity had reassured him that the world could be predictable and benign. And beautiful in a prosaic, cyclical way he could learn to appreciate and enjoy without the stimulation of chemicals.

He looked at his wristwatch. He had a drinks appointment at 7 p.m. and didn't want to be late for it. When time was short he'd discovered you became economical with it in a way he hadn't been before. He'd been a man who habitually and unapologetically kept people waiting. He didn't do that now.

Will Davies was already in the bar. The man from the *Mirror* looked about five years older than his picture by-line but that was a modest deception by the standards of Fleet Street, where most of the mugshots topping the stories were decades old. Abercrombie looked older than his own publicity shots, he knew. But then he'd been ageing in recent months with carcinogenic acceleration. The stock shot of him Davies' paper had used had been taken only a year ago.

The bar was quiet early on an early summer evening, as he had known it would be. It was why he had chosen it. He shook hands with the reporter, accepted his offer of a drink and sat down. He was sipping a double measure of single malt and felt relaxed when the first question was asked of him. The pilgrimage paid to the two most important London locations in his adult life had delivered him a sense of calm.

'Heard of a guy named Andrew Carrington?'

'Not ringing any bells,' Abercrombie said, after a pause. 'Illuminate me.'

'I was sent a pamphlet, something written in the early seventies and published by a small independent press in Oxford. It was sent anonymously.'

'Anon,' Abercrombie said. 'That's one prolific author.'

'It was written under a pseudonym. I did a bit of research. Three or four people could have written it. It concerns Gregory of Avalon and the Forest of Mourning?'

'Continue, brother. I may even subscribe. This is all news to me.'

'I reckon this guy Carrington wrote it.'

Abercrombie sipped and shrugged.

'He's a professor of mythology. At least he was. He's semi-retired. In the pamphlet he makes some fairly wild claims about the forest and its inhabitants. Actually, he makes some pretty wild claims about one inhabitant in particular.'

'Again, brother, you're gonna have to shine a light.'

'And you're lying through your elderly fucking skin.'

Abercrombie grinned. 'I don't have to take that shit,' he said.

'But you're still sitting there.'

'Why haven't you pursued this story? I'm genuinely perplexed about that.'

'People are less interested in forests than you'd probably think. Even in yours. They'd rather get irate about wind turbines.'

'That's not the real reason.'

'Picture a young woman,' Davies said. 'Blonde, a bit vapid, skinny, smokes too much.'

'You've just described half of Soho, brother.'

'I've just described Isobel Jenks. Since I stopped writing about you and your fucking forest, she's stopped following me. And my stereo system doesn't choose its own playlist. And my car radio behaves itself.'

'David Baxter was your source? Jesus, I can't believe I didn't work that one out.'

Davies grinned. He said, 'You're not a well man, Mr Abercrombie. But if you restore the Forest of Mourning, you might rejuvenate someone who can change that for you. And evil bitch that Carrington says she is, she might just be grateful enough to do it.'

Abercrombie drained his drink. 'I thought you'd be more sceptical about that kind of supernatural shit,' he said.

'I was,' Davies said, 'until Isobel Jenks gate-crashed my life after hers was supposed to be over.'

Abercrombie had left the bar and was walking past a Greek Street sex shop with his mind on the Fitzrovia restaurant where he intended to dine when his mobile rang. The number on his display belonged to Tom Curtis.

'Tree Man.'

'You've got Alfred Crawley's account of events at Loxley's Cross, haven't you, Saul?'

'Who told you about Crawley?'

'A professor named Andrew Carrington.'

'This Carrington guy is becoming a royal pain in the ass.'

'What?'

'Nothing, and yes, I've got Crawley's account. What of it?'

'I'd like to read it.'

Abercrombie sighed and looked at his phone. 'Then I'd better tell you where it's kept,' he said.

There were three of them. They were all in their late twenties. The leader among the trio, the one who suggested they do it, was a Russian from the Black Sea port of Odessa. The second of them was originally from County Cork. The third was a Pole from Danzig. Their shared passion was fishing. They worked on the dayshift driving the JCBs that filled the holes around the tree root systems before hand-held jackhammer teams moved in to tamp down the ground.

The work was repetitive and sedentary for these drivers. It was well paid and there was cause and effect to factor in; the fact that what they were doing amounted to something visually spectacular that literally got bigger every day. The food was excellent, the dormitory rooms were warm and dry and the beds were comfortable.

But the camp had about it an air of confinement. Entertainment amounted there to cracking a few beers and sharing in a communal sing-along. Otherwise it was hunkering down with your laptop or listening to something you'd downloaded through your iPod buds. It got boring after a week and tedious after two and after that it just depended on your temperament. Fights had broken out. Feuds had begun to flourish. Despite the limited opportunities communal living offered to do things in private, affairs had been started.

The Welsh men and women among the workers coped best because well-remunerated work was a novelty in this depressed part of their country. They were earning and not spending and they weren't so far from home that the isolation got to them the way it did to some of the immigrant labour force. They counted their money and counted off the days and weeks till completion of the project.

The Russian, Peter, was less sanguine. He thought that a little night fishing might be just the thing to improve the situation. He had smuggled an inflatable dinghy on to the site. It fitted, with its pump, neatly into a backpack designed for the purpose.

He'd brought his gear too – telescopic rods that fitted into a cylindrical case less than a metre in length. He'd discussed his plan with Alex the Pole and Sean the Irishman and they were all very much up for it. And then the night came when the weather was serene and the cloud cover sufficient for them to cross the three or four miles of open ground before the concealment of the forest they were helping create enveloped them and concealed their progress to the cliffs and the shoreline completely.

'What do you reckon we'll catch?' Sean said when they reached the cover of the trees. They'd plotted a route that would steer them well clear of the fresh planting progressing through the night to the north of where they walked.

'Mackerel,' Peter said. 'But this is fishing for sport, my friend. We don't have to eat our catch.'

'Flat fish, too, in these waters,' Alex said. 'Very tasty flat fish, I should think. Dover sole and the one you call hake.'

Sean said, 'What do you fish for in Danzig?'

And Alex laughed. 'The harbour waters are too polluted to support any life but eels,' he said. 'They're filthy and they're ferocious and you wouldn't want to eat one of them, my friend.'

Ferns brushed quietly against their legs. It was funny, Sean thought. The forest was so dense and silent that it seemed to have been there for centuries. He hadn't seen any ferns planted. There was ivy too growing on the trunks of mature oaks and cedars and willows in such abundance that it seemed to have been there since its hosts had been saplings.

That wasn't the case. Every single tree of whatever age and provenance had come in clean of parasites. And ivy was a parasite, however pretty it tended to look in a context such as this.

It wasn't completely dark. A full moon glowered somewhere behind the thin cloud cover above them and it provided enough washed-out, gloomy light for them to see as they got nearer to the cliffs. There was no scent of the sea yet in Sean's nostrils, they weren't close enough. There was no on-shore wind and the land they tracked was too dense with forestation to smell of anything but bark and lichen and leaves and a mouldy suggestion of moss.

'It's getting foggy,' Peter said.

Sean chuckled. 'Focky?'

'Yeah, and fuck you, Mr Linguist. How's your Russian?'

'OK, point taken.'

'My point, smartass, is that there's a mist descending.'

'We'll be OK,' Alex said, 'so long as it doesn't thiggen.'

'Fine,' Peter said. 'Poles are supposed to be stupid.'

Alex said, 'Only in Ameriga.'

'Guys, guys,' Sean said, pausing, 'there's a serious point at stake here. If the fog really is thickening, do we want to be in an inflatable boat at sea when no one knows we're there and the only distress tool we have is mobile phones?'

'Fuck, yes,' Alex said.

'You heard the man,' Peter said, 'come on.'

They reached the cliff edge, the margin between land and sea, about twenty minutes after that exchange. They were about a thousand metres to the south of the Puller's Reach cairn. But that was a landmark none of the three men had ever laid eyes on. It lay by now at the heart of a large cluster of yew trees in a part of the forest's edge that had not required their efforts to flourish and expand.

It was safe to use a torch. The work going on that night was several miles to the north of them. A night trawler might see their light twinkle from out in the wastes of the Irish Sea. But they were confident no one else would be alerted by its beam. They used it to search for a pathway down to the shore. The cliffs were not particularly high at the spot from which they had emerged, perhaps eighty feet, but it was still a descent that required caution. They wanted to fish, not to maim or kill themselves.

After ten minutes they identified a route and then took it, deliberately, carefully, perhaps aware that though the mist hadn't blanketed their path to the beach, it did seem to be growing denser.

They each had on a backpack. Peter's held the craft they intended to fish from. Alex's was filled with lures and barbell hooks and jars of the worms they'd collected from the earth during their working day and brought along as bait. Sean's was filled with a case of beer. And as Peter inflated the dinghy they cracked open a Heineken apiece and discussed the threat the worsening weather represented to their planned night of recreation.

'What was that sound?' Sean said, when their discussion ended and the rubber boat was taut with air.

'It was your empty beer can, moron, which you've just tossed on to the pebbles,' Alex said.

'I don't think it was,' Peter said, frowning. 'It sounded like a splash.'

'Fucking fish are throwing themselves out of the sea in their eagerness to be caught,' Sean said. He belched, happily. 'Kamikaze mackerel, boys. Hake suicide squads.'

'Flounder, floundering,' Alex said.

And Peter raised his can in a salute earned by his Polish friend's impressive facility with the English language.

There was another noise, which they all heard. It sounded through the roiling mist like the dull slap of something heavy on the sand and stones where the waves broke in the opaque vista before them.

'I'm not totally liking this place,' Alex said.

The splash recurred. It was more of a heave, laboured, substantial in size and somehow hurried.

'I'm liking it here less and less,' Peter said.

Sean had become aware of a smell. It was more of a stink than a smell, something fundamentally rotten, decayed and corrupt and somehow wrong, like a sick joke made at the expense of nature itself. It was a contradictory stench. It was to his assaulted senses, the odour of death living. It crawled through his nasal cavities. It filled his soul with a sick sort of dread.

He sensed something loom and then lumber out of the fog. It was massive and when its barnacled maw slathered against his exposed neck it was cold and rough in the brief nightmare the rest of his existence had abruptly become. He felt the skin seared away and sensed the arterial rush of his blood sucked hot and greedily out of him. It had wrapped limbs or tentacles around him and they bound with a grip that was inescapable.

He struggled, screaming, hearing the dying screams of his companions as the fog thickened further and the stinking creatures overwhelmed them and emptied them of life.

NINE

This is my account of the events at Loxley's Cross. They will seem strange and outlandish to you, their reader. Every word written is written truly, though, in horror now and with the heaviest of hearts. Those events began in hope in the spring of 1862. They ended tragically in December of the following year.

Our arrival at our new home was not straightforward. There was a delay caused by the depth to which the well had to be sunk to enable our family to draw clean water for our dietary and household needs. It draws from a prodigious depth and was expensive to bore. But it was done eventually and we took up residence in our unique and spacious house in that desolate part of Pembrokeshire.

For me this relocation fulfilled of course a yearning I had endured since my student days, when I first read the chronicle detailing the exploits of Gregory of Avalon and the defeat of his mythic foe.

My fascination with English and Celtic folklore is too well known an aspect of my character for me to bother to dwell on it here. Suffice to say that it had, until two years ago, dictated much of the curious and curiously nomadic pattern of my life thus far. I went to Pembrokeshire principally to look, to study and to learn. I believed at the outset that this land, despite its open features, concealed secrets waiting for discovery.

The account of Gregory's quest to slay the sorceress and her acolytes in the Forest of Mourning is familiar to scholars of antiquity. He was summoned by a magician or magus or an alchemist. In the terminology of our own advanced age, they would all be described as scientists.

This scientist had no specialism. He was presumably adept

at many of what were then considered the more mysterious arts. But he sought the courage and resourcefulness of Gregory in solving a problem he had failed to tackle effectively by means of his own devices. Probably he was the source of the legend of Merlin. I believe he was, because Gregory came from Tintagel, which of course in my considered view was Camelot. But this Arthurian link is conjecture and a theory that will always remain unproven.

His protagonist in the ensuing conflict was described as malevolent almost beyond belief. It manifested itself in the female gender. It had disguised itself as a comely woman through millennia and caused chaos and tragedy wherever it chose to settle and thrive. Many authorities on mythology through the centuries had concluded that ever since the Fall, this creature has been living her antic, alien and destructive life, always at the expense of common humanity.

When Darwin's *Origin of Species* was published four years ago I read it avidly. Indeed, I read it several times over, agreeing with almost all of his conclusions regarding natural selection. I see no contradiction whatsoever between my own beliefs and the scientific orthodoxy of the great observer of nature who has coined the term, the survival of the fittest.

I think it arrogant to assume anything about the natural world. Apparently we humans are the dominant species. But what if there are other species, equally or more intelligent, though not as prevalent as us? We humans breed as prodigiously as mice. But numbers alone do not endow us with superiority. If it did, the residents of the ant hills of the African continent would govern the destiny of our planet. It would be them or the great shoals of unimportant fish populating oceans.

I have examined and explored the myth of the Green Man. I have read all the accounts of the Pendle witches. I have been to the lake where I believe Gawain finally and reluctantly threw Arthur's sword into the waiting hand of a being probably best described in theological terms as an angel.

My point, put simply, is this. I do not think we are the only species on our planet able to boast manifest superiority to the great apes. The world is shrouded in darkness for much of its life. And the sunless time it endures enables elusive creatures to pursue their own ends. Perhaps they avoid discovery because they fear us as much as we, in our folkloric stories, fear them.

They are capable of magic. We abandoned magic in the Age of the Enlightenment when rationality superseded the old ways with the methodology of the laboratory. What is magic? Magic is a door to which we have lost the key. But the door is there. Were it not locked, it would open on to wonders.

This was my reasoning upon our arrival. With that established, I will give a plain account of what took place when I committed the foolish sin of delivering my innocent family and most particularly my two beautiful and blameless daughters to the inherent evils of the place history knows as Loxley's Cross.

There was an iron signpost a furlong distant from where I had the house constructed. It pointed to three destinations. They were Raven Dip to the south of it, Gibbet Mourning to the north and to the west, on the coast, Puller's Reach.

The more I saw that signpost over the first weeks after our arrival, the more redundant it seemed to me. The nearest Welsh settlement to us was seven or eight miles to the east. No one crossed or visited the land we occupied. It had become the custom of the country thereabouts to stay away and rural customs become deeply ingrained and then followed without question until they achieve the status almost of rules.

One discovery that delighted Rachel and the girls was the small Saxon church at Raven Dip. It was derelict, in the sense that it wasn't used. There was no priest or vicar present there. There were no services held. The church must have been deconsecrated, perhaps in medieval times or in the upheaval of the Reformation in the 1500s. That was the period when King Henry closed the monasteries, after all.

The church was tiny and always chilly, but it was in excellent repair, completely intact once beyond its ancient oak door. It was devoid of the paraphernalia of worship. I have not yet mentioned a congregation and you will have assumed from what I have said that there wasn't such an entity. But there was. There was a congregation of one, which is how Rachel and the girls came to meet Amelia.

To get to the church at Raven Dip meant enduring a journey of eight or nine miles each way from the village where Amelia told the girls she came from. But that journey was only a practicable penance for a devout worshipper to whom her faith, she told Rachel, meant a great deal.

She got on with the girls immediately. It became her habit each Sunday as spring progressed into summer to share a picnic with the three of them in fine weather on the rise to the east of the Dip in the open air after church. That was a glorious period of golden sunshine, looking back. So their picnics were leisurely and enjoyable affairs. They broke the monotony for Rachel and the girls, and alleviated too the solitude.

It was Amelia I had to thank for alerting me to the stained-glass depiction of Gregory at Raven Dip. It was done in the style made fashionable again over recent decades by the Pre-Raphaelite school. It was genuine, to my eye, but still accomplished several centuries after the gory event it commemorates.

The monster is gruesome. I attributed that at the time to the imagination of the craftsman who completed the piece. Gregory is what a medieval scribe would have called fair. He looks noble and resolute and is armed in a manner too modern for his actuality. The window struck me principally as a reminder of the way in which legends are embellished as they endure down the centuries. It occurred to me that they cannot help but gain in drama.

Eventually Amelia was invited to the house. She told us that her father was a surgeon. She spoke only with the slightest of Pembrokeshire lilts to a voice with a sweet, clear timbre. She was twenty-two, she told us. She was unattached. She seemed far too attractive a young woman to be on her way to spinsterhood and that was not a fate Rachel wanted to conspire in having her meet.

Nevertheless, we discussed offering her a position as something between a governess and a companion for the girls. They had by this time greatly taken to her. She was educated, impeccably mannered and seemed entirely someone of good character. She was also local. She was knowledgeable enough about the history and mythology of the region to be of help to me in my researches. She knew the location of the cave in which Gregory had earned his posthumous fame.

I cannot clearly remember the moment when Amelia introduced the idea of the maze. Certainly the suggestion pre-dated her employment with us. But it must have been after her first visit to the house. She must have remarked to Rachel or to myself or both of us that the desolate landscape would be the perfect location for such a feature.

It would entertain the girls. It would brighten the prospect through our windows. It would attract nesting birds and they would pollinate the ground and more vegetation would grow across the barren wilderness we had made our home.

'Regeneration,' Amelia said. 'It is what nature does.'

The phraseology struck me as strange. She sounded almost as though she was quoting what she said. But I could not argue with the sense or the sentiment. And so I had privet cuttings purchased on my behalf and delivered by a team of wagons and we dug the channels and bedded them ourselves to a design I sketched one evening inspired probably by too much claret drunk at dinner.

The planting itself was joyous. We toiled excitedly in the strengthening sun and then when our shift was done, slaked our thirst with cool lemonade and our hunger with ham sandwiches. It took about a month, from start to finish, if my recollection is correct. I'm honestly vague on the specifics. A mood of giddiness possessed us during those days and weeks of horticultural industry and it prevents me remembering the exact detail. Then the day arrived when our maze was done. That would have been sometime early in July.

Its rate of growth was unexceptional at the outset. Its shrubs grew thicker and taller and more substantial. But one would expect that of any cuttings sown assiduously into fertile ground and then regularly watered.

The girls never truly took to the maze. They never mastered its intricacies. They were not at first afraid of it, but wary of its complications and the way in which as it got taller and thicker, it became more impenetrable to light. Once it was two or three feet over the height of their heads, they were reluctant to venture into the labyrinth without an adult hand to hold.

They would only do so comfortably when the sun was positioned directly overhead.

I should say something here about the general health and demeanour of the woman our family knew and had welcomed into our household as Amelia. She was slight and not strong. She tired easily, for a country girl.

It occurred to me more than once that her doctor father might justifiably have prescribed her a blood tonic. She seemed slightly anaemic. She was quite beautiful, but wanly so. A little like the painted Ophelia with which Millais failed to delight the Royal Academy, she sometimes had the tired aspect of a willing victim of the fates.

She did not need to be physically robust. The girls accompanied me on walks around that considerable wilderness when they grew restless in their need for exercise. We bought them a pony apiece. Rachel would saddle her gelding Jupiter and they would ride for hours, the three of them.

With Amelia they read stories, or they did embroidery, they spoke in Latin and French, learning the languages with which she was conversant. They learned history from her, of which her knowledge seemed almost encyclopaedic. They played with their doll's house and their puppet theatre and she taught them tricks of illusion. They sketched and painted and rode in the trap. I observed during this time that she always found a febrile sort of energy for the maze, but thought little of that apparent contradiction.

Eventually I explored the cave in which legend insisted Gregory had fought his noble fight against his demonic protagonist. It was truly an awful place. After meandering at the start to ensure no light spread through its length, it ran east and dead straight for well over a mile of fetid and absolute darkness.

At its conclusion there was a gallery, scooped somehow by nature out of the stone. This was, I supposed, the dismal spot where Gregory had done his bloody deeds, despatching first the creatures that guarded her and then their inhuman mistress. You could not but wonder at his courage and resolution in reaching the spot, let alone summoning the martial strength to complete his victory in so emphatic a manner.

With my back to the direction in which I had travelled to the gallery, I saw that there was a crack in the rock to my left that might lead to some other avenue or chamber. I had brought with me a hurricane lantern to light my way and in my pack, two Davey lamps of the type with which miners equip themselves as spare sources of illumination. I had also brought a length of rope attached to a grappling hook.

I placed my hurricane lantern carefully on the cave gallery floor and hooked the grappler and used the rope to climb up the eight feet or so of rock face to the crack. I levered my way through it and lit the Davey lamp I had put in my jacket pocket for the purpose.

I found myself in a roughly circular chamber about ten feet high and perhaps thirty across. The floor was loam, rich and springy underfoot. There were fungal growths, pale and mushroom-shaped and larger than any native species with which I was familiar. They gave off a musty and corrupt smell.

Most of the walls were stained by splotches of thick moss and over these afflictions, stretched the silvery gossamer of spiders' webs. The spiders that had spun them scurried to escape the light I had introduced to their grotesque home. I am unafraid of spiders generally. These were the biggest I had seen outside the tropics and looked venomous.

Most curious in that horrible place was a sort of bier, constructed at its centre out of what I took from its dominant characteristic of smooth erosion to be driftwood. This had been meticulously put together and provided with a mattress made from reeds. The reeds had been skilfully knitted but the bed coldly abandoned a long time ago, I thought. I shuddered, unable to picture how unimaginative or low might be the spirit of someone content to shelter there.

It was not just the profound solitude and silence and darkness of the spot, though all three of those incurred sensations were almost overwhelming in their force. There was a sense of menace in the cave which almost pricked the skin palpably. Whatever bleak spirit could endure it? They could surely share none of the fears and instincts and loathing of isolation that generally typify mankind.

I climbed back down to the gallery with a shudder. Some

instinct made me remove my jacket. A large spider squatted across its back. I kicked the beast way with a grunt of disgust and it scuttled rapidly into the shadows.

I put my jacket back on, picked up the lamp, freed and coiled my rope and walked the long and lonely route out of the cave. I confess it was all I could do not to run. I am not an overly demonstrative man. Yet when I rounded the dog-leg near its entrance and saw an oval of brightness I knew to be daylight, I could have wept with honest relief.

My whole purpose in coming to Loxley's Cross was to locate Gregory's burial plot. I still believe he is buried there, but confess I never found what I was looking for. I believe he took trophies when he defeated the forest's malevolent ruler. If they were still in his possession at the time of his death they would have been buried with him.

I now believe the tomb likely to have been plundered. Hindsight is a wonderful thing, is it not? I spent days and months searching for some posthumous clue as to the real nature of the creature this noble warrior defeated, artefacts I thought would lie intact and esoteric and wonderful with his helm and broadsword amid his mortal remains.

Gregory had two sons. The elder, David, became a priest led by a vocation that eventually took him to Rome. Thomas, the younger, was a complete contrast in his unruly nature. He fought and caroused and sowed his seed with sufficient enthusiasm to father several Welsh bastard sons and daughters of his own.

History does not document all of his bad habits, but if he was extravagant, or if he gambled, he would likely have got into debt and, with David set to inherit, seems to me the likeliest culprit should his father's tomb indeed have been ransacked for whatever treasures lay with him. Thomas could have sold them to an ambitious chieftain or even to a king. They could have gone to one of the powerful Saxon realms such as Wessex or Northumberland. They would have possessed the assumed power of religious relics and been highly coveted.

The most difficult period before the final tragedy at Loxley's Cross occurred in the late summer of 'sixty-three, when both of our beloved girls were stricken with diphtheria. We fetched doctors from Cardiff and then summoned an eminent London physician but the fevers did not abate and the girls surrendered to weeks of semi-consciousness and delirium. It seemed that nothing could be done and we despaired.

I think now that Amelia got them through it. I do not know how she accomplished it and I am still not sure of her motives in doing it. She did not employ medical expertise learned on his lap as a child from her doctor father. There was no doctor father, we later discovered, when we also discovered that she had never been heard of in the village from which she claimed to have come.

She damped their brows and sang to them in a dialect alien to me through night vigils when we could hear our maze crackle beyond our porch and windows with unruly growth and the world seemed in thrall to a strange sort of enchantment.

We held our breath. What we had planted swelled to monstrous size. Our girls hung on and time itself seemed frozen and perpetual. And then one morning, suddenly they were well again.

'It's a miracle,' my wife said at breakfast, uncertainly.

'It's something of the sort,' I said, unwilling to subject this strange cycle of events to rational analysis.

It was by now September. 'I don't want to winter here, Alfred,' Rachel said. 'The prospect is too bleak.'

I nodded at her from the other side of the breakfast table. She was right, in both senses.

Our daughter Dorothy came into the parlour. I asked her, 'Where is your sister?' She looked quite well. It is remarkable how resiliently the young recover from illness, I remember thinking.

She said, 'Muriel has gone with Amelia to choose a spot at which to begin her wood.'

I said, 'What wood is this?'

'Muriel wishes to plant a willow tree. She might also plant a silver birch.'

'Might she indeed. Was this Amelia's idea?'

'It was Muriel's, father. Amelia said that if she plants a single tree, others will grow around it. She used a long word to describe how. She said it is what nature does.'

I glanced out of the window at the wall of hedge grown to the height of a rampart bordering the eastern extremity of our maze. It was so high now that when the sun set, its shadow stretched almost to the fence around the house. 'Regeneration,' I said.

'That's it precisely.'

'And do you, Dorothy, have ambitions to reforest the land hereabouts?'

'I would like an apple orchard.'

Her mother laughed. It was an unhappy sound. She dabbed at her mouth with a napkin. She said, 'One can only speculate on the size to which the fruit would grow.'

Rachel sounded more than defeated. She sounded afraid. I resolved in that moment that we would leave for somewhere entirely different before Christmas came upon us. I have always been intrigued by myths. I did not wish to find myself living trapped in the midst of one. And that is how it did feel that day at Loxley's Cross, claustrophobic, despite all the stupendous space around us.

There is only one route out of a maze. To put it another way, a noose will tighten, even if the scaffold it hangs from is sited in a wilderness. That is what nooses do. That is their bleak and only purpose. I had the feeling of being led, bound, to somewhere I did not wish to end up. There was a tingle down my spine of trepidation not far removed from the feeling of dread.

'We have to get rid of her,' I said to my wife.

'Indeed we do,' she said, emphatically.

She made no fuss. She asked for no explanation. I offered to pay her wages until the end of December but she refused to take a single penny more than was her due. She went and we never saw her again and the girls grieved for her in their sad, subdued way until the excitement of the prospect of relocation came fully to occupy their thoughts and youthful imaginations.

A sweet-natured Welsh grandmother called Mrs Owen took charge of our daughters on those rare occasions when some social or commercial obligation necessitated our absence from the house. This happened only a handful of times before the fateful evening in Cardiff when we attended a recital and decided to make a romantic night of the event.

We returned on the afternoon of the following day. It was getting dark, as it does early in late December. By then most of our belongings had already been packed and shipped and were in storage in London. The house had an empty aspect to it, as though we had lived there only in our imaginations; as though it had never really belonged to us at all.

Mrs Owen was lying rigid on the cold slate of the kitchen floor, the victim of a stroke from which she died without regaining consciousness. The girls were nowhere to be seen.

I think I knew where I would find them. And find them I did, wrapped in one another's arms in death's embrace in the folds of that monstrous privet folly we had planted the previous year, their pitiful corpses pale and not remotely life-like in the flare of yellow brightness provided by the lantern I used to determine my path through the labyrinth.

We had loved and cherished them and so we mourned them. But the loss was easier to bear than might be thought. I am not a callous man. My wife is not a woman without maternal feeling. Life is precious and none more so than that of Dorothy and Muriel, taken at so heartbreakingly tender an age.

But the fact was that they should have died of diphtheria at the end of the summer. That was their poignant, natural fate. They had been predestined to die young of a fatal illness and had only survived it because nature had been obstructed in a way unnatural and perverse. Both Rachel and I knew this. We knew it in our heads and hearts and did not even need to discuss the matter. Some truths are obvious, even if only in retrospect.

We left the house at the end of December as planned. We moved for a while to my brother's villa in the village of Bonchurch on the Isle of Wight. Philip is a gifted botanist and I charged him with an experiment in hybrid growth he pursued with enthusiasm. He had a hot-house full of species from the rainforests of Central and South America and it was seeing these one afternoon that gave me the idea.

I went back to Loxley's Cross twice. The first time was at the end of January, when I returned to supervise the razing of the house I had built and the destruction of the maze we had planted. The latter had grown to gargantuan size and the uprooting was accomplished by steam-driven machines used usually for the lifting of large cargoes from the holds of transatlantic ships. It was an expensive procedure. I would have paid ten times what it cost.

Once uprooted, the vegetation was burned to ashes and the ashes ploughed under. I was satisfied only when no trace of our occupation remained at the spot. A ball and chain swung from a mighty crane arm reduced the house to splinters and rubble dust, also burned and riven in the earth.

I went back into the cave. It was worse than on the first occasion. This time there was a rank odour of decay that increased in strength with every step I took into the darkness. It was thick, this stench, miasmic, almost something you could stickily touch.

I heard her. I heard her singing. I knew that I was listening then to what the ancients warned of as the siren song. The singing stopped abruptly. 'Mr Crawley?' she said. 'Welcome.'

Something large and heavy slapped and slithered in the gloom ahead of me. It grunted and squirmed along that granite corridor through the pitch blackness. I could sense the eagerness of its appetite. I reeled at the assaulting stink of it.

I fled. I have always been fit and strong, agile and quick. I boxed at Oxford where I exercised frequently on the gymnastic rings and parallel bars. I was considered more eccentric for doing so than for my morbid interest in mythology. But it was time profitably spent in terms of my physical conditioning. A terrified man can run in a straight line and that is what I did, out of that hellish place, not stopping until I was a mile along the beach in daylight, lungs at bursting point, exalted just to be still living.

Philip nurtured his thorny little creation. It had an interesting genesis. It was bred from an insect-eating plant, a parasitic vine and a variety of thorn bush that moves on only after it has strangled into extinction the host on which it feeds. My brother doted on this botanical abomination. He fed it sulphur in potash mixed with snake venom. When it was only the size of a bonsai tree, it first hissed and seemed almost to snarl.

My brother has his specialism. But his interests are far reaching, his mind broad, his knowledge arcane and his skills considerable. He had been enormously fond of his dead nieces and I had told him the story of our Welsh sojourn and he had decided it would be far better if nothing was allowed to grow in the region where Amelia had planted in the mind of poor Muriel the idea of rooting willow and silver birch.

'Drop it down the well you had dug, Alfred,' he instructed me.

'Does it not need light to grow?'

He laughed. 'It will find everything it needs,' he said. 'It will not stay in the well. It will only begin there, once it has gathered strength and appetite.'

'You talk almost as though it possesses a measure of intelligence.'

He seemed to muse on this. 'Not intelligence,' he said. 'It's more a sort of cunning when it comes to the business of survival.'

He placed the plant, potted, in a tea chest. He wrapped it in gun-cotton. He did so warily, his hands protected by heavy leather gauntlets. 'There,' he said, patting it, satisfied with his work, when he had nailed down the tea-chest lid.

And so I returned for the last time to that awful place. I did not linger for longer than it took to do as my brother had instructed me and then conceal the well cover with sods of earth.

Again, nothing remained of us. We left a hole in the ground as our legacy. My wife and I have a hole in our hearts. We believe, as I have said, that our daughters were destined to die in childhood. At least they were buried in the family plot in Oxfordshire, far from that baleful place. It is some comfort.

I write these words partly to try to exorcise the experience from my mind and memory. But there is another less selfish motive in describing this strange ordeal and it is to caution inquisitive men against dabbling in that which they do not and cannot comprehend. Some aspects of the world are blackly unknowable and best wholly avoided. We live on this earth. It allows some of us to flourish. We deceive ourselves if we think it is ours to rule.

I look at the artwork that survived the Dark Ages. We rationalise the monsters depicted in some of the surviving etchings and carvings and pictures as metaphors. But I think now that the monsters were real.

Our ancestors fought a grim fight against spirits bent on destroying humanity. I believe I came across one baleful spirit that survived the struggle. I encountered it weakened. It took a fabled warrior to effect the weakening centuries ago. But it lives. Restored to strength, I believe it would do all in its power to return to the lightless time in which it revelled and it succoured and destroyed.

Written entirely in God's truth,
Alfred Randolph Crawley

Curtis finished the account and looked at his wristwatch. It was ten o'clock. He'd read it in his room. He had a few questions he wanted to put to Dora Straub. But first he wanted to talk to Saul Abercrombie. Saul would have finished his dinner by now. He wouldn't be enjoying the cigar he once would have with his postprandial brandy. Smoking had given him throat cancer and his prognosis was as bleak as that of a seven-year-old child stricken by diphtheria in Victorian times.

'You're a slow reader, Tree Man.'

'You're replanting the forest because you think she'll be grateful to you for restoring her domain.'

'It's a fair assumption.'

'Grateful enough to cure you, Saul? It's a stretch. She doesn't strike me as overly compassionate.'

'She cured those girls.'

'No. That's only what Crawley thought. That's his assumption. And even if she did, it wasn't out of altruism.'

'Why do you think she did it?'

'If she did it, she did it to earn the gratitude and trust of Alfred and Rachel. That plan backfired though, pretty spectacularly. She was influencing the girls. Muriel's sudden passion for horticulture struck both parents as sinister.'

'She needs the forest. It's the source of her strength.'

'I'd say the real source of her strength was the things Gregory took from her and Crawley assumed were buried with him.'

'Even without the forest, she had the power to save the girls.'

'But not much more than that, Saul. She was weak, denuded. Maybe she's dead. Crawley's account was written a century and a half ago.'

Abercrombie laughed. 'She isn't dead. She was around before we came and she'll be hanging out here long after we're gone. It's as convenient for us to endow her with a gender as it's convenient for her to adopt one. But she's no more human than those trees you're planting.'

'You really believe in her.'

'If you don't, Tree Man, you're more stupid than you look.'

'It's hard to credit you led your own daughter willingly into the cave, after reading about whatever it was that came after Alfred Crawley. I mean, how long have you had Crawley's account, Saul? Are we talking years, decades?'

'I didn't lead, brother, you did. I followed. I wasn't enjoying my best day health-wise. But I take the point you're trying to make and think it way off key. We're doing what she wants. Why would she wish to harm us? Everything is cool. Everything in the Forest of Mourning is completely simpatico. Agreed?'

'No. Not fucking remotely. When do you get back here?'

'I'll be there by dawn tomorrow. I've chartered a chopper. That helipad you had built is an idea I should have had long ago myself, Tree Man.'

Dora was on the sofa in the lounge, drinking beer, eating popcorn and watching a movie on a projection screen with Pete Mariner. The movie was an old Hammer horror from the look of the costumes and the blood and thunder soundtrack. It occurred to Curtis that his co-workers had made themselves very much at home. He assumed Francesca was in her studio. Then he remembered she only painted by day. He recognized the actor, Peter Cushing, in a cape on the screen.

Dabs of light from the projection painted velvety patches on Dora's skin. She was dressed in jeans and a ruched top made of some clingy black fabric. It exposed her cleavage and then clung below it to the weight of her breasts. Her lips were dark and glossy, full and half-open. He was noticing more and more just how potently alluring she was. It had started in the cave gallery where she had lied to him about what she'd climbed up and seen.

'I need to talk to you, Dora.'

They both twisted from where they sat to look at him. Dora stood and brushed popcorn debris from her lap. Pete got up and went and switched off the projector. Dora followed Curtis outside, to the terrace. He didn't sit. Neither of them did.

'When did you meet Amelia?'

'On the morning of the day we explored the cave.'

'Did you tell her we planned to do that?'

Dora frowned. 'I might have. I can't remember the specifics of the conversation.'

'That's not like you.'

'I know it's not. She was beautiful. She told me Dora was an ugly name.'

'Where did you meet her?'

'It was by the cairn at Puller's Reach. She said something about some family claim to the land here. It's vague, Tom, as though my memory is foggy.'

She lit a cigarette. She pulled on it and the skin grew taut across her cheekbones. She exhaled and the smoke plumed from her nostrils and shaped a brief halo around her head and hair. Curtis thought it a dirty habit, but Dora smoked like Dietrich or Greta Garbo playing the femme fatale in an old film. She was as powerfully seductive as a screen goddess from the golden age. The tip of her tongue caressed her upper lip, giving it a ruby glimmer. He felt a swell of arousal plump his groin.

'You lied to me about what you saw when you climbed to that crack in the cave.'

Dora frowned. 'What did I see?'

'More than you admitted to.'

'I don't recall seeing anything at all. I swear to you, I don't, Tom.'

'How did Amelia strike you, Dora?'

'I've told you, Tom. She was young and beautiful. She was altogether really quite enchanting.'

She wasn't making any sense. She was always precise and deliberate and so calculatedly self-possessed she was sometimes an intimidating woman. She sounded stoned. But she looked so alluring there in the night lights of the terrace that he felt like nothing more than tearing off her clothes and fucking her raw right out there prostrate on the decking.

Pete broke the spell. The kitchen door yawed open and he came out scratching his armpit and said, 'I need to talk to you, chief. There's some of what our employer would call serious shit going down in Dodge.'

Dodge. It was what they had come to call the workers' compound, after Dodge City, which had sprung up in the Old West in response to the Western Gold Rush. Curtis nodded, absently. In front of him, wet-lipped, Dora Straub smoked and smouldered. Even after Pete's intervention, he could barely lift his eyes from the grapefruit swell of her breasts.

'With you, Pete,' he heard himself say.

'Later, darling,' Dora said, her eyes a hard and unreadable glitter. Curtis wrenched his gaze away from her and followed Pete back inside the house.

'We're losing people,' Pete said.

'And your response is to sit here with Marlene watching old Peter Cushing movies?'

'Who's Marlene?'

'Never mind, bad joke. How long have you known this for?'

'About two minutes. One of the gangers at Dodge just called me. They're losing about thirty a day.'

Curtis shook his head. 'Jesus,' he said. It didn't make sense. The pay was good. The work was physically arduous, but the conditions and morale in the compound were excellent. You sometimes lost a proportion of immigrant workers but the Poles and Lithuanians generally stuck it out and the Welsh workers they'd recruited had seen the job as a godsend in a depressed region of a depressed national economy.

'Where are they going?'

Pete shrugged. 'The gangers and foremen are fucked if they know. There's no job on anything like this scale anywhere else in the country right now, if there ever was. They're incredulous that people are walking away. But if they're not, they're disappearing into thin air, which is just impossible.'

'They've got National Insurance numbers,' Curtis said. 'If they sign on for another job, they'll have to register those and it'll be on a database somewhere. There's the Government Department of Work and Pensions. Everyone who works legally in the UK can be tracked and monitored. You can't avoid it. They do it to make damn sure we all pay our taxes.'

'That's the weird thing,' Pete said. 'None of them has. In Dodge they're calling them the Disappeared. There's quite a few people there getting pretty freaked out about it.'

'Where's Francesca?'

'She went out.'

'Out? Where the fuck is out, Pete? There is no out. This is a fucking wilderness.'

'No, it's not, Tom. If you could bear to drag your eyes away from Dora's rack, you'd see that quite a lot of it is forest now.'

'That's unfair.'

'Not tonight, it's not. If you could have tit-fucked Dora tonight, my money wouldn't have been on you doing much else. You were mesmerized.'

'I'm not mesmerized now. Where's Francesca?'

'She went to Puller's Reach. I asked her why and she said instinct. I asked her not to go, I reminded her of the night when she was scared by something outside her window, but she wouldn't be deterred. She's the boss's daughter, all said and done. She can do what she likes.'

'She didn't want you to go with her?'

'No. She was on a mission, seemed like.'

'I'm going to go and look for her,' Curtis said.

'Take a gun, Tom.'

'I don't like guns.'

'That's hardly the point,' Pete said.

Which Curtis knew it wasn't.

But he didn't take a gun. He took a torch and rode a quad and as the land unfurled yellowy in his headlamp beam, he pondered on the word Pete had just used describing his reaction tonight to Dora. Even if you factored in Pete's pretty much permanent crush on the woman, which made him biased, he'd been right, hadn't he? Mesmerized was the word he'd used. And Curtis remembered the previous autumn and Isobel Jenks and the way he'd felt then, similarly bewitched.

His memory of the whole episode with Isobel Jenks was incomplete, foggy, in the phase Dora had earlier that evening used. He had never had the intention to be unfaithful to Sarah and he honestly didn't think he had possessed the desire. He hadn't even found Isobel likeable. She'd been smart and energetic but she'd done nothing for him physically and had a self-centred character he had actually thought quite repellent.

He'd asked himself often what had led him into that disastrous liaison with its heartbreaking consequences and he had never come up with a satisfactory explanation. He was not faithless by nature. He had a healthy libido and he liked women generally but he had never been a man to let his dick do his thinking for him, even in his adolescence.

Dora was an attractive woman. She had a hauteur that was slightly off-putting and there was little natural warmth or spontaneity to her. She was glamorous and good-looking and shapely, could be mordantly witty and she was intelligent.

But she had embodied all those qualities for the half-decade for which he'd known her. Nothing about her had changed. Drunk or sober, at work or play, she'd never had this effect on him before. They were spellbound, weren't they, she with her conveniently impaired memory, he with his increasing physical desire for her. And the magic would only get stronger. The Forest of Mourning was returning in all its dark and potent force.

Francesca stood talking to her mother. It was her mother's ghost of course and not her mother at all but there was no question in her mind about the authenticity of the experience. She had felt compelled to come to the cairn and her mother had been at the spot, waiting for her in the thick cluster of yew trees now flourishing all the way to the cliff edge. She looked a bit pale and monochromatic in moonlight. But there was nothing spectral about her mother's ghost.

She was struck by the resemblance between them. It was a poignant reminder of where she had come from and the wounding extent of the loss. She had never been angry at her mother for taking her own life, only sad that she hadn't had the opportunity to prevent it. And of course she missed her mother. She had missed her, she realized, seeing her standing there in her familiar cream coat and suede boots, every day since her death.

'Thank you for coming.'

'I felt compelled to.'

Susan Abercrombie smiled. 'Yes. That's one of the tricks I've learned since my departure. I've never used it before. I've never felt the need.'

'Why here, Mum? Why now?'

Her mother looked around. The leaves of the trees rustled slightly in the salt breeze. The cairn crooned a soft accompaniment. Francesca could hear waves breaking gently below them at the edge of an invisible sea.

'I took my life because your father's selfishness became unbearable. My death didn't change him. He was remorseful, filled with guilt for a time. But we don't easily change our natures. He wants to live forever. I embraced death with a degree of relief, to be perfectly honest with you. He will do anything to cheat it.'

'I don't believe you chose this moment just to point score against Dad.'

Her mother smiled. 'You asked why here and why now and the obvious answer is that it's easier here.' She lifted and widened her arms. Francesca couldn't but notice how beautifully tailored the coat was. Susan Abercrombie had lavished money on her clothes.

'I've always thought this place was haunted.'

'It's becoming a domain of ghosts, Fran. Saul is making it so. It's always been a hazardous place, never really safe for the living. But you'll be in mortal danger if you stay.'

'You came to warn me?'

'Death isn't the end of love, darling.'

A sob escaped Francesca. It surprised her. She hadn't expected it. She reached out a hand. 'Can I touch you?'

'No. But you can make me happy, Fran. You can do it by leaving this place.'

'I can't. I can't abandon Dad.'

Her mother tilted her head. Her hands were by her sides

again. The attitude in which she stood was somewhere between resignation and defeat. It was familiar to Francesca, who remembered it from life.

'It's vital you get away. No good can come of your father's antics here.' She looked around swiftly, just a flicker of her eyes. 'Quite the opposite, Fran.'

'I can't just leave Dad.'

'Then make him leave. You all have to get away from here and there's very little time. This place isn't regenerating, darling, it's reverting. It will become darker than you can imagine. The consequences hardly bear thinking about.'

Faintly, Francesca heard the approaching buzz of a quad bike engine. She turned around and saw the uneven glimmer of a headlamp distant through trees.

'It's that cute chap your father brought here. Sadly, I rather think his number's up,' her mother said. She turned back sharply but saw that she was now alone at the spot. Of course she was. Ghosts weren't cabaret performers, were they? She was pretty sure of that, though she had never seen one before.

It was Tom Curtis. Francesca was grateful to see him. The apparition hadn't frightened her but the warning it had given had been horribly ominous. Metaphorically, she probably needed a hand to hold. Physically, she thought she definitely needed a hand to hold. He did more than that, though. He took off his helmet and dropped it on to the ground and put his arms around her and hugged her hard in the fold of his arms.

'I'm sorry,' he said, when the embrace broke. 'I shouldn't really have done that. It was what you looked like you needed though, to be honest.'

'It was exactly what I needed,' she said, sniffing away more tears. She kissed him quickly on the cheek. She had no romantic designs on him anymore. He wasn't to her mind a single man. But she liked him a lot. She was becoming aware of an aroma, released by their booted feet as they shuffled apart. It smelled musty, decayed. She looked down. The ground where they stood was pale and crumbly in the depressions their feet had made with a trodden carpet of toadstools.

TEN

Curtis and Pete Mariner were both up before dawn the following morning. They intended to find out what it was that was leeching away their workforce. Pete had scheduled a meeting with the gangers for seven a.m. to see if they could provide any enlightenment. Bafflement had been the tone of the call Pete took from the compound the previous night, but they'd had time to sleep on the mystery and things always seemed clearer in daylight.

Francesca was in the kitchen already in her coat when the two men came down. She was going to drive to the helipad to meet her father and ferry him back to the house. It was the sort of routine task Sam Freemantle would have handled back when he'd lorded it on the estate, probably with a loaded pistol in the glove compartment of the Land Rover he drove and a shotgun in the rack behind his seat. He'd had an unendearing swagger about him that the weapons had encouraged.

Freemantle Theory was the name they'd given to their joke solution to the puzzle of the multiplying trees. But the real, enduring puzzle was the way in which Sam Freemantle had vanished so entirely. His departure had been as abrupt as it was inexplicable. Were the workers their fellows in the compound dubbed the Disappeared going the same way he had? They'd have to try to find out.

Dora came down about five minutes after Francesca had left. She had on a cream satin dressing gown paler than her tanned skin and was clearly wearing nothing underneath it. Her hair was unbrushed, giving her a blowsy, wanton look that forced Curtis to swallow involuntarily. His heart had begun to pound at the sight of her. He didn't think it was the caffeine. She poured coffee from the pot on the hob as she habitually did before going out on to the terrace to light her breakfast.

Curtis followed her. She sat toying with a pack of Marlboro

Red at the terrace table back-lit by the rising sun, teasing cellophane off the box with her fingertips.

'We're going to the compound for a meeting with the principle guys. We're losing people. It's a worry.'

She shrugged. 'Hard labour isn't for everyone. You get dirty and it's repetitious. What's the strength of the workforce now?'

'Six hundred, give or take.'

She looked westward, in the direction of Puller's Reach, where Francesca had told him matter-of-factly the previous night about the warning given by her mother's ghost. She said, 'You're going to lose a few. I'd say it's inevitable.'

'They're not signing up for a wage anywhere else.'

'They've probably used what Saul has paid them to buy a flight to a beach. It's late June, Tom. You earn and you spend and when you're broke, you look for another paycheque. It's the modern way.'

He nodded. She might be right. On the other hand, she might be wrong. 'What's your schedule like?'

Dora smiled. 'Is the boss concerned I might play hooky?'

'No. Hooky would bore you.'

'I've got some saplings that need testing for the Ash Dieback virus. Then I'm supervising the planting at Raven Dip. Rather a delicate task, the Dip.'

Curtis nodded. This was true. Abercrombie had decided the church should remain intact in its dense portion of woodland to the south. That meant planting the right trees. They had to be substantial enough to blend in with the rest of the forest, but they needed to have root systems that wouldn't reach and undermine a stone building a thousand years old. It was the sort of aesthetic arboreal challenge Dora liked to take on.

This morning, dishevelled and not yet dressed, he thought she looked rather like a supermodel might after a debauched night of champagne and nightclubbing. She was actually a tree expert with a professorship. But if her name was ugly, it was the only ugly thing about her.

'See if you can clear that foggy memory of yours,' Curtis said. 'It would be helpful if you could remember more of what happened when you met the woman who calls herself Amelia.'

She treated him to a rueful grin. 'Yes, boss,' she said.

They took quad bikes because they were better through the trees. The forest had not yet extended to the eastern border of the estate, along which the workers' compound had been constructed. That would be planted last. It was why Dodge had been built there. But if their meeting with the foremen failed to provide conclusive answers, Curtis and Pete planned to split up and go and look for clues as to where and how the Disappeared were disappearing from Abercrombie's domain.

Eventually they got to land churned and scarred by the caterpillar tracks and giant tyre treads of the big machines. The tonnage of some of the plant they were using was immense. The sheer volume of vehicles was staggering. Curtis had early on toyed with the idea of building a railhead, like they had in France in the Great War for transporting the shells fired from the big guns in a Somme offensive.

He'd decided against it. The delicate balance between infrastructural upheaval and ecological integrity would have been destroyed had he elected to do that. Nevertheless, the impact on the virgin land of what they were doing was profound and damaging and more difficult for them to travel over the closer they got to their destination. The ground was so deeply rutted in places the quads struggled to cross it at all.

None of this was a surprise to Curtis. He'd been living with it on a daily basis for weeks by now. But he felt conflicted by the assault on this domain. It looked like they had gone to war with the land and that was contrary to everything he had accomplished before this project in his entire professional life.

He pondered on Amelia. He considered what poor Alfred Crawley had written and what Andrew Carrington had warned him against. He thought about Saul Abercrombie and his employer's reluctance to accept the hand dealt him by fate and more compellingly by his own destructive habits. He thought about Fran. She had suggested he call her that, considering him a friend she said, his pillion passenger the previous night. And he wondered whether he believed any of it.

He did. Dora was the ironic proof. In her presence he could think about none of the things that really mattered to him or to his life or to his future fulfilment. Or he couldn't without herculean effort. Had Amelia done this as part of some recip-rocal bargain with Dora? If so, Dora had been made to forget the bargain's striking. If so, it had not been done for Dora. It had been done to distract him from what he ought to be doing to stop this stuff from happening.

And it proved she wasn't strong. She was spreading herself rather thin, was Amelia. She was covering a lot of bases or juggling a lot of balls or whatever platitude you wanted to use. But she wasn't strong. Not invincibly strong, anyway. Not yet, she wasn't. He made a mental note to call Carrington. He should do that as a matter of urgency. He should have done it already, he knew. He should have done it the previous evening, the moment he had finished reading Crawley's account of the events at Loxley's Cross.

They were there. To Curtis, Dodge looked like a high-end shanty town, constructed as it was of Kevlar-toughened fabric ribbed and framed with titanium rods and girders. They'd been really lucky with the weather. Twice in the decade before their daughter was born he'd been with Sarah to Glastonbury when the festival held there had become a quagmire. Here it had hardly rained since they'd begun. They could be wading through mud between the buildings on earth that was instead bald and hard with the wear of booted feet.

Their meeting was inconclusive. They'd done a roll call that morning. They'd lost another dozen people from the night shift.

Pete said, 'It's always at night that they go?'

The gangers sitting around the table in the logistics suite just looked at one another. There was a chart on the wall detailing the progress of the job. There was a computer bank dedicated to arboreal stock control and fuel supply monitoring for the vehicles and predicting meteorological conditions in advance of the weather they faced. There were software programmes for ordering food rations and carrying out a laundry cycle and ensuring everyone was paid on time. None of any of it addressed this particular problem.

'So,' Pete said, 'they disappear at night. We know that the fence hasn't been breached anywhere along its length. We know from the security guys that they're not departing through the gates. What does that leave?'

Again, silence. Curtis thought about making a sarcastic crack about the missing people descending the cliffs and swimming away. But he thought it would be tantamount to workplace bullying. He could say what he liked only because he was in charge. It would be a joke made at the expense of the people around the table. They were not to blame. None of them were paid to be gaolers. And he had an ominous feeling about the fate of the missing by now.

One of the gangers, Carter, spoke. He was a picturesque individual, both of his burly arms heavily scrolled in Celtic tattoos, ears elaborately pierced, hair pony-tailed. Curtis had worked with him before and knew him to be both honest and completely professional.

'The worrying thing is that they're not taking anything,' he said. 'There's been the odd incidence of petty pilfering here in Dodge. That goes with the territory. But nothing valuable has been taken from the site and when people disappear, they generally take stuff with them.'

Curtis nodded. So did Pete. What Carter was saying was true.

'We haven't lost a vehicle. Land Rovers are a big temptation. So are bikes. But nobody's mislaid a single one. It's not like anything I've ever experienced before.'

Curtis noticed that Carter was wearing a heavy silver crucifix on a silver chain. He hadn't figured the man for a Christian. Maybe he was, or maybe it was just another of his adornments.

A little later that morning, Sarah Bourne went to the Riverside Café. She rightly assumed that the café's proprietor would have a contact number at which she could reach Professor Carrington. He was on friendly terms with his regular customers. She could have gone through the university switch-board but regarded her business with the professor as personal and didn't want to approach him that way.

She called him and arranged to meet him at his home. He gave her an address on Kingston Hill. She had ridden her bicycle to the café; it was a sunny June day and theoretically a pleasant one on which to ride. But she felt increasingly troubled about events going on in Wales. Charlotte was sleeping better, but the sketches had grown more lurid and disturbing. She had a painting rolled into a cardboard tube in her pack she wanted to show to Carrington.

The sun shone and the birds sang in the trees on her route. The pedestrians were bright in their summer clothes and Sarah noticed none of it. She was a mother who monitored what her daughter came into contact with assiduously. She knew that the images in her daughter's mind were not coming from a computer game or site or some nightmarish DVD she'd been allowed inadvertently to watch. The problem was neither did she believe Charlotte was just dreaming them up.

The blood bond, Carrington had called it. To Sarah's ears the phrase had sounded medieval. But that had just been her prejudice against a crusty scholar discussing folkloric myths. That sort of stuff held no interest for her and never had. Unfortunately though, it had involved her. And the blood bond between father and daughter wasn't mythic at all. It was an undeniable biological fact.

His house was a chaotic mess. There were books and maps and pamphlets piled indiscriminately in every room. Everything lay under a patina of dust. There was an odour of stale pipe tobacco. He insisted on making tea before they spoke and presented it with some ceremony on a silver tray. Her cup was decorated with the Willow Pattern and didn't look particularly clean.

'I thought you were going to Wales.'

'I am. I'm expecting a call from Tom Curtis. It's pointless me going until he invites me. He's probably reluctant to do so. He seems to be quite a stubborn man.'

'Very,' she said.

'But he's also a man who wants answers. And he's in dire need of help. Unless he leaves it too late, he'll call me. And then I'll go to Wales. And it might already be too late. I'm doing the best I can to remain optimistic.'

'Surely the invitation needs to come from Saul Abercrombie.'

'Fate took Tom Curtis to the Forest of Mourning. It's from your husband that the invitation needs to come.'

'He's not my husband.'

'He's the father of your child.'

'Who painted this,' Sarah said, picking up the cardboard tube from where she'd placed it beside her chair and handing it to him.

Carrington wore a pair of spectacles on a chain around his neck. He put them on and unfurled the picture in the tube, taking it over to the window of the room to examine it in daylight. The glass was not terribly clean, Sarah noticed. But the mid-morning sun shone strongly through it.

'What is that?'

'In Norse mythology they were called the Eaters of the Dead. They're leech-like creatures. They feed the way a Lamprey does, on a host. But the process is rather quicker because they're large and they're thirsty.'

'It looks revolting, and terrifying. I knew my daughter hadn't dreamt it up, but I don't know where she would have seen something so disturbing.'

'Collective memory,' Carrington said.

'You've just said those creatures are mythic.'

'So is the creature they served.'

'Please don't speak in riddles again.'

'There are myths and there are myths,' he said. 'Some are completely fantastical. I never expect, for example, to encounter a mermaid.'

Sarah gestured at the picture. 'While you think you might encounter one of those?'

'Tom Curtis had an ancestor who did.'

'You mean that Gregory guy?'

'There will be people vanishing on the domain Abercrombie deludes himself is his. That's the meaning of your daughter's painting. It's a warning for her father he will never get the chance to heed.'

'That's a bit contradictory,' Sarah said.

'Why?'

'Because the forest is what's required by this Eve person. That's what you told me. Why would creatures who serve her kill the people restoring it?'

'A tipping point has been reached. The land is reverting. There are more trees every day than they are putting in the ground.'

'That's impossible.'

'Ask Tom Curtis if it's impossible. It's a conundrum he'll be aware of, though I'd imagine he regards it as the least of his problems.'

'I'm not ready to speak to him.'

'You're as stubborn as he is.'

'I don't want monsters in my daughter's head.'

'She's his daughter too. That's what's putting them there.'

'I want it to stop.'

'One way or another, it will stop soon enough. Matters are reaching their conclusion, I feel. Whatever the outcome, things will be resolved.' He rolled the picture with a visible shudder and fitted it carefully into the tube. He offered it back to her.

'Keep it,' Sarah said, 'with my compliments. Please don't bother to see me out.'

He took the picture outside into his garden after her departure and burned it in his empty leaf bin. Isobel Jenks, the ghost of Isobel Jenks, watched him do it, leaning against one of his poplars with a scowl twisting her wan features.

She wanted to interfere with him. Of course she did. She served someone malevolent to a degree beyond the human capacity to comprehend. She wanted to harm him but the precautions he had taken prevented her from doing so.

He honoured the old Gods. He was punctilious and faithful in this and he believed they protected him as a consequence. She could scowl at him in the garden. It had become startling at night sometimes when her face loomed out of the darkness to stare palely into one of his windows. But she could not get into the house and she could not hurt him. Andrew Carrington wasn't confident of much concerning this present woeful business, but he was sure about that.

He had almost just now mentioned the nuisance Isobel had become to him to Sarah Bourne. Charlotte wasn't the only innocent casualty of the work being done in Wales by Tom Curtis. He had decided against doing so because Sarah had obviously been so badly hurt by the business in the autumn and, though tact didn't come naturally to him, he liked her.

He liked her despite her making it fairly plain that she didn't much care for him. That was all right. Honesty was a quality he respected. And he'd never for one moment in his entire life felt the all too common craving to be popular.

He had entertained Sarah in his lounge. It was the tidiest room in what he regarded as a pretty neatly kept house. He cleared up the tea things noticing that she hadn't drunk hers, which was a pity because he made a rather good cup of tea.

He went from the kitchen after washing up the cups to his study and picked his way through the unsteady pillars of books rising from the bare board floor and opened his strong box. He took the pendant and the amulet he had stolen from the Ashmolean and examined them, as it had become his habit to do three or four times every day.

He had thought about polishing them, but their dull lustre was the best clue as to their ancient provenance. They had been taken from their owner a very long time ago. He could only imagine the gleam in her eye should she ever lay eyes on them again. He thought he might see that expression for himself in a moment swiftly approaching. He did not delude himself he would enjoy the protection he did from the trivial nuisance Isobel Jenks had become when that confrontation occurred.

Pete decided he'd look for clues on the beach. The meeting had left him feeling embarrassed and frustrated pretty much in equal measure. He didn't like to look stupid in front of Tom Curtis and keeping the workforce up to strength was one of his specific areas of responsibility.

He was generally good at keeping people happy. He had a way of cajoling more out of people than they thought they had to give. It was a happy knack that had made him valuable as a core team member on a number of projects to Tom in the past. He couldn't really understand what would make people walk away from this particular gig. There was nothing he could identify that would make people unhappy about the work.

Parts of the estate were a mite spooky. You could call them atmospheric, but they were more than that. You might even see them as sinister. The bush at Gibbet Mourning had been positively monstrous and had freaked him out pretty badly.

But the people paid to transport and excavate and plant hadn't had to deal with that – he had, together with Tom.

When the people they'd employed worked in the dark they did so under floodlights. There were large areas of woodland now and some of them were very dense – and, by definition, isolated. But the missing weren't being hunted down, were they? It wasn't like there were bears in the woods.

The gangers should have told him sooner that people were deserting the job. It was their failure and they'd no doubt tried to keep it that way until they had realized it was a problem beyond their resources to solve. So it had been elevated with no warning whatsoever into his problem. That was fine. He'd deal with it. If he didn't, it would become Tom's problem and he'd have failed and he wasn't about to let that happen.

He rode to the southern gate. He chatted to the security guys for a couple of minutes and verified that people weren't streaming out on foot with packs on their backs. That wasn't the sort of exodus these people would miss. Once outside the perimeter, he rode along the fence west to the area beyond Abercrombie's land that led to the shore and had reminded him when he'd first arrived of a golf links built for giants.

He thought about Dora. He'd pretty much reached the unhappy conclusion that she was completely out of his league. He'd known that when they'd first met, obviously. But he thought he'd matured over the years since their first encounter and had hoped that might make a difference on this project.

He'd been hurt when she'd laughed at his coming to Fran's aid when Fran had been freaked by the paw print on her bedroom window. He thought he'd behaved pretty coolly, that night, all in all. Dora had been alone in seeing a comic side to his heroics. But she was the one he had hoped would be impressed when the tale was related the following morning over breakfast. She hadn't been.

He'd scarpered out of the cave, on his first experience of the estate, on the day of his arrival. His undoing had been in telling them all about that. He should have restricted the information to the discovery of the cave and said nothing about imaginary wildlife. He'd been unnerved on the subsequent cave expedition. Dora had pressed on with Tom to the bitter end. The end had actually been more mundane than bitter, but Dora had been the one to brave any possible risk.

She wasn't frightened of Rottweiler dogs. Tom had been the one to say that. He could have added that Rottweiler dogs were probably afraid of her.

Maybe he should turn his attentions to Fran. She seemed to like him. She was easy on the eye and sweet-natured, too. It was a stretch, though, to imagine himself with a billionaire's daughter anywhere else but there. Escort her to London and the paparazzi would be in tow. He couldn't really see Fran Abercrombie sharing a packet of salt and vinegar crisps over a half of lager in his local. She was down to earth, but her life beyond her father's orbit was an exotic one.

What he should actually do, he thought, was concentrate on the job in hand. He was being well paid to work on a once-in-a-lifetime project. They were well over halfway to pulling it off successfully. There were a couple of snags, a couple of fairly weird anomalies, but they were gathering momentum by the day. Soon he would be able to start thinking about his bonus and ways in which to spend it. Speculating on that was likely to be more fun than being lovelorn. Maybe he would splash the lot on a babe-magnet car. There were worse investments.

He rode relaxed, the rising cliff face to his right, the sea to his left, the quad much more stable on the mixed surface of pebbles and sand than his own bike had been on that day weeks earlier when he'd got lost on arrival.

His plan was to ride all the way to the north-western extremity of the estate. He didn't think that the beach had anything to do with the disappearances but it needed to be checked out. Some of the missing workers had vanished from the area on the cliffs to the north of Puller's Reach. It was possible they'd gone for an after-work swim and got into difficulties and drowned.

Their work was hot. The summer weather was warm. People swam spontaneously. It was something you could do on a whim if there was a beach handy. It was free. There were routes down the cliffs to the sand and when it glittered in the late afternoon, after a long shift, the water could look more inviting than the trudge back to Dodge and beer and card games in a stuffy compound dorm, with its June aromas of diesel spillage and stale human sweat and whatever the galley was frying for supper tonight.

He'd been tempted to have a swim himself. He'd seen a couple of body boards drying, leant against the Dodge recreation block. Someone had taken then out and then shoved them on to a vehicle tailboard and driven back with them. Someone, probably several people, had been for a dip in the sea.

So he was looking for corpses, wasn't he? It was a grim thought at odds with the beauty of the vista and the day. The beach really was in Enid Blyton mood, with its blue water and golden sand and orange pebbles glittering with dried salt crystals. It smelled wonderful. The last thing he wanted to do was find a rip-tide victim stiff and dead in the surf. But he had to look. He wouldn't be doing his job properly if he didn't do that.

There was a figure on the beach. She was slight and, as he approached, he realized that he didn't recognize her. She wasn't dressed in the regulation outfits the women planters wore. Anyway, they weren't planting on the beach. She wasn't wearing a swimming costume either. She didn't fit his skinny-dip theory. He brought the bike to a halt about a dozen feet away from her and switched off the engine.

She looked to be in her late twenties and when she smiled at him he noticed that she was exceptionally pretty. 'You must be Pete,' she said.

'Correct. You've got me in one. But I have absolutely no idea who you are.'

She frowned. 'That's strange. My name's Amelia. I'm one of Dora Straub's students, from Hamburg?'

'And you're doing what here, some kind of fieldwork?'

Amelia coloured. 'I can't believe she didn't mention me. It's all been cleared with Mr Curtis and Mr Abercrombie.'

Pete held up his hands, open-palmed. 'Relax,' he said. 'You've just slipped under the radar, Amelia. We've had a couple of issues sidetrack us and Dora has a hell of a workload. I'm sure she will mention you. I'm sure you haven't been entirely forgotten about.'

She smiled again. She was a post-grad student, he assumed, obviously smart and really exceptionally good-looking. Just for a moment he wondered how Dora would react to his hitting on one of the girls she taught.

'Where are you staying, Amelia? It isn't particularly safe out here. You're not in Dodge, are you?'

'I'm not in what?'

'You're not in the compound. It's to the east of here. That's not where you're staying.'

'I've a refuge on the beach,' she said. 'It's sheltered and it's dry. It's a cave. Dora told me about it.'

Pete nodded, thinking, *of course*. He would have paid his entire bonus from the Abercrombie job personally not to have to endure a single night in the cave. But that wasn't how Dora thought at all. To her it was an innocent geological feature. It probably made perfect sense to her to tell a cash-strapped student doing fieldwork it was a place she could doss down in for free.

He assumed Dora to be unaware yet of the disappearances. He'd been alerted to them by the gangers and he'd told Tom Curtis but they'd only found out the previous night and, to his knowledge, Dora was still out of the loop. Tom might have told her or he might not. Pete didn't know. Until they discovered what was behind them, the beach had to be regarded as a hazardous place. Everywhere on the estate did.

'I don't want to alarm you, Amelia, but for now at least, you're better off out of the cave.'

'My things are there,' she said.

He looked at his watch. It was approaching noon. He said, 'I plan to ride as far as the north-eastern border of the estate. I can be back here in less than two hours. I'll give you a lift to the compound and you can quarter there. You can't stay here.'

'But I need my things,' she said.

He nodded. He looked around. Everything seemed not just safe but nursery-bookishly benign. It was a scenario ripe for raft-building and lashings of ginger beer. The waves broke at the edge of the sea. The sun was hot on his back. The gulls in the blue above him wheeled and cried contentedly. The idea that this young woman might be in immediate danger seemed an absurd one. That said, she was alone in a remote place and people were vanishing.

'I'll come back for you.'

For the third time, she said, 'I have to have my things.'

'Fine, I'll come back to the cave for you.' He glanced at the water to his left. 'Don't go swimming in the meantime.'

'I can't swim.'

'Good.'

He took out his mobile. He thought he should call Dora as extra insurance, just as back-up. But there was no signal on the beach. It didn't really matter. Dora already knew Amelia was there, didn't she? He put the phone back into his pocket and switched on the quad's engine. 'See you in a bit,' he said.

She smiled again. She really did possess a lovely smile.

Curtis was on his way to Gibbet Mourning when he felt his mobile vibrate in his pocket. It was Carter, the picturesque ganger. 'We've found a body,' he said.

'Shit!'

'Not what you're thinking, Tom. This guy's been here a while.'

'We need to tell them at the house.'

'I already have. We found him an hour ago. I've been trying to get you since then. This is the first time you've registered any signal. I called the house landline and told Francesca Abercrombie forty minutes ago.'

'Where'd you find him?

'Nearest landmark is the Puller's Reach cairn. The grave is about a thousand metres inland from those Freemantle Theory yews we didn't have to plant.'

Curtis grimaced. He liked Carter but was getting weary of Freemantle Theory jokes. They'd never been funny and they got less so as parts of the forest they weren't responsible for continued stealthily to grow. 'I'll be with you in about twenty minutes,' he said.

Saul Abercrombie and his daughter were already at the site when he arrived there. The earth-mover had taken the top off the tomb very cleanly. The skeleton was intact on its back in an oval depression about eight feet below where the surface of the ground had been. The double-edged blade of a battleaxe was plainly visible laid next to Gregory's remains. Even some of its wooden handle had survived, preserved by the rawhide binding which the warrior had gripped to wield the weapon. There was the bronze boss of what Curtis assumed had been a wooden shield.

'The grave's been ransacked,' Abercrombie said. 'Crawley got that part right, Tree Man. There'd have been jewellery, guy of his station in life. He'd have been buried with his treasures and mementoes. He deserved a more dignified end. He deserved to rest in peace.'

'Amen,' Curtis said.

'This is becoming a place of ghosts,' Francesca said. It was what she'd told him her mother had told her the previous night and Curtis couldn't argue with the observation. He'd seen Gregory's ghost on his first visit to the shore below Puller's Reach. The dead weren't resting in peace in this part of the world. Something was preventing it. He thought that if he saw Alfred Crawley's daughters walking palely through the woods together hand in hand he wouldn't be surprised. He'd be shocked, but not surprised.

To Saul, Curtis said, 'Will you call in an archaeologist?'

'There's no archaeology left, brother. The second son saw to that. Badass offspring, just like Crawley said. What I'll do is have a proper grave dug at Raven Dip.'

'The church is deconsecrated.'

'It was consecrated once.'

'I should tell Dora. She's overseeing there this afternoon. I'll tell her to hold off until you've decided exactly how you want it done.'

He looked down at the remains, thinking, *We all come to this eventually*. Gregory hadn't been much less than six feet in height, by his rough estimation. That was tall for the period but then he'd been described as physically formidable. He'd been broad-shouldered and he'd had all his teeth. Not much sugar in the diet back then and anyway he'd probably have died before the rot had a chance to set in. Life expectation in those days had been brutally short.

The grave was shaped like the hull of a boat. Its planks had been planed smooth and sectioned and time had petrified them into something closer to stone. The bones lying there were age-mottled and brittle-looking. Once they had been strong. Time had made them fragile. Exposure to fresh air would quite rapidly render them nothing more than dust.

'It happened, didn't it?' he heard himself say. 'The legend isn't a legend at all. It's historical fact. It's the truth.'

'Yeah, Tree Man, it's the truth,' Abercrombie said. 'How cool is that?'

Curtis looked at Francesca. She looked very pale. She said, 'I don't think finding him now is something that's happened by chance. I think it's a warning.'

Abercrombie chuckled. 'A grave warning,' he said.

Francesca shot her father a glance momentarily full of fury and frustration.

'We'd have found him eventually,' Curtis said. 'It was inevitable.'

This wasn't true. They wouldn't have found him if he'd been under the yews at the cairn or in a dozen other spots where trees had multiplied without them having to dig. Finding him did seem symbolic. It signified something. There was something ominous about the timing of this discovery. He remembered his promise to himself to call Andrew Carrington. He would do that just as soon as he carried out the business at Gibbet Mourning he'd been diverted from.

He took out his mobile. This close to the shore, he didn't have a signal. None of them would have just then. It came and it went. To Carter he said, 'I need you to tell Dora to delay the Raven Dip work. We can re-schedule when the guy down there's finally at rest.'

'Shouldn't take more than a couple of days,' Abercrombie said. 'Know anyone who can do it, Tree Man?'

'Eddie Stanhope's people could do it.'

'The crew laid my helipad?'

'They're quick and they're all ex-forces blokes who know how to keep their mouths shut.'

'They do graves?'

Curtis had turned to leave. 'They sometimes excavate swimming pools. It's the same principle.'

'Where are you going?'

'To look for another forgotten hole in the ground,' Curtis said. To Carter, he said, 'Phil?'

Carter walked around the grave and across to where Curtis stood. They were out of earshot of the others.

'Dora's in the lab still doing her Ash-back thing,' Carter said. 'I'll get over to her right away.'

'Never would have figured you for a believer, Phil.'

Carter fingered the crucifix around his neck. 'You mean this?'

'You're decked out like someone scared of vampires.'

'A lot of the guys are wearing them,' he said.

'Since when?'

'Since the disappearances started to become something we couldn't rationalize.'

'Where are you getting them from?'

'One of the guys in Dodge used to be a silversmith.'

Curtis shook his head. 'So Dodge is down to one sane resident.'

'Dodge has some seriously spooked residents Tom,' Carter said. 'And on this gig, more and more of them are voting with their feet to walk away.'

Dora got an email requesting she call her doctor without delay just before eleven o'clock in the morning. She was in the lab and the work was serious. The Ash-back virus was always fatal to the host tree and its spread was something no one had discovered a way to impede, never mind stop. It was worse than Dutch Elm Disease, the last great arboreal pestilence to strike the British mainland. It was worse than acid rain. But Saul Abercrombie wanted ash trees in his forest and what he wanted, he tended always to get.

She was working on saplings rather than mature trees because Curtis was insisting on planting species at all stages of development. He wanted the forest to reflect faithfully the way woodland developed in nature. The Disneyland version wasn't for him and Abercrombie was in agreement with the principle. The morning had gone well. Every sapling she had examined had been healthy. The consignment had come from Italy, which was allegedly virus-free.

Then she heard the ping of the email and read the message and remembered the X-rays she had undergone during her short spell at home in Hamburg between the job on Wight and coming to Wales. And she keyed in her doctor's number with a more than averagely anxious thumb.

It had been the bicycle ride from Ventnor to Freshwater Bay that had done it. More specifically, it had been the long ascent before the steep descent into the bay. It had left her feeling tired and breathless. She had always been fit and strong, but there had been a hollow sort of feeling to the breathlessness. She had recovered OK, after her Coke at the café and her stroll on the beach. She had ridden back the route she had come without really struggling. But she had decided to get herself checked out, just as a precaution.

Her doctor cleared his throat. He was a sometimes colleague at the university, where he'd done microbiological research. He was a handsome man and she'd slept with him once, after a faculty party. He did triathlon in his leisure time and had a nice body. But he'd been a disappointment in bed.

A tumour about the size of a tennis ball, he told her, the sporting analogy registering with her as typical of him. Inoperable, probably too late to remove the lung, every likelihood that the disease had spread to major organs, though further tests would be needed to determine that. Given the size and malignancy of the growth her chest was harbouring, he didn't give her any real chance of living beyond the end of the year. He was sorry. He was truly very sorry.

Dora ended the call. She was aware of a buzzing in her ears that was the sound of numbness. Her iPhone felt alien in her hand. She could smell wind soughing through the verdant land. Everything looked brightly coloured, like stage props, too big and garish, too rudely obvious to be anything but unreal.

She fumbled the pack out of her breast pocket and lit a cigarette. Of course she did, she thought, smiling inwardly, sucking the smoke deep, relishing it, grateful for the calming nicotine hit.

She had smoked since she was fourteen. She was thirty-seven. She'd had a two-pack-a-day habit for the best part of twenty years. Some people got away with it. Others didn't. Was it fair? It didn't matter whether it was or it wasn't. She was at the young end of the spectrum but she certainly wasn't blameless.

She had smoked unrepentantly. She had never wanted to give up and so she had never tried to. Now she wouldn't have to, because smoking was giving up on her. She would be a statistic. That was her legacy and on that day and in that foreign place it seemed bitterly trivial to her.

Her whole life seemed suddenly trivial. Her principle ambition in going to Wales had been to fuck Tom Curtis, who to anyone with half a functioning brain was obviously still in love with the woman who had thrown him out in the autumn of the previous year. She hadn't accomplished that, a sexual conquest that now didn't matter to her in the slightest.

What had she achieved? The answer was nothing. She'd lived for the moment and some of those moments had been sensationally enjoyable. But her accomplishments were pitifully few. She'd written one or two well-received academic papers. She'd contributed to a couple of books on the subject of ecology. She'd recently saved a clutch of ancient oak trees for a grateful man who'd had the means to pay her generously for doing it.

She was toiling in a sort of half-trance on a vanity project of grotesque size in a location polluted by magic. The Abercrombie domain was awash with enchantment. They were all spellbound there, weren't they? But it was a spell she would break, Dora thought with a grin, crushing out her smoke on a laboratory bench. She would break the spell if it was the last thing she did. She would do it while she still felt strong and able.

She took one of the quads from the motor pool at the compound. Nobody turned a hair. She turned a couple of heads, but she was used to doing that. She'd been doing that ever since her adolescence. Nobody challenged her right to the bike. She was high up in the chain of command. To her own mind, Dora was already history. To the people around her, she thought ironically, she was still somebody, deserving of respect and even deference.

She rode to the woods. It was a perfect June day. On the way to the woods the air was rich with grass scent. Smoking had never noticeably impaired her sense of smell. The forest was cool and dark and she twisted and turned through what all their industry had created with dapples of light painting the loamy earth through the leaf canopy. Her senses tingled. The air was syrupy with birdsong. She didn't honestly know when she had felt more alive.

Eventually Dora came to the cliffs. She paused in the bike's saddle to appreciate the boundless view and then dismounted and walked the cliff edge until she came to a spot where she could safely descend. She was agile, gifted with excellent balance. It didn't take her long to reach the beach.

She crouched and sifted a handful of sand through her fingers. It was fine and yellow and there was a quartz sparkle to it in fragments infinitesimally small. The world was complex and beautiful.

She had tried to preserve the beauty of the natural world and in some small ways she had added to it. That was an accomplishment of sorts. It would have to do. There wasn't time for further achievements. Illness was ugly and debilitating and when it was terminal, it didn't enable the hope ambition required. She could do no more, really, than she had already.

At the edge of the sea, Dora took off her clothes. She had lost a little weight. She had put that down to the rigours of the work but now knew it was the tumour feeding hungrily on the healthy parts of her. She still looked good. Her skin still had the tawny spring tan she had acquired during her weeks of false summer earlier in the year on the Isle of Wight. Her muscle tone was good. She was firm and slender and golden and still, apparently, flawless.

She walked into the water. It was surprisingly warm and so buoyant with salt that she felt almost weightless when she was immersed only to her waist in it. When it reached her chest, she started to swim. She was an excellent swimmer and swam front crawl with a determined rhythm and a metronomic stroke.

She stopped once. She looked back to the shore. She was a long way off the beach by then. Treading water, she thought she saw a slight figure, a dark shape against the pale grey of the cliffs. But it could have been a shadow or smudged trick of perspective from that distance. If it was a figure, it didn't move. It stood entirely still.

The sea or perhaps the distance she had swum through it from the land sluiced away the enchantment. It felt a little like waking from a nap she'd been lulled into unexpectedly. Clarity returned to her mind for the first time in what felt like weeks and she remembered what she had seen when she'd clambered on to Tom's shoulders and levered herself through the crack in the cave gallery wall.

Who could inhabit such a place? If Amelia sheltered contentedly in so dismal a refuge, what sort of creature did that suggest she was? Yet she did shelter there. It was her refuge. And Dora had kept her secret as she'd been requested to do in return for future favours only hinted at.

She'd been mesmerized. The trees were spreading malevolence across Abercrombie's domain and Amelia was at the dark heart of it all. People were disappearing. She shivered, the unplumbed void beneath her feet feeling chilly and fathomless. They weren't buying flights with what they'd been paid, the people vanishing. She'd been wrong about that in her desultory exchange of the morning with Tom. It was Amelia's doing, wasn't it?

She was rather glad that it wasn't her problem. She thought it might be too much for cute, hapless Pete Mariner to handle. She thought it might be too much for Tom Curtis to deal with, strong and capable as he was. The owner of the land was dying and his titular claim was being called into question. His pretty daughter was a sentimental fool incapable of doing anything but decorating a room with her vapid prettiness. All in all it was a bleak situation. She thought it probably hopeless.

Dora turned and swam on. Sometimes people left notes, didn't they? She hadn't been close enough to anyone to leave a note. Maybe that was a sort of indictment, but it was also a fact. A note would have been melodramatic and absurdly personal, addressed to Tom or to Pete. It would have been completely inappropriate.

She swam. There was a swell, the further out she got and the water grew darker and cold. She was a good swimmer but in that wilderness of water, exhaustion eventually took her and when the moment came, she surrendered quite gratefully to the enveloping embrace of the deep.

ELEVEN

C urtis first went to the spot from where Crawley's thorn bush had ripped itself from the earth on its journey to devour the yews at Puller's Reach. It had only made a thousand metres or so south by the time they'd burned it to carbon and ash. He remembered the way it had risen, like some arachnid creature threatened and poised for a venomous counter-strike. He wondered if it had also sunk something of itself at that moment.

He found the place. Once it had been marked by Freemantle's abandoned Land Rover and the empty casings of his shotgun cartridges. They had long vanished from there but it was easy still to identify the area he was looking for. The hole was narrow, not much wider really than one of his arms. He'd brought a plumb line with him and he fed it into this cavity in the earth. It was just over eight feet deep.

That was probably deep enough, he thought. Heat rose, didn't it? It was a scientific truism that heat rose. If the bush had thrust something of itself eight feet deep when they'd incinerated what they could see of it with the flame throwers, then it could have survived. Pale in the rich earth, that root could flourish. It could grow strong and push up into the light and then it could begin to roam again.

He thought it probably had. Crawley's brother had said he'd endowed his hybrid creation with a cunning gift for survival. Crawley's brother, a gifted botanist but a man Crawley had hinted dabbled in darker and less precise arts than botany. He'd been a man who'd doted on his nieces. He'd created his vicious plant as an act of retribution not just against the land, but specifically against the creature which had killed them.

It was just a theory. Curtis thought it plausible only because he had encountered the bush himself. He'd tried to avoid the temptation to endow it with qualities beyond those possessed by a plant. But he'd thought it crafty. He'd seen a show of its barbed malice. He'd counted the avian casualties impaled on its lethal spikes. If it didn't think, it possessed instincts he'd only otherwise seen in life forms with a measure of intelligence.

If it had survived the burning, he was pretty sure he knew where it was. It had retreated to its original home to gather and grow and replenish itself. It had returned to the dark, deep shelter of the well Alfred Crawley had dug when he'd first come here and then returned to after the death of his daughters. That had been its first real home, a hundred and fifty years ago, when it had only been the size of a bonsai tree, different from a bonsai tree because it hissed and shivered and thick gauntlets had been required even then to handle it.

Curtis had brought a tool with him. Saul Abercrombie sometimes walked with the use of a stick. There was a small collection of them. They resided, when he wasn't using them, in a tubular metal holder under the coat rack in the hallway of the house. Curtis had taken one he'd never seen his employer use and therefore didn't think he would particularly miss. It was silver topped and made of black polished hardwood. He thought it probably Victorian, which was really quite appropriate.

He used it when he got to Loxley's Cross to try to locate Crawley's well. He knew that the hatch over the well was turfed. There was a chance the wood underneath had rotted. If he plunged suddenly through turf and crumbling timber, he'd have found what he was looking for. He might plummet through darkness to a watery death. Or he might descend suddenly into the snarling embrace of the growth he had tried to destroy, which had become strong and sinewy and massive and quite bloodily vindictive again.

He quartered the ground. He walked methodically. It was almost an hour before his tapping was rewarded with a sound more hollow than the meek thud of a walking stick's rubber ferule on solid earth.

He determined where the edge of the well-cover lay. Sound told him this, his gentle tapping signalling through its percussive response that the hatch was circular and about six feet across. It was a generous size for a well, but Crawley had been a prosperous man and he had been ambitious to live there in some style before events in his life took the disastrous turn they did. He'd bought ponies for his daughters. He'd planted his monstrous maze.

Curtis put the walking stick down and lay on the ground so that only his head and arms were over the hollow place. Then, with his elbows on solid earth, he pried the grass and soil away in a small patch and revealed the thick tongued-and-grooved oak boards of the well cover.

He heard a skittering sound. It came from inside the well. It sounded like the hasty clamber of giant limbs up the length of the stone pit on the brink of which he lay. Then it stopped. It stopped completely and there was no sound at all. They would be very pale, those groping limbs. They had re-grown in the pitch darkness.

He heard the slow, deep scrape of what he thought might be a single thorn against the wood; a single, probing finger of fibrous intent. The well cover trembled and rose very slightly and then eased flat again. He shuffled back in a careful retreat on his stomach, picked up the stick, rose to his feet and crept away from the spot.

He was a mile from Loxley's Cross when he took out his mobile and saw that he had a signal. He called Andrew Carrington.

'You've taken your bloody time.'

'People are disappearing. And you were right about Crawley's thorn bush. We weren't successful in destroying it.'

'I'm afraid this is one of those rare situations where being proven right offers me not a shred of comfort, Tom.'

'We found Gregory's tomb this morning. It's all true, the legend.'

'Of course it's true.'

'She's here.'

'You've aided and abetted her.'

'Gregory's tomb had been robbed. The things he took from her had been taken from him.'

'And I know by whom. And I know who bought them from his thieving wastrel of a second-son. And God help me, I know where they are now.'

'You should come here.'

'Are you inviting me?'

'I'm asking for your help.'

'You'll have to pick me up from a convenient station. I don't drive. I'll work out the route and text you later with the time of my arrival. Trains permitting, I'll see you early tomorrow afternoon. It's probably too late.'

'Too late for what?'

'Too late for any of us, Tom.'

Had Pete progressed beyond the cave mouth on his return south along the beach, he would undoubtedly have seen Dora's abandoned clothing at the water's edge a few hundred metres further on. He would have recognized them and, because mobiles never worked on the beach, he would have gone as fast as the quad bike could carry him to raise the alarm. But Dora was already dead by that point and Pete didn't get beyond the entrance of the cave before stopping.

There was no sign of Amelia. You couldn't see the cave mouth until you were almost upon it because of the angle there at which the cliff face was configured. But he had confidently expected to reach the place and see her sitting on the sand with a bulging student backpack ready for her lift to civilization. Or at least ready for her ride back to a cold drink, a square meal, a hot shower and a comfortable berth.

Was Dora's graduate student an ill-mannered ingrate, or had she decided to stay for stubborn practical reasons? She hadn't said specifically what it was she was studying. Maybe she needed to be close to the spot where she was doing her field-work. On the other hand, maybe she was just late. Women sometimes were. Dora, emphatically all-woman, was the exception to that particular rule. But Amelia might have got into a flap, packing. It had happened to other girls he'd known in the past.

He dismounted and walked into the cave mouth. He peered through the gloomy interior as far as the dog-leg, but there was no sign of her and there was no luggage either. He called out her name through his cupped hands and he heard it bounce and reverberate, echoing along the stone like a fading rumour.

'Here,' she said, from beyond the dog-leg. 'Come here, Pete. I've got something for you.'

She had a voice as pretty as her smile. There was just the hint of an accent and a huskiness that made her sound slightly exotic. Tension slipped out of him and his shoulders dropped slightly. He realized that, without consciously knowing it, he'd been a bit worried about her. It had been cavalier to abandon her on the beach earlier when they still didn't know the cause of the disappearances.

He walked along the cave, through the dog-leg, unshocked when it confronted him with the reeling blackness of the cave interior beyond because this time he was prepared for it. He had his mobile in his hand and he'd switched on its torch.

She was standing before him half-naked. The curve of her breasts had a luscious weight in the light of his torch beam. Her nipples were small and pink and proud. Her skin was very smooth and pale and her hair hung in dark blonde tresses falling down to her shoulders. She licked her lips. They were full and ripe and looked almost black in the bleached light he played across her face and body.

'I want you to fuck me, Pete,' she said. She reached out a hand. Its fingers twisted undone a button of his shirt. The hand trailed down his chest and stomach and she stepped towards him and cupped his groin and squeezed. When she spoke, she whispered and her breath smelled lightly of cinnamon and musk. She said, 'I haven't been fucked by a man for a very long time.'

She turned abruptly and began to walk back along the cave and he followed her, seeing the shape of her back, her perfect shoulder blades and, below the base of her spine, the youthful switch of her hips with each step under the cream gossamer of the skirt clinging to her pert behind.

He almost stumbled. He slithered on something that gave off a faint stink. His mind felt gluey with lust, his breathing was shallow and his cock bulged throbbing in the confinement of his jeans. He'd never felt so aroused. He thought that the cloth pressing against his erection, just the rhythmic friction of walking might make him come before they got to wherever she was leading them.

'Calm down,' she said, reading what passed in his sluggish mind for thoughts. 'I don't want a single drop of you wasted, Pete.'

He couldn't remember the last time he'd had sex completely sober. There was always a drink involved somewhere in the preamble. He knew that he should have felt nervous, but the throb between his legs suggested that erectile dysfunction would not be a problem and he was too filled with the gobsmacking wonder of the moment to care.

They didn't require a drink. He knew with a tingling thrill of expectation that sexual inhibitions weren't Amelia's thing at all. She wanted to be fucked and he'd be happy to fuck her senseless.

Something lumbered and splashed in the distance. Pete paused. Fear clarified his thinking momentarily. Instinct fought the intoxication and a bewildering sort of terror clutched at him. He felt cold. A shiver convulsed through him. It was a trap, wasn't it? He'd been lured there. *Oh, no*, he thought. *Please God, not like this.*

Amelia turned and pounced, fumbling the phone from his grip and hurling it at the cave wall, smashing it to fragments, casting them into absolute blackness, her laughter light and cruel as she walked past him back in the direction they had come, her retreating steps blindly confident as he heard something maul and slither from the end of the cave, approaching him.

They were cold and clammy and their skin was rough and barnacled when they reached him. The stink of them made him void his bowels in the moment before he felt the first rude, assaulting touch.

Then they were on him.

He was a strong man. He loved life. And so he struggled and fought and screamed until the blood loss brought unconsciousness and death. And Amelia, who had brought him there for them, was made by them to be as good as her word. They didn't waste a single drop of him.

*   *   *

That was the last day on which anyone was able to fool themselves that things were well or even normal among the workforce on the Abercrombie estate, or across the domain generally. By the following morning, everyone knew that Dora Straub and Pete Mariner were now numbered among the missing.

Dora had been more respected than liked. She'd turned heads, though, as she'd rightly observed on her own account. She was an immediate and conspicuous absentee. So was Pete, who had been popular in a way Dora had never cared to cultivate. It was clear when those two disappeared that whoever orchestrated the vanishing was no respecter of rank.

Even more damaging to morale in Dodge, though, was the disappearance during the same night of Phil Carter, the picturesque ganger with the tattoos and the piercings. He'd been charismatic, hugely popular and the compound's leader in all but name. He was an expert at his craft and physically formidable.

He still went, leaving no trace, as he supervised the twilight rescue of a birch, planted too close to the cliff edge and threatening to topple unstably down on to the shingle and sand a hundred feet below. He went down the face on an abseil rope and he never came back up. His silver crucifix proved a talisman incapable of saving him when the moment came.

The great machines fell silent after that. To Curtis, it was as though the Forest of Mourning was staging a silent vigil for the latest of its victims. He harboured a gloomy certainty that Pete was dead. The same was confirmed about Dora shortly after dawn when her clothing was discovered by a search party. It was not long after breakfast when the guards at the western gate called him to tell him that the workforce were deserting in numbers that made them look like a column of fleeing refugees.

The tracking device on Pete's quad bike led them to it at 10 a.m. By then Curtis felt like the sheriff in a frightened town trying and failing to raise a posse to confront the bad guys. It was just Fran Abercrombie and him. Saul was by turns ailing and tinkering in the comms room pretty much like someone under house arrest. Gregory's remains awaited burial under the protection of a tarpaulin staked at his grave's edges in the ground. Eddie Stanhope had said his boys were all far too tied up with a convenient backlog of jobs to come and intern him afresh.

Curtis didn't want to go into the cave. He was tired and shaken. He'd had no stomach for breakfast and he had the cantankerous Andrew Carrington to endure meeting later in the day. But Pete had been his friend and he'd had and still had a duty of care towards a man he'd personally recruited. He had to explore the cave to its gloomy conclusion in looking for anything that might survive of him now. He felt certain, but he still had to make sure.

He made Fran wait on the beach. He thought she'd be safer there. He didn't think she'd be safe – nowhere on her father's domain was any longer safe. The work he'd organized had seen to that. It was corrupt, enchanted and malign. It was a place of deliberate danger. But it seemed safer in the sunshine against the glittering backdrop of the sea than it did in the stone sepulchre nature had tunnelled underground. It was light versus darkness, an equation an infant could solve.

The walk underground was the longest mile he had ever travelled in his life. He'd brought a Maglite torch. Like Alfred Crawley before him, he'd brought a rope attached to a grappling hook. He'd also overcome his own distaste for them and brought along a gun.

He had a semi-automatic Sig-Sauer pistol strapped into a shoulder holster. It carried seventeen nine-mil hollow-point rounds. He was an inexpert shot, but he could slip off a safety catch and squeeze a trigger and there wasn't much space in the cave for bullet dodging. Saul had told him sombrely an hour earlier that the weapon would put an exit wound the size of a dinner plate in anything he hit. He hoped not to have to test this claim.

He reached the gallery eventually. He clambered through the crack as Alfred Crawley and Dora Straub had done before him and he saw with the same sinking heart as Crawley the dismal refuge of the enchantress he had described and Dora had been spellbound into forgetting about.

Nothing with any belief in life or hope or light could have

endured residing there. It was a resting place for a creature without a soul. Soft and loathsome, the fungus grew and blossomed palely to grotesque size all around the driftwood bier. The walls moved furtively in his torch beam with insect life. Something, a large moth or possibly a bat, skittered across his scalp. His gorge rose on a surprised gulp of the reeking air. He had to get out of there. He felt at once wretched and afraid.

He slipped a few times on puddles of slime on his return to the beach. Once or twice his own heightened senses conjured noises for him to hear. But nothing had followed him in, nothing had lurked inside and nothing followed him out of the cave. And he reached the dog-leg and the sunshine only with the chill certainty he'd felt all morning that Pete Mariner was never coming back.

He thought Francesca brave. He also thought her loyal. She was loyal to her father but she was also the only ally he had left in whatever was happening here. She had accompanied him there. It had been a comfort to have her travel the route at his side through the malevolent kingdom of trees he'd created. It was a comfort to see her, concern etched across her lovely face, when he emerged back into daylight. She smiled and then she brought her arms wide and hugged him.

He thought he might lose his composure at that. Pete had been easier to love than Dora but he had grown to love them both really over the years they had worked and laughed and bickered and drunk together. He had cherished memories of both of them that would never now grow beyond the point they'd already reached. The loss was abrupt and deep and he couldn't shake the sense that he'd been not just complicit in their destruction but the cause of it.

'Thanks,' he said, returning Fran's embrace.

'I owe you one,' she said.

'Well, not anymore.'

'It isn't your fault.'

'I'd have to beg to differ on that.'

'Dora took her own life, Tom. She left her clothes behind. God knows why she did it, but she drowned herself.'

'Pete didn't. Neither did Phil Carter or any of the others.'

'I didn't believe it until yesterday morning. I didn't really believe any of it until I saw the proof of Gregory's remains. You didn't either. I could see it in your expression, Tom. That was the moment you finally became convinced of it.'

'Trees don't breed the way rats do, Fran.'

'Freemantle Theory?'

'There's nothing theoretical about it. It's hard to quantify from the ground because of the sheer magnitude of the job. But we had the aerial evidence almost from the start. Something unnatural has been happening here from day one. It's gathered momentum ever since.'

'My mother – my mother's ghost – said the place is reverting.'

Curtis only shrugged.

'Can it be stopped?'

'There's a fellow arriving this afternoon might have the answer to that. If he thought it was no, I don't think he'd be coming.'

'You've invited some kind of occultist?'

He laughed. 'A university professor,' he said.

She looked suddenly crestfallen. She said, 'My dad doesn't want it stopped. He wants to be well again. He's prepared to pay any price to buy that particular miracle.'

'Your dad needs to wake up and smell the coffee,' Curtis said.

'You'll be the last she'll take,' Fran said. 'You were never going to need that gun just now. You're Gregory's descendent. That's why the likeness is so strong. She brought you here. It was always going to be you and it was always coming to this. And she's always known it.'

'Yeah, well. She doesn't know everything,' Curtis said. He shivered. They both did. The sun had gone briefly behind a cloud. She smiled at him and he thought her courageous and clever and worth more than what fate probably had in store for both of them.

'You could leave,' she said.

'No, Fran, I can't. I started it. I have to do what I can to make it stop.'

Saul Abercrombie injected himself with the last vial of the solution his Harley Street Doctor Feelgood had concocted for him. He rather felt that the moment had come. A tipping point had been reached. Events had accelerated to the point where there was really no going back to how things had been when the land he owned had been a wilderness.

He'd just accessed and then studied some satellite pictures he'd had taken at considerable expense that morning. They showed the extent of the forest. It covered the whole of the coastline now and all of the territory inland at the southern extremity almost to Raven Dip. To get to Puller's Reach from the room where he studied the pictures meant crossing two miles of open country and then five of densely planted wood. There was woodland to the north, west and south of Loxley's Cross.

Only to the east did the forest falter. And falter wasn't really the right word because the regeneration was occurring at pretty staggering speed. More than sixty per cent of the land he owned lay in the cool and loamy shadow of leaf canopy. What had been that phrase he'd used with Curtis at the outset? 'Broadleaf, brother, far as the eye can see.' They'd gone and done it and taken overall what they'd accomplished was pretty fucking cool.

It was time to make contact with the original owner of his domain. It was time to call in the considerable favour he'd done her in restoring what she had capered among and capriciously ruled back in ancient times.

He knew about the disappearances. He felt personally quite sad about Dora Straub. He'd known she taught at a university and thought her way too cool for school. She'd been drop-dead glamorous and he'd enjoyed her laconic sense of humour. It hadn't hurt that she'd flirted back with him. Ten years younger and in decent health he'd have made a serious play for Dora.

He regarded the disappearances generally as collateral damage. You had to expect something of the sort. There was a price to be paid for tampering with the natural order and that was just the way it was. There'd been no bodies and itinerant workers were nomadic by nature. He didn't think any of them would be returning any time soon but without a corpse there was no crime and he didn't think anyone would have any real success in trying to offload blame on to him.

One very singular occurrence had decided him on action today. He didn't think he had an awful lot of able-bodied time left to him, but it hadn't been that spurring him on to do what he was about to. It had been something revealed on the satellite pictures you wouldn't yet see from the ground.

One of them had been taken above Loxley's Cross. And it detailed in a darker green than the surrounding grassland the precise patterns and turns of a hugely substantial maze.

The privet was no taller than the grass still covering most of the open land at the Cross. Probably it wasn't yet as tall as the grass or someone would have noticed it over recent days and called this phenomenon in. Curtis would have known and would have told him about something so curious. But he hadn't, because it had only just occurred.

It was symbolic of her growing power and confidence. It was a defiant retort to what Crawley had done to her in preventing her original scheme from being fulfilled. She had influenced Crawley's daughter Muriel to want to plant willow and silver birch. Now Saul Abercrombie had seen to it that those species were planted across this richly forested land in their thousands and he wanted the reward owing him for doing so.

He wanted recompense. As they said so often in those eighties cop dramas he was actually secretly quite fond of, it was payback time, baby. He put on his steampunk goggles, adjusted them over his eyes and kicked the quad under him into snorting life.

He was in no great hurry that day to get to her. He felt pretty confident that she wouldn't stand him up or blow him out. Paying your dues was a principle well known to the players of the medieval world. She'd expect him to demand something. And he wasn't demanding much. She could probably accede to his request with a single benevolent thought. He didn't anticipate potions and spells. She didn't strike him intuitively as some occult drama queen. She was the real deal, a one off, a class act.

He belched. He had breakfasted on a fry up of his own clumsy devising. Jo and her kitchen people had departed at some point during the night. His staff had gone, finally too freaked out to stay. Things were a little weird. They might even be frightening, unless, like him, you were firmly in the loop.

They met Carrington at the railway station at Haverfordwest. He didn't seem at all put out to Curtis by the fact that Fran Abercrombie had come along. He sat in the back of the Land Rover and told them blithely about his theft of priceless artefacts from a museum. Then he asked if he could smoke his pipe, a request Curtis didn't reasonably think in the circumstances he could refuse.

He told them about the cosmological map etched in tin and buried with the king who had bought the items in his bag from Gregory's wastrel son. Then he took them out and Fran, in the front passenger seat, examined them. 'They're engraved with planetary symbols,' she said. 'What does that signify? Do you think Amelia came originally from another world?'

'Amelia isn't a person, dear. People don't live for a thousand years. We'll never know where she came from but what she'd be more accurately described as is a force, like gravity or the tide.'

'Only more destructive,' Curtis said.

'Certainly more antagonistic,' he said. 'She's neither a natural nor a neutral force in that she's deliberately harmful. She relishes human pain and destruction.'

'She appears in the guise of a woman,' Fran said.

'That's both her strength and her weakness,' Carrington said. 'It's what seduces her victims. It's why protagonists through history have tended to underestimate her. It's also a flaw we can exploit.'

'Crawley thought there were lots of monsters, or demons or devils,' Curtis said. 'He thought the fight in the Dark Ages with demonology was real.'

'I think he was absolutely right,' Carrington said.

Fran said, 'Warriors like Gregory were schooled. They were formidable and well-prepared. We're totally out of our depth. We haven't really got a hope, have we?'

'Gregory wasn't invincible,' Carrington said. 'He wasn't that Pre-Raphaelite sap in stained-glass and shining armour you've seen staring piously from the window in the church at Raven Dip. He probably fought very dirty and used every trick in the book.'

Curtis said, 'Such as?'

'He was summoned by a magus or warlock to help with the struggle against the creature who calls herself Amelia. For a start, he would have done something to protect Gregory from being devoured by the parasites that guard her.'

Fran said, 'Something magical?'

'Only a very practical sort of magic that owes something really to common sense,' Carrington said. 'This chap would have possessed an apothecary's skills. It's my belief he would have polluted Gregory's blood to deter them from feeding on him, deliberately infected him with something. They'd have sniffed out the corruption. It would have acted as a repellent.'

'We don't have polluted blood,' Curtis said.

'We will have,' Carrington said. 'I have three doses of flu jab in my bag. We'll be polluted when we've injected it.'

'That will act as a repellent?' Fran asked. She sounded unconvinced.

'Practical magic,' Carrington said, who sounded up for the fight.

The phrase put Curtis in mind of Crawley's thorn bush.

'The other important thing is choosing the ground,' Carrington said. 'Gregory had no choice over that. He had to enter her lair. It was a frontal assault. We by contrast have some things she wants very badly. We can stay away from the shore and away from the trees. We can make her come to us.'

This prospect didn't sound welcome to Curtis – it sounded terrifying. He swapped a look with Fran and saw that she felt the same. They were going to deliberately goad and defy an ancient and malevolent creature. They were going to try to trick and defeat it. The outcome would likely be painful and grotesque.

'Courage, my friends,' Carrington said from the rear seat. 'We're going to need all our strength and resolution for this.'

'Amen to that,' Fran said.

'I have a letter for you, Tom,' Carrington said, fumbling an envelope from his jacket pocket, reaching it forward.

Curtis opened it one-handed in his lap. The single page contained just three words and a signature. The signature was Sarah's. The three words were *Come home safe.*

He thought he'd take a look at the camp. It was deserted now, but he'd never seen Dodge and he'd paid for its construction and was curious to see the Kevlar and titanium township his money had enabled.

His route there was a trawl through thickening vegetation. Ferns were growing densely everywhere. Saplings were poking their slender vertical paths upwards from what had been virgin ground.

Here and there mature trees he knew hadn't been planted by Curtis and his people loomed stately out of a slight layer of mist. There were pale clusters of toadstools around their trunks. The smell of bark and leaves and air-borne pollen permeated the air and something else, some other smell he couldn't readily identify. It wasn't the sea, the smell of ozone drifting inland. It was slightly sour and sulphurous and he thought it was probably the odour that had risen from this land a thousand years ago. It was returning to itself, wasn't it? It was reverting.

Dodge was looking already pretty ragged with neglect. Ivy in heavy clusters had begun to spread over its buildings. It groped across windows and doorways and masked interiors from the light. He pried a vine away from one window, looked inside and saw that fungus had claimed the floor of a gloomy interior, swollen around chair legs, bloated and yellow under a sheltering tabletop.

He rode to Loxley's Cross. The maze was clearly visible by now. In the time since the satellite pictures had been taken at first light, the privet had grown to a height of a couple of feet. He dismounted and switched off his engine and walked among its leafy avenues. He could hear it grow. It was a rustle, almost like speech, the furtive language of something urged into life by enchantment.

He passed abandoned machines. Ivy afflicted these too,

looping and coiling through their cabs, wrapping their steering wheels and gear levers, congealing across their caterpillar tracks in deep green clusters and swathes.

Eventually he reached the trees. Saul Abercrombie felt the fond embrace of the forest. The gloom of its permanent twilight was grey and opaque in the mist he had first noticed in Dodge and thought now slightly thickening, the closer he got to the coast and his destination.

He was headed for Puller's Reach, for the cairn and the spot where weeks earlier the first tree had been planted. She would find him there. This was her land now. He had restored it to her and would claim his rightful reward from her before departing forever. He would take Francesca with him, treat her to some of the energetic fun for which he'd had such a gift and which had been so tediously absent from her life over recent months.

Curtis was still around too, somewhere. He'd have to remember to write Tree Man a cheque. The job was completing itself now the tipping point had been reached. Curtis had done as much as he needed to. He'd earned his fee and played his part in restoring his employer's health, which had been the whole point of the whole gargantuan project. What happened to him afterwards was a matter of complete indifference to Saul Abercrombie.

He dismounted when the foliage got too thick for him to continue to ride through. He would walk the last hundred or so metres to his destination. The stuff he'd been given by the Harley Street guy would give him the stamina to do that. Soon, he would have no further need of such expensive and temporary help.

She was there, waiting for him, as he'd known she would be, standing beside the cairn on the cliff edge, looking out over the water, the sea pale green and calm in wan sunshine through the mist. She had a shawl wrapped around her shoulders and she was a slighter figure than he'd expected. Her loosely worn hair was a dark blonde lustrous even in the matt light.

It worked both ways, didn't it? He had restored her strength and vigour in the way she was surely about to return his.

'You want me to make you well.'

'It's all I've ever wanted from you.'

He heard something rustle behind him. He could afford to ignore it. There was surely no danger here, with her.

She turned around. She was beautiful, clear-eyed and, when she smiled, kindness came off her like radiant heat on a cold and wintry day.

He heard the rustle again. It was a loud, rude noise through the branches of yews, a squirming, eager sound. And there was a smell, too, wasn't there? Something corrupt, decayed.

She held his gaze. She said, 'It's done.'

And he felt it. He felt a great weight unshackled from him, actually felt his own cellular integrity returned as the blood coursed purely through him from the heart pumping strongly in his chest. For the first time in months he tasted saliva, performing the swallow reflex without a grimace of pain. He could feel his own firm musculature. He felt solid and exuberant and alert and almost youthful. He was himself again. The frailty had been suddenly and completely drained away from him.

He heard that noise again, smelled the stink, which seemed to be strengthening and coming at him from every direction but the one he faced.

'Thank you,' he said.

'I did it only because of a lesson harshly learned,' she said.

'I'm truly grateful.'

And her expression changed. It became as bleak and dark as an eclipse and with a belated clutch of dismay in his soul, he caught a glimpse of her age.

'It was a practicality, Saul. I can't feed tainted meat to my followers,' she said.

They returned to a mantle over the land of thick and sulphurous fog. It wasn't sea fog. It was a phenomenon remembered from a murkier time and restored in celebration of something bleak and awful. The domain had a new ruler and she was as cruel as she was regal. That was the impression Curtis had, looking at the canted gate through their headlight beams, seeing the deserted post where the security guys usually sheltered. He felt the same certainty he'd felt about Pete and about Dora. Saul Abercrombie, he suddenly knew, was dead.

'Christ, look at the fence,' Fran said.

He did. They all did. Ivy covered the wire and wooden posts in a verdant maul. To the right of the gate its weight had made the wire stretch and the fence sagged there, greenly breached.

Curtis said, 'You haven't read Crawley's account of his time at Loxley's Cross, have you, Andrew?'

'I've always suspected it existed. I'm glad it's survived. Reading it will be a scholarly treat I'll indulge if we survive till the end of the day.'

'He concluded with a warning. He pretty much predicted this. He said it would spread and that other spirits like Amelia might revive as a consequence. He didn't give us much chance against them.'

'It will spread,' Carrington said, 'like a contagion. This place is afflicting the land around it already. It won't be contained, I'm afraid.'

They drove in. The ground felt spongy underneath them and Curtis knew from the strong chlorophyll smell that their tyres were crushing ferns as they progressed. They passed trees he hadn't planted looming like leafy phantoms out of the mist.

Fran asked, 'Are we going to the house?'

'No,' Curtis said. 'One way or another I think we should get this over with.'

'I think I know what you intend to do,' Carrington said.

Fran said, 'I wish I did.'

'You'll have to wear them, Francesca,' he said. 'You'll have to put on her pendant and her amulet. We have to make her furious at the indignity done to her by our defiance.'

'She doesn't sound very much as though she needs much help with fury.'

'Will you do it?'

'If you two tell me the plan, I will. That's if there is a plan. Please tell me there's a plan?'

'There's a plan,' Curtis said. 'I think it's our only hope.'

The drive to Loxley's Cross took forty minutes. The Land Rover's headlights were powerful and the fog grew no denser. It was strangely even, the absence of detail and light. Uncannily so, Curtis thought. But the land kept throwing up unexpected obstacles: copses and stands and clusters of trees where none had been even the previous day. Crushed ferns mired their axles in sharp-smelling pulp. Stray branches swatted out of nowhere at their windscreen.

Eventually they arrived, each having submitted to their flu jab, Fran having adorned herself too with her new jewellery. Or more accurately her old jewellery, Curtis thought. She had been wearing a sweater. She'd removed it, the better to show these trinkets off. She was wearing only a T-shirt and jeans and the gold pieces looked dull and incongruous, like half-hearted theatre props on an actress unconvincing in her role. She shivered, getting out of the car, either feverish from the jab or frightened, the way he felt himself.

Curtis peered to his left.

'She isn't here,' Carrington said. 'We'd smell the stink of her entourage.'

'She won't take them everywhere.'

'Just everywhere she feels threatened,' Carrington said.

To Curtis, Fran said, 'What are you looking at?'

'Crawley's maze is back,' Curtis said.

It was. They walked towards it. It was a hedge wall, perpendicular to them and it marked the eastern boundary of the maze. It stood about eight feet high and closer to it they could hear the strain and crackle of exuberant growth.

'Fucking hell,' Fran said.

'Quite,' Carrington said.

'Magic should stay on the stage,' Curtis said, his voice a confidential murmur. 'It has no place in real life.'

Carrington said, 'You invited it here.'

'That's not strictly true, Professor,' Fran said. 'The truth is it never left.'

They followed Curtis to the spot. He located the well cover. He poked around until he found the hinge. Within the well there was only an ominous silence. At a point opposite the hinge, he gouged the turf with the heel of his boot until he'd exposed enough of the cover's wooden rim to give him sufficient purchase.

Would the thorny creation lurking in the shaft remember him? Would its horny protrusions flay him alive in revenge?

He thought the threat at least as plausible as it was ridiculous. Nothing seemed fanciful anymore in this fog, in this place. It was its own universe of weirdness and perversity. Logic never prevailed. Reason had been exiled. He had been concealed beneath a protective suit and mask when he'd attacked it. Anyway, he didn't have a choice.

'Help me,' he said to Carrington.

'Look over there,' Fran said, her voice struggling not to shake.

Both men looked to where she pointed. Two young children stood hand in hand about twenty feet away, staring at them incuriously. They were girls wearing white nightgowns of the sort used in the days when people lit their path up the stairs to bed with a candle. They turned in the direction of the maze and walked away, the fog swallowing them.

The cover was heavy. Crawley had described himself as strong, but hadn't had to lift the circle of oak encumbered under its weighty concealment of soil and sods of grass. He'd laid the turf only before his final departure. They lifted it to forty-five degrees and then walked carefully to either side of it and swung it back where it landed with a mist-dulled thud before stepping away carefully from the black maw of the shaft.

For a moment, nothing happened. Curtis thought barbed limbs might dance and skitter up the shaft attracted by the light. But the bush moved slyly, didn't it? The animal quality its clever creator had endowed it with, of all animal attributes, most resembled cunning. So it was cautious. It was careful. Given its maker's sombre mood of grief when he'd brought it into being, it might even possess a lethal sort of patience. Victorian grief was persistent. The anguish was endured over a long period of mourning.

Fingers of growth probed carefully into view. They snaked over the lip of the shaft and caressed the grass and trembled, testing the air. Perhaps because there were seven of eight of them, they reminded Curtis a little of octopus arms. But then the bush became bolder or more curious and they extended and thickened. There were black protrusions glistening sharply from sinewy white limbs and he was looking at a monster of an altogether greater magnitude.

It retreated. It gathered or recoiled and they could see

nothing of it from their cautious distance a dozen feet away. Curtis swallowed fear and walked to the edge of the shaft and looked down upon the antagonist he thought he'd burned into extinction.

It rested there, a few feet from the surface, massive and poised, the barbed violence of its thorns a malevolent promise it waited to fulfil, biding its time, perhaps testing the space and the novelty of light or just relishing the prospect of further provocation in its fortress home. It writhed down as far as the eye could determine any detail, a far greater complication in the complexity of its vicious coils than it had ever been at Gibbet Mourning.

He turned around. All three of them did. The air had tainted suddenly and assumed a darker caste. She was there. So were her guardians, but they were not so close as to be visible. She was slight and serene-looking and quite beautiful. She was bare-headed and she had on a purple cloak clasped ornately in silver and ermine trimmed.

'You're wearing what belongs to me,' she said to Fran. 'You'll suffer for that. Your father's recent death was mercifully quick. Yours won't be.'

'My God,' Carrington said. 'You're real.'

She smiled. 'The meddler from the south,' she said. 'You'll watch the wench perish and in so doing witness your own fate.'

'You're lying about my father.'

She reached inside the cloak. Her hand reappeared holding the strap of Saul's steampunk goggles. One of the lenses was smashed. Both were spattered with blood. She dropped them disdainfully on to the toadstools carpeting the ground at her feet.

'Do it, Fran,' Curtis said.

Fran took off the pendant and amulet. She slipped the chain from the pendant before tossing both artefacts lightly into the well. They heard the precious items clatter and fade to silence as they slipped and tumbled the length of the shaft. She'd taken off the chain so the pendant wouldn't snag on a thorn within easy reach. They'd discussed the need for this during their approach, but it was still impressive, Curtis thought, that she'd possessed the cool deliberation to remember to do it.

To Curtis, Amelia said, 'Your death will follow theirs. You're as comely as your ancestor. I hope his ghost is here to hear you scream.'

'He beat you.'

She laughed. 'He tempted my followers to feast on pigs the tinkerer he served had fed a sleeping draft. He slaughtered them while they slumbered helplessly. He seduced me – the only man to do so. Gregory sowed his seed in me and while I slept, stole my things like a base thief. It was trickery, not valour.'

'Fascinating,' Carrington said.

There was a blur of movement then, a sudden rising bloat in the air of decay and the professor was hauled abruptly into the mist by something huge and moist and barnacled in the brief monstrous vision they had of it. They heard his screams. Fran covered her ears, but could still hear them until they abruptly ceased.

'It wasn't fascinating,' Amelia said. 'It was low and unjust. Like the low trick of coming here, all three of you, bearing some affliction.' She grinned and gestured in the direction Carrington had just been dragged. 'I've cured you. Congratulations, you're all healed and whole.'

'You were going to kill me first,' Fran said.

'I changed my mind. I believe it's a woman's privilege.'

'You're not a woman.'

'What I am matters little to you.'

She walked to the edge of the well. She looked down the way a skilled mountaineer might, studying a tricky descent. She slipped out of her cloak and draped it on the ground. She said, 'I bleed, but not easily. I'm more agile a creature than you people could imagine and stronger, of course. This won't take long. You can try and escape if you wish. You'll just perish in the same manner, but sooner. I don't really care either way.'

She looked grimly at Fran, dead-eyed and hollow-cheeked, the age of her dismayingly apparent suddenly in her pallor and the savagery of her spite. 'You'll pay dearly for this impertinence,' she said.

She dropped deftly down on to the topmost limbs of the bush. She began to weave a nimble path through them. In the silence, as they watched her, Curtis heard the sobbing of infant girls away in the maze through the mist. Lost, he thought. They all were. Amelia twisted and contorted down the depths of the well. She became obscured to sight from above.

They would join other ghosts. They would join Dora and Pete and Saul, who had tried and failed to live forever. There would be troubled Sam Freemantle. There would be Andrew Carrington, who had least of all deserved his ghastly fate. Older than all of them would be Gregory, who had been neither as brave nor as noble as his enduring legend insisted. Together they would people this ancient land. They would add to its spectral, sinister atmosphere. They would be exiled in the Forest of Mourning to grieve forever for their own perished lives.

Amelia was deep into her descent before the bush finally reacted to her presence. It shivered and emitted a gasp that sounded exultant and then with a spasm of swift movement it scraped down the shaft in on itself, its thorny mandibles contracting and becoming denser as it wove a sinewy prison for its precious captive that was too intricately complex to escape.

It writhed and shrank back and the spaces between its fibrous tangles became small and suffocating. The rising aroma of sap filled the air above the well as Crawley's bush cut and wounded itself in its eagerness to complete the task for which it had been born. It had waited a long time. It had endured a vigil of a century and a half, hungering all the while for this destiny. The wounds would heal. Curtis thought, in the circumstances, you could forgive the bush its zeal.

It thrummed and shivered. It creaked and moaned like the hemp rigging of a vast ship under full sail in a storm. It fought her. Curtis thought her true voice would rise coarsely upward in a foul eruption of ancient oaths. But that didn't happen. She struggled silently within the barbed bonds of her confinement. An odour rose fungal and corrupt and he thought about what she'd said about not bleeding easily and knew that she was bleeding now.

He waited with dread for her to escape it. He waited for the smirk of triumph on her pale oval face as it emerged from between the sharp, shackling tentacles so tightly binding her. He waited while a minute became two and then while five took an endless time to double into ten. But she didn't emerge. She didn't come up. She had boasted that she was strong. The thing now confining her was evidently stronger.

'The girls have stopped crying,' Fran Abercrombie said, eventually.

They both looked towards the maze. They could see it more clearly, he realized, as though the mist had lost some density. He walked up to the wall of privet and then walked back and said, 'You can no longer hear it grow.'

'That stink has gone. I think she might have lost her followers. Do you think she's dead?'

'No, she'll never be dead. But for now she's powerless. She didn't retrieve her treasures. She's trapped down there and the well is deep.'

'She'll escape the thorns. The bush will perish eventually and she'll be free of it, won't she?'

'Not in our lifetimes.'

'No. We're rid of her, even if the world isn't.'

'Your dad was right about that. She was here long before us and will remain long after we're gone.'

She shivered. She said, 'He was right about most things. What he did here couldn't have been more wrong.'

'I'm sorry he's dead.'

She smiled. 'He was dying anyway. His death from his disease would have been grotesque. She said it was quick, instead. I believe her.'

'I do too.'

Lastly, Fran helped Curtis close the well hatch. There was a sigh as it descended through space and crashed back into place. It could have been the sound of corrosion in an iron hinge. It could, though, almost have been human.